Cuffed & Collared

by

Samantha Cayto

Book Three
Boston's Brave

Cuffed & Collared

Contact Information: info@thewildrosepress.com

Cover Art by *Diana Carlile*

The Wild Rose Press, Inc.
PO Box 708
Adams Basin, NY 14410-0708
Visit us at www.thewilderroses.com

Publishing History
First Scarlet Rose Edition, 2015
Print ISBN 978-1-62830-816-7
Digital ISBN 978-1-62830-818-1

Published in the United States of America

The hunt for a killer, a submissive witness, and the Domme in charge of both...

"Sergeant Malloy…or should I say Mistress Regan?"

"I didn't give you permission to kiss me," she replied in a cool tone.

Kyle twitched a little, as if to gauge the strength of her hold on him. "We're not having a session, Mistress Regan." He sounded annoyed but not too annoyed. His obvious ambivalence egged her on.

"Aren't we? I make the rules, remember?" With that warning, Regan grabbed a fistful of his hair with her free hand and, pulling him away from the wall, frog-marched him into the kitchen.

"Now what?" he demanded through gritted teeth.

She shoved him against the countertop over the dining space and made him lay the side of his face on the cool, granite surface. "I didn't give you permission to speak, either," she admonished before letting go of his hair.

He made no effort to get away during the short trip from the hall, and he still had a hand free to try something. Even with her expert training, she knew a man with at least fifty pounds on her could give her a run for her money. He wasn't fighting her because he didn't want to. He wanted her to control him and to dominate him.

The knowledge sent her pussy into overdrive. "You're a very disobedient boy, Kyle."

"Yes, ma'am," he agreed in a cheerful voice that grated on her last fucking nerve.

"And you're enjoying this entirely too much."

Prologue

Her victim quivered beneath her, a mixture of fear and excitement. Soon, his movement would change. It would become more frantic, a desperate attempt to avoid the agonizing pain, and his feelings would be pure terror. Or, would they? Perhaps he would enjoy this final act of submission. Maybe it was what he had been looking for all along.

She didn't know, and sometimes, like now, right before she began her serious punishment, she wondered was it really possible to derive pleasure from pain? All her victims seemed to believe so. They craved the sensation. They wanted to be at her mercy. They begged for it. Some even paid for it.

But no, she couldn't imagine it. That feeling was not for her. She was a Domme, a sadist as some might call her. She was destined to inflict pain, not receive it, and she loved doing it. She loved every stroke she delivered, every grunt and groan and, yes, scream she pulled from her subs, especially at the first moment they realized she had changed the rules of the game. That moment when they understood she had turned play into reality.

Her breath quickened in anticipation. Her cunt tightened, and her body flushed with heat. She was wet with desire as her sexual excitement mounted. This was it. It was time. The urge to find her release was strong, yet she restrained herself. Rushing things ruined the fun. She needed to be patient, to take her time, let it last. And she could, she would, because she was the best.

She was the Mistress of them all.

Chapter One

Sergeant Regan Malloy squatted beside the king-sized bed to get a better look at the victim's face. He was such a handsome man, and unlike the rest of his body, this part was unmarred by violence. She wasn't going to insult the poor bastard by saying he looked peaceful in death, but she could say he looked relieved. After all the pain that had been inflicted upon him, she could imagine he had welcomed the moment of death. With the crime scene well-documented, she felt free to reach up and unstrap the gag from the back of his head and pull it away from his rigid mouth.

"You know what we have here, don't you?" a voice asked behind her.

Regan looked over her shoulder at her partner, JoJo Mathers, an African-American woman several years her junior. "A serial killer."

"Mmm hmm," the woman replied through tight lips. Her gaze was fixed on the victim, thirty-eight year old Joseph Xavier Bennington, III.

As she stood, Regan looked at the man, too. He lay face down, covered in nothing except welts, cuts, and a large quantity of his own blood, on his massive and stylish bed. The killer had tortured him with a variety of as yet unknown devices for hours, by the coroner's estimation, before neatly castrating him. Regan couldn't tell just by looking, but she'd bet anything the ME would find the poor man's private parts stuffed inside his rectum. A final act of violation and contempt by the killer, before, in a perverse act of mercy, lifting Bennington's head and slitting his throat.

The M.O. was precisely the same as used in the murder of Eugene Morales. Even with only two victims to go by, Regan was sure they had a serial killer on their hands.

She turned to her partner. "Two men, both good-looking, fit, socially active yet single, wealthy and with powerful jobs. Both were killed in their own beds, tied up and gagged, but with no signs of forced entry or a struggle, implying they let their murderer into their homes and probably their beds as well. And having done so, they were both tortured to death in a sadistic, sexual ritual, and raped, although with what is unknown. Morales was straight by all accounts. We'll check it, of course, but I bet Bennington was too." Regan shook her head. "We can't blame these on a Ted Bundy or a Jeffrey Dahmer. This time, it's one of our own."

"You're convinced it's a woman," JoJo observed as they walked away from the bed and the sad remains of Joseph Bennington.

"I'm certain of it." Regan was. It only made sense, and the idea turned her stomach more than any crime scene ever could. Being a woman who had achieved a measure of success in a profession still dominated by men, she felt strongly that women had a duty to wield their power wisely. If they didn't, the world would be no better off than it was with only men in charge.

"It seems pretty clear," she continued, "that we have a killer among the Femdom crowd. We know

Morales was into the scene, and if we can determine that Bennington was as well, we should be able to establish what clubs, groups, and friends they had in common. Ugly as it is to have a second victim, it may give us the break we need for both murders."

They walked into the hall and headed toward the living room. The victim's apartment was a fancy and expensive one located in a high-rise building near the Theatre District of Boston. Although Regan's knowledge of quality in furnishings and art was limited, she knew the price of real estate and could tell the guy had been loaded, with refined tastes, just like the first victim. Apparently their killer liked to prey on the well-heeled. Was it resentment for the wealthy, or was she one of them?

"Go ahead and bag him," she said quietly to the attendants waiting in the living room.

"I guess the best source of information now may be his friend," JoJo said with a toss of her head.

Regan followed the direction to the far side of the room into a dining space. Seated at the long, elegant table was the man who had called in the crime. Kyle Ramsey, according to the young uniformed officer beside him. The kid was giving the witness as much privacy for his grief as possible while keeping an eye on him. Until he was questioned, Ramsey was technically a suspect.

"I'll talk to him," she said to her partner. "Why don't you start digging through the victim's effects?" Although she phrased it as a suggestion, as the senior detective of the two, she was in charge.

The other woman nodded. "The vic had the second bedroom set up as a home office. I'll start there. Good luck with Mr. Hottie," she added with a smirk.

"Please," Regan sneered in response. This was hardly the proper time to drool over a man, even though JoJo was right. The witness was as gorgeous as his unfortunate friend. When she first arrived on the scene, she'd caught a glimpse of him. Tousled blond hair on top of a face made of perfect angles. From afar, his male beauty had been easy to see. Close up, it was even more so. His profile would have done any coin of the realm justice, so straight was his nose, so square his jaw. Every plane was refined, yet not soft. Majestic was the word that came to mind and sexy, of course.

With the possible exception of her three gorgeous cousins, Regan only saw faces like that in magazines, not in real life. Then again, she ran with rough and tumble kind of guys. A man like this was out her league and a good thing, too, because she was working a case, and he was part of it.

Regan approached the dining table on soft cop feet as if she were stalking prey. In truth, she was, although it was the killer she sought. This man with his hands clasped tightly together on the table top, head down, jaw clenched, was probably only a means to an end. But you never knew. Cops took nothing for granted.

He must have heard her approach. When she was only a few feet away, his head jerked up and he stared right at her. She was careful to keep her steps steady and her face blank, but, oh mama, did Kyle Ramsey pack an extra wallop up close. Given the color of his hair, she would have expected blue eyes or maybe green. Ramsey's eyes, however, were a deep, rich, earthy brown. Although they were a little red from crying, they still had the capacity to entice and arouse.

Oh, yeah, this guy was definitely fuckable.

Regan adjusted her leather jacket to make sure her sudden interest wasn't showing by way of erect nipples before she stopped at the table. Ramsey stood in greeting, startling her. She wasn't used to such gentlemanly behavior, but she wasn't bothered by it. Her mother had always told her there was nothing wrong with good manners so long as they weren't being used as a substitute for genuine respect.

"Mr. Ramsey, I'm Detective Sergeant Malloy of the Boston Police Department." She held out her hand, glad her voice was clear and didn't betray the effect he had on her.

"Sergeant." His voice was deep and mellow and a bit rough with emotion.

His obvious grief over the death of his friend was even more appealing. Maternal instincts rose to mingle hotly with her arousal. She wanted to wrap her arms around the poor man and sooth away his hurt. She could picture pressing his cheek against her breast while she ran her fingers through that tangled flaxen hair.

"Sergeant?" His voice was stronger this time, and it snapped her out of her reverie.

Regan coughed once to clear her throat and her head. What an idiot she was being. Now was hardly the time for hot fantasies about a man, especially when the body of his friend was being wheeled out behind her. Ramsey's gaze flicked in that direction, and he briefly closed his eyes. He opened them again and focused on her this time.

"I need to ask you some questions, Mr. Ramsey," she said, her mind now firmly fixed on her duty.

"Yes, of course."

"Please have a seat." She gestured toward the chair he'd occupied before she arrived and took her note pad and pen from her pocket. Flipping to a clean page and clicking her pen ready, she noticed he wasn't moving. She felt annoyed at his immediate lack of cooperation before realizing he wasn't sitting because she was still standing. Okay, now his manners were getting on her nerves. She liked to move when questioning someone yet knew she'd get more from a relaxed witness. So she sat with a suppressed sigh.

"Go see if Detective Mathers needs any help, officer," she said to the kid in uniform. Her line of questioning was going to be dicey and most likely embarrassing to Ramsey. Another person hanging around and listening would only make it more difficult.

"Yes, ma'am," the officer replied and walked away.

With a silent, deep breath to steady herself, Regan looked straight at the man sitting beside her and tried not to get lost in the deep brown of his eyes.

Concentrate on what she's saying, not on how she looks. Even as he admonished himself, Kyle knew he was wasting his internal breath. Sergeant Regan Malloy was impossible to ignore. Not even the memory of his friend lying dead in his bed was enough to keep this woman's proximity from stirring his blood and his cock. Christ, had she seen his hard-on? He didn't think so. She had stared him directly in the eye the whole time they stood, piercing him with her strong, intelligent gaze. This was a woman who took no shit from anyone, he could tell.

He understood his reaction to her was partly fueled

by his heightened emotions over his friend's death and an almost desperate need to be distracted. Anything that could supplant in his mind the hideous images of what he'd found would be welcome.

Sergeant Malloy certainly fit the bill. She was tall and lean with a high, firm rack that caused her leather jacket to jut out. Although cut short, her auburn hair was far from boyish. It was doing wild things around her oval face. She had kelly green eyes and pale skin with a smattering of freckles around the bridge of her small nose. Irish, of course, with a name like Malloy, and yet she didn't look like a sweet, friendly girl from the Emerald Isle. She looked like a tigress on the hunt, and she was. She was hunting a killer.

"Mr. Ramsey," she began in a low voice that held only a hint of a Boston accent. "What exactly was your relationship with the deceased?"

Shit! At the reminder of why he was there, the images of blood and gore returned. His eyes began to water again. He blinked back the tears. He had cried enough, although strangely he felt it would be okay for him to let go in front of this woman. As strong as she appeared, he knew he wouldn't be embarrassed to be less than stoic with her. Strange, he had never felt that way before about a woman.

Still, it would be counterproductive to give in to his grief. Time for that later when he was alone. Right now, he had to help the police catch the butcher responsible for this horror. He swallowed hard and cleared his throat to ensure his voice was strong.

"Jazz and I are—were—old friends and also law partners. We're both at Mayberry and Howard." He had to look down at the table, the one he helped pick out. It was easier to talk if he didn't look at her.

"Jazz?"

"Sorry, I meant Joseph. Jazz was his nick name."

"I understand." Out of the corner of his eye, he saw her scribbling in her note pad. Her fingers were long, but the nails were short, not the useless painted talons like other women's. "How is it that you came to find him?"

"Uh." He snapped his concentration away from her fingers and back to her questions. "He didn't come into the office this morning, and he didn't call. That wasn't like him. His secretary was beside herself, because he had missed a client meeting. She couldn't get hold of him. I tried, too, and then I decided to come over." He paused to gather his wits. It was harder to talk about than he thought it would be.

"How did you get in?"

"I have a key, for emergencies, and I guess it's a good thing I do."

"Yes, it is." He liked how her voice remained low and matter-of-fact. It was soothing.

"Anyway, I was worried. I used my key when he didn't answer the doorbell. I…" His voice caught, and it was a struggle to continue. "I could tell as soon as I stepped into the entryway that he was dead. I followed the smell into the bedroom."

Kyle had to stop again, and he hated how weak he was being. Christ, he thought he was tougher than this. His father certainly would be disappointed if he could see how his son was choked up and nauseated over the memory of his mutilated friend. But he was. He had never seen anything like it, not even in the movies, because he never went for that sort of entertainment. He wanted to be stronger. He really did. He simply couldn't.

"Here." A glass of water appeared on the table beside his hands. He looked up into the detective's concerned face. He hadn't even noticed she'd gotten up he was so wrapped in his misery. "Have a few sips. It helps."

"Thanks," he whispered and did as she suggested. Once again, he tried to avoid staring at her. She was proving to be a distraction, and he needed to pull himself together to answer her questions. "Sorry," he said and was happy with how steady his voice had become. "I found Jazz on his bed. I knew enough not to go into the room and disturb any evidence, so I came back out here and called 911 on my mobile phone." He shrugged. "That's really all I can tell you. I mean, I have no idea who would do something this vile to him, or anyone."

"Was Mr. Bennington married?"

"Divorced, no children. God, someone should tell Felicity before she hears it on the news."

"We'll take care of notifying next of kin," the cop assured him. "Unless you are particularly close to Mr. Bennington's ex-wife?" The question was asked without innuendo.

Kyle shook his head. "No, not at all. I haven't spoken to her in the three years since they split up. She's friends with my ex, though." The admission surprised him. Why had he bothered to bring up Julie? Was he trying to tell this cop he was available? How crazy was that? She wasn't his type. He liked sophisticated, demure women, not an obvious ball-buster for all her compassion. And even if she were the kind of woman he went for, she was working a case, not angling for a date.

"Okay, Mr. Ramsey, let's back-up and talk about Mr. Bennington in terms of what happened prior to today."

He angled his head toward her. She was sucking on the end of her pen, riveting his eyes to her lips. They were free of lipstick, yet as bright and lush as any he had ever seen. "What do you mean?"

"I mean what can you tell me about your friend's social life? Was he seeing anyone?"

"No, no one lately. He hasn't actually dated seriously since the break-up."

"But when he does date, where does he go to meet women? What does he do to relax?"

Kyle struggled to come up with a useful answer. The truth was, he didn't know much about Jazz's sex life. "When he wanted to relax, he golfed with me. Other than that, he worked very hard. As partners at Mayberry, we keep very long hours. I suppose he met women the same places I do, through friends, at charity events, the occasional professional meeting, sometimes the health club."

"I see." She nodded and wrote, the pen going in and out of her mouth depending on whether she was speaking or he was. He couldn't bring himself to look away. "What kind of women was he attracted to?"

Kyle frowned. "I'm not sure what you're getting at, Sergeant. What does this have to do with his murder? You can't think a woman did that." The idea was ridiculous and repulsive. His friend had been tortured and mutilated.

The cop didn't answer right away. With pursed

lips, she gazed at him as if weighing her answer. Finally she said, "Actually, I do."

Flabbergasted, Kyle sat back in his seat. "With all due respect, Sergeant, that's crazy. How could a woman overpower him enough to tie him to the bed? Or do you think he was drugged?"

"We're looking into every possibility. But to be honest, because I really do hope you, as Mr. Bennington's close friend, have answers I desperately need to catch his killer, I believe he knew the woman who killed him. He either let her in or brought her here and allowed her to tie him up. Unfortunately for him, he didn't know at the time she planned on killing him."

"You're saying he was having kinky sex with her, and it got out of hand."

"It didn't get out of hand for her. She intended to kill him from the moment she met him, I'm betting." With a sigh, she crossed her arms on the table and leaned into him. "Look, Mr. Ramsey, I'm going to take the chance of telling you something I shouldn't, something confidential. Mr. Bennington appears to be the second victim of a killer who struck only two weeks ago."

The shock continued to grow. He could hardly take in the implication of the Sergeant's words. "Are you talking about a serial killer?"

"Yes, quite possibly."

"I can't believe it. And you still think it's a woman?"

"Yes, even though it's very rare for a woman to be a serial killer. It fits in this case."

"How so?"

"For one thing, all the evidence in both cases

points to compliance by the victim, at least initially, with the killer. Was your friend gay?"

"No!" The denial came out too forcefully, and Kyle realized it made him seem defensive when really it was a function of how overwhelmed he felt by the entire thing. "No," he repeated more evenly. "I've known Jazz since prep school. Nothing he ever did indicated he was gay, and he did a lot to demonstrate he wasn't. Besides that, we have another good friend who came out to us in college. So he knew he could have told me and it wouldn't have mattered."

She gave him a small smile he read as approval. "Fair enough. The other victim also appeared to be straight, so if neither victim was inclined to get naked and in bed with a man, it means the killer was a woman."

She stopped abruptly and gnawed at her lower lip. It drew his attention back to her lips, damn it all. He felt his body go hot, and even though his tie was already loosened, it was as if something were making it hard for him to get a decent breath.

"Go on, please," he choked out, in order to put his attention back where it belonged.

"There's something else."

He could sense her reluctance to continue. "Tell me," he urged, and without thinking, he leaned forward and placed his hand on her arm. All he got was a handful of soft leather, yet his cock pulsed in response to touching her. Her eyes widened, then narrowed again, and her cheeks flushed. Those ripe lips parted, and the point of a pink tongue darted out to wet the lower one. She stared at him for long seconds before pulling away from his grasp and standing.

"The other victim belonged to a certain type of club," she said in a breathless voice while she peeled away her jacket and tossed it on the chair she'd just vacated.

Kyle's gaze was immediately drawn to the hard nubs pushing out the thin fabric of her blouse. So, he wasn't the only one hot and bothered in the room.

"What kind of club?" He watched her pace the length of the table.

"A club where men can go for a little—discipline." She turned on her heel and gave him a pointed look.

"I'm not following you." Was she talking about a health club? He and Jazz belonged to the same one, and he couldn't remember his friend picking up a woman there recently, although it was possible, even likely.

"I guess that means Mr. Bennington never mentioned being a member of a special club, then." She was stopped, one hip cocked in a *fuck me* stance. At least, that was the message he was picking up.

"No, he didn't. You're being deliberately vague, Sergeant."

She quirked her lips. "Yes, I suppose I am." She walked toward him and placed her hands on the back of her chair. "Let me be blunt. Was your friend into the BDSM scene?"

"BDSM, as in bondage, discipline and sadomasochism?"

"That's right. Particularly, did Mr. Bennington enjoy being dominated and punished by women?"

Kyle laughed. He couldn't help it. The idea was so absurd he threw back his head and laughed out loud. The sound was almost a hysterical one given the raw emotions bubbling inside him. He managed to control himself, however, before it degenerated into a fit.

"Sorry, Sergeant, but you don't know how ridiculous your question is. Jazz was a brilliant litigator who tore his adversaries to shreds. He was ambitious and thrived on the kind of stress that would send most people screaming down the street. He was a born leader, too, and the type of guy who frankly always looked for women who needed to be taken care of. He liked being the strong one in a relationship. It was part of what broke up his marriage. He was overbearing. You're way off base with that idea."

"Mmm," was her reply. "Well, the other victim was described in much the same way. He was a banker, a little younger, and not as well established, yet very much cut from the same cloth. However, on his lunch breaks, at night, and on weekends, he frequented a club and went to private parties he found on the internet where he would strip down and let a woman first tie him up, then beat him up. Nothing too heavy, of course. The law frowns on this sort of thing even when it's consensual, at least with respect to the club. What happens in private is harder to track."

Outraged, Kyle shot to his feet, all concerns about his attraction gone, along with his nascent hard-on. Something had finally overridden his desire. "You are way out of line, here." His voice was hard and loud, and he didn't care. He had stood in horror, looking at his battered and bloody dead friend. He wasn't going to stand by while some cop implied that Jazz had asked for it.

"Calm down, please, Mr. Ramsey. I know this is hard to hear, but I need information in order to find the killer."

"You won't find him by thinking Jazz wanted to be tortured."

"Her," she corrected in a stern voice. "And I'm not saying Mr. Bennington agreed to what was done to him. To the contrary, I'm saying he may have had a need to be dominated by women, which was exploited by the killer. I'm not making any personal judgments about your friend's sex life."

"The hell you aren't." He took two steps around the table so he was mere inches from her. He tried to ignore the pull of her eyes and the smell of her heat. He really did try, and his failure stoked his temper. "I'm a lawyer, Sergeant, and as such I'm warning you to be very careful about the accusations you make about my friend."

She snorted contemptuously before gathering up her things. "Thank you for your time, Mr. Ramsey. This interview is now over, and you are free to go."

"That's it?"

"Yes, thank you," she said with emphasis. "We'll be in touch if we have any further questions." She turned and walked away.

"Wait a minute." he called after her.

She stopped and looked at him from over her shoulder. "What?"

"You're wrong about Jazz. He wasn't like that other guy, and if you pursue that angle thinking he was, you'll never find Jazz's killer."

"I appreciate your concern, Mr. Ramsey, but this is my job. I'm actually quite good at it."

"Not this time, Sergeant Malloy," he couldn't help saying. "And I won't stand idly by while my friend's killer runs free."

That got her attention. With a hard look, she said, "If you're suggesting you're going to involve yourself with this investigation, I would strongly advise against it."

Kyle folded his arms across his chest. With a sense of growing purpose, he felt stronger than he had since finding Jazz. "You know, Sergeant, you'll find I'm much like Jazz was. I don't take orders very well, and I don't take shit from anyone."

A teasing smile played across her lips. "Neither do I, Mr. Ramsey. Stay out of my case, or you'll discover just how little shit I do take and what I do to those who try to give it to me."

Kyle watched her walk away, down the hall toward the bedroom. His teeth clenched over her high-handed orders, and his hands curled into fists. He was determined to look into Jazz's death himself, because he was not intimidated in the least by Sergeant Malloy's threat. But he was something else. He was excited by it and that fact just made him angrier.

****

Less than an hour later, Kyle stormed into his condo, flung his keys on the counter, then stopped dead in his tracks. Overwhelming emotion, grief and anger, froze him to the spot. His body shook with the effort it took to keep himself under control before he realized he didn't have to anymore. Here in the safety of his private world, he could let go.

He hated living alone, apart from his daughters, his marriage broken beyond repair. But at that moment, he was glad no one was here to see him break down into the kind of tears he'd learned to suppress in early childhood. He bent at the waist and pressed the heels of his hands against his watery eyes. A sob ripped past his lips, and again, he was grateful to be alone in his misery.

Losing people he loved through old age, accident, and even illness was always hard. This was different. Murder was a kind of violation he'd never expected to deal with. Wrapping his head around the fact, accepting that Jazz was gone for good because someone chose to rob him of the rest of his life was impossible.

As Kyle stood, rocking with his grief, he fought to regain some semblance of rational thought. He wouldn't do Jazz any good falling apart. He told himself all of this, and yet the tears insisted on having their time to spill out and wring him dry.

Long minutes later, he was finally done. With shaky steps, he headed for the wet bar and poured a couple of fingers of scotch. He downed that quickly and refilled the glass before stumbling to the couch. He slouched bonelessly into the cushions, sipping the second drink even though he wanted to knock it back, too. Hollowed out as he felt from his crying jag, getting shitfaced and being hung-over the next day at work wasn't going to help his friend.

Neither would focusing on his residual anger at the cop in charge of the investigation. The woman had been infuriating, believing Jazz had conducted a kinky sex life that had led to his death. How dare she suggest such a thing? The pull of attraction he'd felt in her presence only served to add to his ire. She was flat out wrong in the direction she was heading, and he was an idiot for wanting her on any level.

With his head pressed against the back of the sofa, he pictured the last time he'd been with Jazz in this very room. They'd tied one on months ago when they had nothing better to do on a Saturday night. The evening had devolved into a bitch session, no other word for it, about their ex-wives, how much divorce sucked, and the difficulty of finding women to date or even just fuck given their heavy workload. Or, at least Kyle had complained about his dry spell. He'd also confessed to his best friend that the stress of the divorce and work was getting to him in a way it hadn't ever before.

Jazz had suddenly fished around his pants' pocket and handed him a business card. "I've got just the thing for you, my friend."

Kyle had reached for the card and narrowed his eyes to focus on the tiny writing in stark black against a snow white background. There was simply a name, an address, and a phone number. He raised his eyebrows.

"Club Nemesis? That's the goddess of divine retribution. So, what is this? A strip club or something? Not my style since college, you know that."

"Not a strip club. It's different," his friend had claimed with a sly, drunken grin. "When you get tired of being the big shot litigator, stop by. You'll sleep like a baby afterward, I promise."

Kyle had tossed the card aside dismissively when Jazz wouldn't divulge more. The memory of that night jarred him out of his miserable stupor. What had he done with the card? Reaching over to the side table, he yanked open the drawer. The card lay inside, slightly crinkled. Snatching it up, he studied it again with his more sober eyes. There still wasn't anything to indicate what the club was like or what relevance it might have. Yet a feeling grew in the pit of his stomach that this piece of information might be critical to solving Jazz's murder.

He should call the cop, Sergeant Malloy. Of course he should, but first he'd look into the club himself. He was a man who got things done, and at that moment, finding who killed his friend was paramount.

Chapter Two

"Hi, Pops." Regan sauntered into her father's living room and was gratified to see him sitting in his wheelchair watching television. There was something very comforting in this mundane predictability. It was especially true given the long, wretched day she'd had.

He turned the large wheels of his chair with the power of his massive arms in order to see her. "It's past ten, and I bet you skipped dinner again."

"Since when don't peanut butter crackers out of the vending machine chased down by a cold cup of coffee count as dinner?" she asked.

"Since it's your dinner we're talking about, not mine," her father retorted. Jack Malloy had been a cop for more than ten years before a drug dealer put him in that wheelchair while resisting arrest. "Lucky for you, I ordered take-out."

She had meant to only make a quick check on her father before going upstairs to her apartment on the second floor of his duplex, but the smell of Chinese food lured her into the room. "I suppose a few spring rolls and some sesame chicken wouldn't hurt." Sitting down on the sofa, she snatched up a carton and a pair of chopsticks to dig in. It was just what she needed. Bless her Pops.

Muting the TV with his remote, her father asked, "Got something big going on down at the station, have you?"

"A serial killer," she replied with a mouthful of food.

Her father's eyes went wide. "Christ, Jesus, you're not serious?" Unlike her mother's side or her cousins, the Callaghans, her father was recent to America, having immigrated as a child. He still had a bit of Irish in his voice.

When she nodded to indicate she was indeed serious, he shook his head in dismay, although a glimmer of excitement lit his eyes. It gave Regan great satisfaction, knowing her work added some meaning to her father's otherwise restricted life. With dead legs and a dead wife, he worked hard to keep active and interested in things and not wallow in the house.

"We haven't had such a thing around here since the Strangler. You're sure?"

Regan swallowed hard. "Why does everyone keep asking me that question?" Like her lieutenant. Fuller was a good cop and a good boss, but he was skeptical of her theories. "I'm as sure as I can be with only two victims. The M.O. for both murders is too similar and two bizarre for it to be anything else, unless we find a close connection between the vics to indicate it was directed solely at the two of them," she conceded.

No such tie between Morales and Bennington had been uncovered, however, and her gut told her one wouldn't be. Although the men were of a type, a rare type in her experience, they were too dissimilar to imply a personal relationship between them.

Her father pursed his lips and nodded gravely "There'll be hell to pay when it gets out. I still hear talk of how frightened women in this city were fifty years ago."

Regan bit a spring roll in half, chewed, and swallowed. "Well, this time women appear to be perfectly safe."

"Ah, crap, are we talking little boys, then?"

"No, grown men, and Pops, the killer is a woman." She grinned at her father's astonishment and quickly filled him in on her theory.

"What kind of man wants a woman to hit him?" he mused.

She had been wondering the same thing since Morales' death, and she had no real answer yet. It was simply kink as far as she could tell. The images of her two victims popped up in Regan's head, and because their killer had been careful not to touch their faces, they remained as gorgeous in death as they had been in life. She would have been happy to let either of them into her bed and into her body. Would she have been willing to tie them up and hit them, too? Sure, she felt a little thrill every once in a while when she took down some punk on the street, but this was different. It was cold-blooded—no, make that hot-blooded—and supposedly arousing.

No, she couldn't quite imagine herself doing it. That is, until another image came to mind. Kyle Ramsey, a man in need of a good spanking in her estimation. He was too arrogant and handsome for his own good, or hers. And gorgeous was only the half of it.

There was something intoxicating about that man. She had sat and interviewed him like she would any other witness, and yet all she really wanted to do was toss her notepad and pen away, strip off her clothes, and straddle his body. She had been so wet when she returned to the station that she changed into spare panties and jeans she kept in her locker.

Thinking about him again was having the same effect, which was really gross considering her father was sitting only a few feet away. She gulped down the rest of her food, telling herself that chopsticks in no way represented a Freudian cock before she answered her father's question.

"I have no idea, but JoJo uncovered the best lead we have. Both victims belonged to a club that caters to this type of fetish. I already interviewed the woman who runs it in connection with the first murder and came up with nothing helpful. This time, I'm going in strong and hard. It's got to be the connection we're looking for. For all we know, the killer works there."

"Sounds about right. You want some ice cream?" he asked as she started clearing the empty boxes and left-over food.

"No, thanks," she said with a smile.

"You're too skinny, you know."

"I have to be to chase punks," was her teasing reply. "I'm going to dump these in the kitchen before heading up. Do you need anything, Pops?"

"Nothing, thanks, darlin'."

"See you tomorrow, then." She pressed a quick kiss on her father's head when she passed him.

It wasn't cool, living above her father in Charlestown, her old Boston neighborhood. She had grown up in the duplex, although in a small room in the downstairs apartment where her father stilled resided. Now she occupied the rental part that had helped her parents make the mortgage payments for many years.

Not that she was technically a tenant, because her father refused to accept rent. He didn't need it, he said, and she knew it was true. Her mother's life insurance policy had paid off the last of the home debt.

No, there was nothing fun or sexy about where she lived, and bringing guys home was always tricky. What a good thing it was, then, that she had so little time for what amounted to a pathetic love life. Being a cop was her first and only love, anyway, the one thing she had wanted since she was a little girl.

As an only child, she had been the center of her parents' world, and she had worshipped her father. She still did. Her mother's sister had lived a block away with her cop husband and their three boys. Daire, Ronan, and Finn had treated her as not just an honorary sister but an honorary brother, too. Aunt Sheila and Uncle Rory were gone, cut down in a double murder that still remained unsolved despite her cousins' efforts. Ronan and Finn had started their own families, albeit a hair unconventional ones. Daire still rattled around in his boyhood home, so Regan didn't feel terribly odd living above her father.

Helping her father to get along, now that her mother was no longer around to do it, was no great hardship. It was more than duty. It was devotion, and if at the age of thirty, she was beginning to feel the lack of a husband and children, she only had to remind herself of how getting home at ten o'clock was not an unusual occurrence in her life. There wasn't time for love and family.

There was time for sex, though, she reminded herself as she stripped off her clothes, washed her face, and brushed her teeth. There were enough nights when she went home with a guy or brought one back with her to keep her itch scratched. She had even had several relationships, although work had always strangled them dead. It didn't matter. None of those nice, young men had really satisfied her. There was always something lacking, although she couldn't really say what it was.

Sitting on the edge of her bed, Regan opened the bottom drawer of her night stand. Here was where she kept those men that truly satisfied her. They had beautiful faces and perfect bodies and were absolutely silent. She picked up her tablet, an expensive treat that allowed her to see thousands of men at the mere touch of buttons. She pulled up a relatively new image of a beefy blond lying naked on the beach. She hummed her approval and dipped one hand down her stomach to the junction of her thighs.

As late as it was, Regan wanted to take her time. She studied the model and let her fingers play lightly on the outside of her panties. They were already wet, because she was wet. It seemed as if she had been wet the entire day. She made lazy circles with her middle finger, pushing it just a tad between the slick folds.

She let her fantasy begin, imagining that she was touching not herself but the man in the picture. With her eyes half-closed, she could hear the sound of the ocean crashing against the shore and smell the salt water. In her mind, she was there, lying next to him, the sand rough against her skin. She started with his hair, she always started there, grasping and tugging the blond locks. Blond. She loved blond. It was rare and beautiful. You could get a man's attention by anchoring your fingers through the strands and yanking back to make him look you in the eye. She imagined her fantasy man doing just that, giving her a look of invitation when his gaze met hers.

Yet there was only so much fun to be had with hair, so her fingers disentangled themselves, slid around his jaw and down his neck to his pecs. She liked a smooth, rock-hard chest and ran the pads of her fingertips back and forth across it, the skin slick from suntan lotion. It was silly for men to have nipples, of course, but they were there, so why not play with them? A caress, a tweak, a nip with her teeth. She loved the look on a man's face when he realized she could arouse him with his nipples. Pressing her finger in to flick at her clit, she imagined she was doing just that.

Regan's breath sped up, and her own breasts tingled with anticipation. Her legs moved restlessly with mounting need. Not yet, it was happening too fast, although there was a limit to teasing herself. She dug her finger in deeper, still separated from her sensitive nub by the layer of cotton, and picked up the pace. In her mind, her hand was on the move down, down, over the abs. Nice but not overly exciting. The good stuff was still to come.

The pubic hair, blond like the head—she liked her men natural—was crisp. She gave it a quick tug and smiled when the man winced. And now she was where she wanted to be, stroking the long, thick cock while massaging the satiny balls. The cock started out soft, so she squeezed and tugged until it sprang up hard and ready for her. The turgid flesh pulsed in her hand as if it were breathing on its own.

Regan moaned and thrust her hips in imitation of the movement of the man's rod. Her fingers slid up and under the waistband of her panties, the desire to touch her own flesh too strong to resist. Oh, yes, she was slick and hot, and her clit welcomed the assault. It begged for more, for harder, for faster. She wasn't going to deny herself much longer, but she still had more to conjure in her fantasy to make it good.

What should it be? Should she suck the tempting cock into her mouth? Should she straddle his prone body and take him inside her cunt? Regan looked at the man's face for inspiration, and damn, it changed. It was no longer the no name stranger, but Kyle Ramsey, and he was wearing that condemning look he had when he accused her of botching the investigation.

"Uh!" she cried out as much from the jolt of pleasure tearing through her as from the sense of outrage that this man should invade her private fantasy.

And yet, the image didn't fade. Dropping the tablet, Regan sunk into her pillows with her eyes closed. The beach scene was gone from her mind. She was back in the Bennington apartment glaring at Kyle. He was challenging her with his eyes, and she was furious with him.

Her fingers picked up their pace.

The man needed a lesson. He needed to show respect. Without further thought, she grabbed his arm and shoved him around, pressing him against the dining table. His gasp of surprise elicited a satisfying grin from her. She noticed as well that he wasn't fighting her. He wasn't trying to use his superior strength to stop her from controlling him. It was because he knew he'd been bad, she thought with glee. He knew he needed to be punished.

Her fingers were drenched now with her own juices. They were slipping around her clit, sending sharp jolts of pleasure shooting up her abdomen.

She lifted the end of his suit jacket, sorry she hadn't yanked it off him. No matter, she merely wished it and all his other clothes away. Naked, he was as perfect as any of the younger men she ogled in her magazines, with rippling muscles down his back, a high, tight ass, and thick, corded legs. His balls, hanging long and loose, peeked out from between his thighs.

She was desperate to get her hands on him. "You've been a bad boy, Kyle, haven't you," she taunted.

"Yes," he hissed out.

She brought the flat of her hand down squarely on his ass. "Yes, what?"

"Yes, ma'am." She could hear the excitement in his voice. He wanted this, and she would give it to him.

Regan's back arched as she pictured smacking him again. His buttocks quivered against the strike, and he breathed out a low gasp. But he didn't move. He didn't try to avoid her harsh touch. He bore it all with respectful courage. Her flesh tingled, in her palm and between her legs. She did it again and again. The only sounds were her flesh meeting his and their harsh breathing. They were in sync, in and out, faster and faster, as Regan spanked Kyle over and over, her fingers gyrating wildly against her clit, the tension mounting until…

With a final jerk of her hips, Regan exploded in climax, every muscle in her body twitching. She whimpered her pleasure, biting her lower lip as her back arched off the bed. Her fingers played out the orgasm until her sensitive folds cried for her to stop.

She lay spent, satisfied, and a little disturbed.

Holy shit, maybe she did understand this kind of kink, after all.

****

Regan slurped down a heavy dose of her morning coffee, ignoring the burning of her tongue. The cool of the fall had set in enough to switch over to the hot stuff. "You want to say that again, please, Lieutenant?"

"What part of 'get inside that club' didn't you understand, Sergeant?" Lieutenant Fuller was a no-nonsense kind of guy, good at his job, and decent to work under. He gave Regan his "I mean business" look.

She couldn't blame the guy for his lack of patience this morning. As JoJo had related it, the mayor had sent the shit rolling downward early in the morning. It had bounced off Commissioner Finnegan, beaned Captain Maher as she walked into work, and now it sat square in the middle of the lieutenant's office. Apparently the idea that wealthy, powerful men, even those with a weird sex life, were being targeted potentially by a serial killer was giving the higher-ups fits. They wanted the Morales and Bennington murders solved immediately, as in yesterday.

Regan squirmed at the idea of what she was about to have to do to shovel the shit out of her way. "You do know, LT, that there are only two kinds of people at that club, masochistic men and the women who work them over."

"I get that point, Malloy," the man snapped back. "But as this club is the only known common denominator for the two victims, it makes sense for someone to go undercover and see what she can turn up. If nothing else, it will give you a better sense of this

31

subculture, and if no one at the club is involved, then maybe you'll gain useful information that will help you find leads elsewhere."

Regan took another gulp of her coffee before responding. "It does make the most sense. I interviewed the proprietor after the Morales murder, and she was eager to be helpful. The last thing she wants is for the police to start hassling her. What she does is barely legal." She grimaced. "The idea of paddling strangers while rigged up as some sadistic Playboy Bunny is still hard to imagine."

"If you're uncomfortable with the assignment, Malloy, you can always have Mathers go in instead. You're the lead investigator, after all. However you want to play it is fine with me."

Regan's partner choked on a mouthful of her Coke. JoJo was a diet Coke drinker twenty-four/seven regardless of the weather. She looked back at Regan with pleading eyes. Regan shook her head with a smile. "No, that's okay. Detective Mathers is a married woman. I think this is best handled by me."

"Fine," Fuller replied.

"What if the club's owner is the killer?" JoJo threw out, looking relaxed now that she was off the hook.

"I don't think she is," Regan said. "Because I remember she's left-handed and the coroner said the throats were slit by a right-handed person.

JoJo dismissed that observation with a wave of her hand. "Everybody watches TV these days. If I were a left-handed killer, I'd deliberately use my right hand to throw the police off the scent."

"Let's hope the killer hasn't seen the same shows as you," Regan replied with a frown. "Anyway, I have to figure all the women working there are going to tumble to who I am pretty quick. The best I can hope for is to flush the killer out by my very presence."

"You're probably right," the lieutenant agreed. "But we have to try. If we are dealing with a serial killer, and I'm still not convinced of that yet, then two dead men in two weeks is pretty quick work. Either she's been killing for a while across the country without anyone figuring out the pattern, or she's new and escalating far faster than the average psycho. However it may be, if she's picked our city to make a stand, we have to bring her down, hopefully before she kills again."

"We'll do our best, sir," Regan assured her boss.

"I know you will, and to help out on the psychological side, I want Mathers to find us an expert in this area."

"You want an FBI profiler, LT?" JoJo asked.

The guy shook his head. "No, I mean someone, a psychologist maybe, who has a handle on this whole Femdom thing. We need to know what was going on inside the victims' heads and the killer's."

Regan winced at the idea. She wasn't sure she ever wanted to know, especially after her bedtime equivalent of warm milk the previous night. The memory of it made her flare up with unwanted heat and longing. If she wasn't careful, she'd end up with more wet panties. Time for a figurative cold shower. Time for a visit to Club Nemesis.

****

"I don't like this idea at all." Veronica Pugh had an unfortunate name, but she was a striking, almost elegant, woman, and Regan imagined she still turned men's heads even pushing sixty.

"I understand your reluctance, Ms. Pugh, and believe me I'm not too keen on the idea myself. However, this is the best strategy we have right now, and I'm sure you'll agree it beats all hell out of another one of your clients getting murdered."

From where she sat behind her desk, Veronica frowned. "You're right, of course, and I suppose if I don't agree, you'll be all over this place driving business away and generally making my life hell."

Regan cocked her head a bit. "Well, you do tend to skirt the law a tad."

"This is not prostitution. There's no sex involved, and if what we do here is illegal, then you better lock up every parent who spanks their child."

"We actually do lock some of those people up. Besides, if it's that benign, then you should have no problem with my playing at being, what do you call it, a Mistress?"

"Hey, being a Mistress isn't as easy as you think. The reason it is benign is because my women are highly trained professionals. They know how to chastise their clients without hurting them. I'm concerned about the liability of having a novice operate here."

"Don't worry about that. I'm a cop. Restraining people without doing serious damage is part of my training, too. I know how to pull my punches."

"Huh!" Veronica seemed less than convinced, but she really had no choice, and she was a smart enough business person to realize it. "I can't guarantee your cover won't be blown. It's hard to keep secrets around here, and pretty much every professional in this scene knows each other."

"I understand," Regan assured her. "I can be your cousin from Paducah if you want. I need to spend some time checking out both the women and their clients."

"None of my gals is a killer."

"You know them all so well? They've all been close friends of yours for years?"

"Yeah, yeah, I get it. Mistresses come and Mistresses go, so you'll check everyone out— discreetly?" When Regan nodded, the other woman continued. "You'll need a name and an outfit. We'll go next door to my adult toy shop for the clothes. I assume the police department will reimburse me for the costs."

"Yes," Regan confirmed in a neutral tone, although she was already cringing at the thought of filling out the requisition papers.

"What are you going to call yourself?"

"Mistress Regan?" she offered.

Veronica shrugged. "Mistress Regan it is."

Within a few minutes, a reluctant Regan stood in Veronica's naughty shop, and the older woman was rummaging through the racks of clothes she kept on the back wall to outfit the new Mistress Regan.

"With your hair, you could get away with red, but I think basic black will suit you just as well." So saying, Veronica held up a black leather dress. The thing was more laces than material, leaving the front, back, and sides exposed. There were even laces on the sleeves. It didn't take much imagination to realize quite a lot of Regan would be exposed. The get-up was clearly designed to entice a man.

"If I'm supposed to be dominant, how come I'm dressed for his pleasure? Shouldn't I try to remind him of his mother or something?"

Veronica rolled her eyes. "You know nothing about this."

"That's true. Educate me." Regan folded her arms across her chest.

"You're dressed to excite him, because this is about his fantasy, not yours. Our clients want strong and sexy women to dominate them. They come in here during or after busy days where they're often responsible for other people, other people's money, and sometimes other people's very lives. They have to make hard decisions and deal with tremendous stress. All they want is some time when they don't have to be the strong one. They're looking for absolution, if you will, but they don't want it from someone who looks like their mother—mostly," she conceded. "Besides, they're going to be either naked or stripped down to their skivvies. Humiliation is part of the scene for them."

"Great," Regan replied, suppressing revulsion over the idea of seeing so much of her future clients. She was pretty sure few of them were going to look like her magazine models, although the killer's victims certainly had. "I still don't understand why they want this."

"You don't have to. Just try this on."

Veronica shoved the dress in Regan's hands and showed her the dressing room. The leather was surprisingly thin and supple, and while it was tight and made her breasts pop out in an alarming fashion, there was no denying it made her feel feminine as well as sexy. Standing in front of a full-length mirror, she gave a little twirl and was pleased with the way the tea-length material cut on the bias flowed around her legs.

There was more, of course. Veronica gave her

black fishnet stockings and black knee-high leather boots with three inch stiletto heels. Regan wore nothing but flat, comfortable shoes on all but the nicest occasions.

As she tottered around the store, she wondered if her *clients* would be happy if she fell on them as punishment. Even small details were attended to by the club owner. Regan's short hair was slicked back and dramatic make-up was applied. The other woman went so far as to glue long, fake talons in blood red to Regan's short nails.

It took over an hour, and when she was done, Veronica stood and stared Regan up and down. "Wow, did you miss your calling, honey. You look fabulous, a natural born Mistress."

Regan couldn't help grinning over the compliment. She looked at herself in the full-length mirror and couldn't believe the exotic creature staring back was actually her. Casual and comfortable was her typical style, and yet the tight, curve-hugging dress felt good, very good. It moved with her like a second skin, and even she could see how hot she looked in it. The thin leather allowed her hard nipples to jut out, and their state had nothing to do with the temperature of the store. A small drop of dew tickled her inner thigh, because the dress didn't allow for underwear. She felt wicked.

But there was more. Being a cop meant feeling strong, confident, and powerful. The badge and gun she normally carried were part of that, as were the muscles she worked hard to keep toned and cut and the kempo karate she practiced. And yet, this was different. There was power in these clothes. She felt as if she could control a man with simply a look when dressed this way.

"You look like a Mistress, but you have to learn to act like one, too," Veronica observed.

"I have no problem giving orders," Regan assured her, unable to stop looking at herself in the mirror.

Veronica snorted. "I bet. There's more to it, though, as you well know. We have a variety of instruments we use for chastisement." She held up a riding crop.

Regan didn't take it right away. She stared at the thing, wanting to giggle almost at the clichéd absurdity of it all. But eventually, she took it from Veronica and weighed it in the palm of her hand. It was fairly light to hold, although it was made of a stiff leather. It would certainly hurt far more than a spanking. She wondered if, when it came down to it, she could inflict this type of pain.

"Try it," Veronica urged in a low voice.

Regan slashed the crop down in an arc and was startled by the satisfying sing it made. She swept it up and down once more. Then she smacked it against the side of one boot, and the sting of it heated her blood and made her breath quicken. Her reaction was not because she enjoyed the pain, but because she now had a sense of what she could do with it to someone else. To a man.

Mistress Regan was born.

Chapter Three

Kyle paced along the sidewalk in front of Club Nemesis, trying to work up the nerve to go in. Christ, what was wrong with him? He was usually decisive and almost fearless, when it came to business anyway. He had a plan of action, carefully thought out, at least as carefully as anything could be with his grief still raw and his mind numb from shock.

Jazz was dead, and the sexy, aggressive cop had been right. His friend had been into female domination.

After a horrid night filled with nightmares of finding Jazz's body laced disturbingly with sexy images of the cop, Kyle had called the number on the card Jazz had given him. One phone call filled with cryptic answers to his careful questioning left him in no doubt as to the kind of service provided at this club.

It was located in what was left of the old Boston Combat Zone, a corner of Chinatown that had traditionally housed lots of strip clubs and adult bookstores. Civic pride had cleaned up most of it, but it was still a part of town where one could spend a mostly legal, yet morally iffy, time.

Kyle stopped in front of the club's door, determined to go in and find out what was going on. He owed it to Jazz, although there was this little nagging part of his mind that kept telling him he should have called Sergeant Ball-buster immediately with what level, he would have. As it was, he wasn't sure he wanted another encounter with her. Not only had she left him seething with anger, she had also left him aching with want and need. An unpleasant combination and one he didn't want to repeat.

Tamping down his doubts, Kyle entered the club and found himself in a fairly sedate and nondescript reception room. It looked not unlike his dentist's office with several chairs, tables and magazines. Only a quick glance at the reading material told him he wasn't going to find Golf Digest or Sports Illustrated in this place. At the far end sat a young woman with white-blonde hair pulled back in a ponytail. She looked young and innocent, and she smiled up at him.

"May I help you, sir?" she asked.

Suddenly, Kyle wondered if he was wrong about this place. Could it really be some kind of kinky sex club? Besides her fresh-faced look, the receptionist had on what looked like a suit jacket with a crisp white blouse underneath. She certainly didn't fit his vision of a Dominatrix. He cleared his voice discreetly as he approached her.

"Yes, I hope so," he replied using the confident and commanding tone he had cultivated in his career. He was used to being in charge, and he wasn't going to let the unknown of this establishment throw him. Stopping in front of the desk, he cleared his throat again, this time for effect, as if he were slightly embarrassed to be there, which of course wasn't entirely untrue. He gave a deliberately charming smile back at the young woman. "A friend of mine recommended I obtain a membership

40

in Club Nemesis." He paused. "I hope I'm in the right place."

"Oh, yes," the receptionist was quick to assure him. "Mr.…"

"Ramsey, Kyle Ramsey." He had decided to use his real name, because he knew it was good enough to get him admitted into any club, and he wasn't going to take any chances in that regard. Besides, this type of business had to be discreet, so he was reasonably sure no one he cared about would find out. After all, he wouldn't have known about Jazz if he hadn't handed over the card in the first place.

"Well, Mr. Ramsey, if you'd please have a seat, I'll let Mistress Veronica know you're here. She'll be happy to help you explore whether Nemesis is the right club for you."

"Thank you," he replied before taking a seat. Because the waiting area was a few feet from the reception desk, he couldn't quite hear what the woman said into the phone the moment he turned his back on her. He assumed she was talking to Mistress Veronica, and he wanted to snicker over the cheesy name of what he assumed was the manager or maybe owner of the club. But there was nothing funny about a mutilated Jazz lying in the morgue this morning, and whatever had happened to him, Kyle believed it had to do with this sick place. No matter what kind of bizarre fantasy experience Mistress Veronica was selling, he intended to buy it.

The magazine lying on the table in front of him was like something one might see in a spoof of kinky lifestyles. A burly man wearing a leather harness was genuflecting on the floor, arms tied behind his back, while a black woman in a red leather bustier stood with her booted foot resting on the back of his neck. The look on the woman's face was one of a conqueror, and despite the picture's obvious staging, Kyle felt his cock stir.

What the fuck's the matter with you? And yet his body continued to respond to the idea of a dominant woman.

His chest rose and fell in a deep breath, his eyes riveted to the scene, and only the sound of a door opening took his attention away. Looking up, he saw an older woman, conservatively, yet provocatively, dressed in a mini-skirted business suit, standing in an inner doorway.

"Mr. Ramsey?" She greeted him with a warm look that managed to make him feel welcome.

Standing, he gave a curt nod. "Yes. You're Mistress Veronica?" He couldn't help the tinge of irony in his voice.

The woman apparently detected it, because she gave him an understanding grin. "Welcome to Club Nemesis, Mr. Ramsey. Please come into my office while we discuss your needs."

She escorted him through the door, down a short hallway, and into her office. Like the reception area, it was nothing unusual. He took a seat in one of the visitor chairs after Veronica sat down behind her utilitarian desk. He crossed his legs and waited for her to start the ball rolling.

Obviously used to men having trouble asking her for what they wanted, she started up almost immediately. "I understand a friend recommended us to you. May I ask who?"

"I'd rather not say, actually," he demurred.

"Of course. However, did this friend explain the nature of our services?" Veronica raised her eyebrows in question.

Kyle took a deep breath and let it out slowly. "Well, he said this was a good place to let loose. You see, I'm a litigator, a partner actually in a large firm here in Boston. My days are filled with tremendous stress. I have to make decisions and take responsibility if they're wrong. It wears on my nerves after a while. I need an outlet. Somewhere I can go and leave the decisions to someone else." He was making it up as he spoke, not really understanding what this lifestyle was all about.

One thing was for sure, though, the anticipation of what he was about to get into was having a stimulating effect on his body. As with looking at the magazine, he found he was becoming aroused, the blood flowing into his cock, making it turgid. He shifted in telltale fashion, unhooking his legs and tugging a bit at his pants with one hand. The movement was not lost on Veronica.

"If you need to relax, there are places where you can get a good massage," she observed with a sly look. "This is not that kind of place."

"I know," he was quick to assure her. "I'm not looking for relaxation so much as correction, absolution, if you will. I need someone to punish me, so that I can live with whatever mistakes I might have made." God, was he saying this right? Was this what men came here for? He didn't know. How could he? He was getting so far beyond what he had ever imagined doing.

It was the right thing to say, apparently. With a

sympathetic nod, Veronica said, "I believe we can help you, Mr. Ramsey. The women who work here understand what your feelings are and want to help you. There are strict ground rules, of course, and we do have a rather steep membership fee."

"Money isn't a problem," he replied.

"Good." She paused a second before continuing. "As it happens, we have a new Mistress, Mistress Regan. Because she hasn't had time to book out her appointments with our members, she's free to give you a session now if you'd like."

If he'd like? Kyle's stomach lurched at the idea. He still wasn't sure what they did here, but he was certain some amount of pain was involved. He worried he couldn't hack it. Although he was used to the kind of discomfort that came from sports injuries, he suspected this would be different—the deliberate and sustained infliction of pain. Could he withstand it without getting angry and giving up?

The memory of Jazz face down on his bed covered in blood hardened Kyle's resolve. And he couldn't deny his cock had gone hard with anticipation. It throbbed within the relatively rough confines of his cotton boxers, demanding to know what the provocatively named Mistress Regan had in store for it.

"Yes," he finally said. "I'd like that very much."

Mistress Veronica couldn't hide her enthusiasm. "Excellent. Now if we could just get the financials out of the way first?"

****

Within thirty minutes, Kyle was rethinking the sanity of his decision. It wasn't the outrageous amount of money he had allowed to be charged to his credit card. He had expected this kind of kink to be expensive, and he hadn't lied when he said money wasn't an issue. No, it was the fact that he was kneeling painfully on a cold tile floor, arms pulled up straight over his head with wrists manacled and wearing nothing more than his boxers.

He was well and truly trussed, although he hoped he wasn't well and truly fucked, as in over his head pain-wise. Not to mention how two men were now dead, having been bound in this way by a sadistic woman. But, no, that was different. They had been tortured and killed at home. This was a business. No one was going to kill him here, but if he was smart and lucky, he might learn who was moonlighting as a serial killer.

Lifting one knee, he winced at the pain already setting in with this vulnerable position. The tether that held his manacled wrists was attached to the ceiling, but it was some sort of soft cord, allowing him if he wished to simply stand up. Mistress Veronica had told him in a stern voice, however, that he was to stay on his knees or risk worse punishment from his Mistress for disobedience. She had suggested this little *scene* as she called it. It was a nice way of introducing him to what he wanted, she insisted, because it gave him some freedom of movement should the session become too intense. Maybe. He wasn't convinced, and he had yet to meet his Mistress Regan, either.

He felt foolish, to be frank. Flexing his arm muscles, he tested the strength of his confinement for the third time, and confirmed once again he was indeed incapable of freeing himself from the tether, his ability to get to his feet notwithstanding. This was no joke. He was really at this mystery woman's mercy. What would she do to him? There was an alarming array of punishment items hanging against the wall—whips, straps, and the like.

A shudder went through him, although it wasn't entirely unpleasant. There was still a frisson of excitement running through his veins, and his erection strained against his underwear. Despite his lack of clothing, his skin felt hot. His heart pounded, and when the door opened, his breath froze.

Regan hesitated, her hand on the door handle, a sliver of the punishment chamber visible through the opening she had just created. It was show time, and she wasn't sure she was up for it. Veronica had said not to worry. The guy trussed up in this room was as big a neophyte as she was. He would have no idea whether she was a good Dominatrix or a bad one, and so long as Regan didn't hurt him, Veronica was perfectly willing to let them bust their Femdom cherries with each other.

Okay, you can do this. It's the job. You always do the job whatever it entails.

With that litany of duty recited in her head, Regan pushed the door all the way open and gasped with surprise, which quickly turned to fury. She entered the room and slammed the door shut behind her, and all the while, her eyes pierced Kyle Ramsey with her displeasure. Her gaze remained locked with his as she approached. Her stilettos made a menacing clack against the hard floor.

"Shit," he muttered.

Shit, indeed. So this was her unnamed client. Veronica said it was up to Regan to establish how she would address the man, and said clients often gave a fake name during the session, anyway. Regan would never have guessed that this arrogant man, who had insisted she was way off base looking into Femdom for the murderer, was the one waiting for her. The obvious question was whether he had lied about what he knew, or had he found out something about the club after the murder and decided to look into it himself. Either way, he was pissing her off royally, and her only consolation was her dominance over him—at least for the moment.

Ramsey's eyes showed his shock at her appearance. He watched her walk toward him with wariness. She found the look satisfying. She also appreciated the vision the rest of his body presented her. Dressed, the man was physically impressive. Naked, the man was magnificent, and he wasn't even completely naked. But what she could see caused the anger to take a back seat to desire.

Long and lean, every muscle in his body was well-developed and clearly delineated. His corded forearms strained against his restraint, a sign of his agitation, she assumed. She liked the idea that her presence unnerved him. His skin glowed a healthy amber color under the soft lights of the room, and there was a slight sheen to his chest, as if he had broken out in a sweat. Even better. Best of all, though, was how his shorts tented in front, telling her he had conflicted feelings about the circumstances.

Good. So she wasn't the only one who suffered from an inappropriate case of the hots.

As she walked toward him, he struggled to stand. She realized, with a quick appraisal of his bindings, that he could and decided she better take charge of the situation and keep him in his place. If anyone other than

Veronica was watching, she needed to act the part of a real Dominatrix, and besides, the condescending bastard deserved it. She quickened her pace and, placing the ball of one foot at the back of his closest knee, pushed him down again before he could get all the way up.

With a grunt, Kyle slammed to the floor. "Son-of-a-bitch!"

"I didn't give you permission to stand, boy-o," Regan said in her best imitation of her father. When he whipped his head around and looked like he was going to argue with her, she made another preemptive strike by squatting down beside him and grabbing a fistful of hair. "You weren't planning on speaking where you?" She tugged a little, just enough to get his attention. "Because I didn't give you permission to speak, either, boy-o."

"My name is Kyle," he said through gritted teeth. The look in his eyes was murderous, but they didn't stay focused on hers for long. Instead, they flicked to her cleavage in typical male knee-jerk reaction.

"Like what you see?" she asked in a purring tone that was meant to bait. "Of course, you do."

With her free hand, she reached over and gripped his rigid cock through his shorts. The quick intake of his breath encouraged her to squeeze the thick, hard length all the way up to the tip. It felt good in her hand, and she could only imagine how good it would feel inside her, filling her completely, rubbing against her sensitive tissues, sending her up and over into ecstasy.

Regan almost moaned at the thought, but she didn't. She couldn't let Kyle see how much he affected her. It was her job to dominate him, and if he was going to be stupid and arrogant enough to put himself into this situation, she was going to make damn sure he appreciated the seriousness of it.

"I asked you a question. You will speak when spoken to." To emphasize her words, she tugged again on his hair and dug her fake claws into his cock.

This time, Kyle hissed in obvious pain. The sound gave Regan a thrill, and she grinned at him. "Careful how you answer me, boy-o. Remember, this is what you wanted."

She meant it as an admonition that he apparently had come to this club to search for answers to his friend's murder and therefore couldn't complain about her treatment of him. If he wanted to keep his connection to the killing secret from the potential murderer, he had to play along with Mistress Regan. She could see by his expression the moment he understood her meaning. Good, she did like a smart man.

"Yes, ma'am," he replied carefully.

For a few seconds, he held her gaze before lowering his eyes in a submissive fashion. He wasn't fooling her, however. She knew he was putting on an act by the hard set of his jaw and his fixed stare. His smooth, gleaming chest rose and fell just a little too hard for a relaxed person.

Nevertheless, and this was the interesting part, his erection remained hard and hot in her hand. Before standing up again, Regan gave the delicious member a teasing stroke. Kyle moaned and closed his eyes, his body leaning into her grip. The blatant request jolted her, because it suddenly occurred to her that she had crossed a line. She was a cop not a Dominatrix, and besides, this was not a massage parlor. She wasn't supposed to be jerking him off, even if it were for her pleasure as well as his.

Regan let go of Kyle and pushed back from him, teetering on her high heels. Running her fingers through her hair, she pulled herself together and recaptured her professional detachment. She was letting it get personal, and that was the biggest mistake a cop could make. She was on the job and needed to remember that fact even when faced with a temptation as great as Kyle Ramsey was proving to be.

She gave the man a stern look, something lost on him because he was still staring at the floor, and laid out the rules the way Veronica had taught her. "I am Mistress Regan. You will call me that or simply Mistress or ma'am, as you did. You will not speak unless I ask a direct question or give you specific permission to ask a question of your own. Is that clear?"

There was a distinct pause before he replied in a low voice tinged with both passion and sarcasm. "Yes, *Mistress.*"

She let the show of ego slide. If this was his first time as a submissive male, he must find the scene more than a little unnerving. She did, and this was only a show for whoever might be watching. It wasn't as if she were going to learn anything useful from the man. At least, she didn't think so. Perhaps he knew more than he had let on the previous night.

"Good," she continued. "Now, you're here to be chastised by me. I get to decide how and when and for how long your punishment occurs. That is my job, not yours. You have no power here and no responsibility, so you can relax, let go."

She was going on a gut level again, mimicking the idea behind Club Nemesis as told to her by Veronica. As she spoke, she paced back and forth in front of Kyle with her hands resting on her hips. The soft leather of her dress was like butter to her fingertips, and the roughness of her fishnet stockings rubbed against her inner thighs with each step. The combination of soothing and agitating left her hot and wet.

"However," she went on, determined to ignore her burgeoning lust. "Because this is all for your benefit, we don't want you to endure more than you're able to. Therefore, you're going to give me a word, something unusual, something you wouldn't ordinarily say even when extremely stressed. When you say this word, I'll know you really want me to stop."

Long seconds ticked by without a response. Regan stopped her pacing and with legs braced apart, she stood in front of her *client* waiting for an answer. Slowly, ever so slowly, Kyle lifted his eyes from the floor. They traveled up the length of her body starting with her pointy-toed boots and pausing at her breasts before reaching her eyes. There was insolent admiration in his gaze and more, a challenge. He ran his tongue across his lower lip in blatant sexual interest. "Yellow. That's the word I choose, Mistress Regan, although I promise you you'll never hear me say it."

Regan ignored the thrill she felt at his use of her name and worked to make her tone match his confident one. "Really? Well, we'll see about that, won't we?"

Turning on one heel, she walked to the wall where the various instruments of punishment hung. She made sure to put a lot of swing in her hips and dangled a forefinger from her mouth as she contemplated her choices. She angled her body, too, so that Kyle had a good view of her provocative pose.

"Hmm," she murmured, as if to herself. "So many possibilities." She pulled her finger from her mouth and caressed a riding crop with the wet digit. "This might be interesting." She shook her head. "No, not this time. It would be too harsh for a virgin." She tossed a smirk at Kyle over her shoulder and grinned widely when she saw the scowl on his face.

Turning back to the wall again, she made her selection based on what she'd found to her liking during her compressed lessons from Veronica. The short, flexible strap was only a little wider than a man's belt, and when she slapped it against her own thigh, it made a satisfying crack without yielding more than a nasty sting. It would do nicely.

Regan played out the trip back to Kyle, sauntering and swaying her hips suggestively, letting the strap hang loose by her side. His eyes flicked back and forth between her face and the method of punishment, as if he were gauging her seriousness. Perhaps he thought she was merely going to pretend to hit, because, after all, she was a cop, not a true Dominatrix. If that were so, he was in for a surprise. She was working undercover and had to be convincing.

Kyle Ramsey was about to get a real taste of being dominated by a woman. The knowledge that it might very well be his first time was exhilarating. Regan liked the idea of being the first woman to bring this otherwise alpha male to heel, and her feelings about what she was going to do both surprised and frightened her. She had never been one of those cops who got carried away with her power, beating suspects and throwing her weight around gratuitously. This was different, however. She wasn't sure why. She just knew it was.

In one respect, though, it was the same as the power she wielded as a cop. It came with responsibility. Because she effectively controlled Kyle at this moment, she owed him a duty of care. She had to be very careful to protect him from herself as well as any other dangers that might be lurking in this strange environment. So she needed to exercise restraint. Her fingers gripped the leather strap with sudden nervousness. Could she do it? There was only one way to find out.

"Eyes down, boy-o," she commanded as she came to stand beside him.

He hesitated long enough to convey to her that he wasn't afraid, and that he was only doing it because he chose to. She admired his bravura the same way she admired how his cock still stood at attention and the way his magnificent muscles flexed against his restraints. She raised the strap and slid it gently across his back like a caress and watched how those same muscles shimmied in response to the unexpected touch. He had been bracing for a blow, probably, and now he would get it.

Without warning, Regan straitened her arm and brought the strap singing down across Kyle's taut ass. He grunted and jerked, the only signs he gave of the assault. Two more strokes elicited more of the same, but the fourth time she smacked him, she saw his fingers grip his tether in white-knuckle fashion. By the fifth stroke, his grunt had morphed into more of an exclamation of pain.

Regan held the strap in check. She was starting to

pant, more from excitement than exertion. As much as she hated to admit it, even to herself, this was the most fun she had ever had on an undercover assignment, or on any assignment for that matter. Still, she was there because of two gruesome murders, not to play, and as much as it pleased her to also take the arrogant Kyle Ramsey down a peg, there was that pesky sense of duty to adhere to.

"Is there something you want to say to me?" she asked. Now was the time for him to stop this pointless game they were playing. He would save himself from a beating, and she could get on with her investigation. They had done enough to satisfy the curious.

Kyle shook his head once in an almost violent move. "No, ma'am." Like her, he was breathing hard.

Okay, then. If that was the way he wanted it, then that was the way it was going to be. Regan resumed the punishment.

Chapter Four

"So, Dad, you're coming to back to school night, right?"

Kyle stuck the phone in the crook of his shoulder in order to turn the salmon fillets while talking to his daughter. It was almost nine, the usual time for him to get home from work even when he didn't spend a large chunk of his day in a sex club. But he hated being a clichéd divorced man living off of take out. He cooked for himself almost every night that he didn't go out on a date or with friends.

"Of course, I am, Emma. Have I ever missed a back to school night?" It was a point of pride to him that he never allowed work to interfere with being a good father. It was especially true now that he and Julie had split up.

"No-o," the twelve-year old replied. She didn't sound convinced, however, and he supposed it was simply par for the course with an adolescent. Nine-year old Stephanie was more trusting.

Satisfied that the fish was cooking properly, he put the phone back into his hand. He turned around without thinking and leaned against the countertop of his kitchen. The sting of the hard granite against his still sore ass caused him to gasp and pull away immediately.

"Dad, are you okay?"

"Yeah, sure," he fumbled to reply, walking farther

into the room. Not that the movement was much better. He was wearing worn jeans, but the fabric still rubbed his sensitive flesh in a painful way. And yet the pain had the strangest effect on his cock. It sprang to life immediately as it had been doing all day, and as it pressed against his the rough denim, his dick produced a pain of a different kind.

Kyle closed his eyes to savor the feeling before he remembered who he was talking to and how inappropriate it was to be sporting a hard-on when talking to one's daughter. Clearing the passion from his throat, he struggled to remember what they were talking about. School, right.

"Look, Emma, I love meeting your new teachers and seeing what you'll be doing all year." Christ, that was rather a lie. Although he took an avid interest in his daughters' education, sitting in classrooms with other parents never appealed to him. Besides, Emma's new school had been Julie's choice. He'd wanted his alma mater, but Julie had had her way, as usual. His ex-wife had always been demanding in a passive sort of way, except in the bedroom. There she had been wholly passive, if not indifferent. Not that it mattered anymore, and not that his poor sex life with her mother was anything involving Emma.

"Besides," he continued, "I have you girls that weekend. I'll ask Mom if you and Stephie can stay Thursday night, too. After back to school night's over, we'll pick up Stephie and get ice cream before coming here."

"Yeah, okay." There wasn't a lot of excitement in his daughter's voice. He blamed Julie for that. The woman watched her weight obsessively and was already stoking the same concern in their daughters.

"The next day, we'll go shopping at the Pru after school." He knew he had her now. Since the divorce, he had moved into a condo in the Back Bay, within easy walking distance to the trendy shopping mall. Like her mother, Emma could always work up interest in having money spent on her. And while it was a shameless bribe for a divorced father to make, he hated living apart from his daughters, and it was only a matter of time before first Emma and then Stephanie would balk at staying with him at all on the weekends.

"That would be awesome, Dad," Emma replied with genuine-sounding enthusiasm.

Kyle smiled at the tone despite his aching ass. The gesture reminded him, however, of the smirk Mistress Regan sported too often during their session that afternoon. Oh, man had he nearly shit himself when she walked into the room. He thought she was still chasing down other leads and was feeling guilty about not letting her in on the club, but she was way ahead of him. Working undercover, no doubt, although if he hadn't known she was a cop, he would have been convinced she was the real deal.

She'd been totally hot and fuckable in her Dominatrix outfit, and to his chagrin, his cock had proclaimed the fact loud and clear. She certainly knew how to wield that strap, too, although he had taken fifteen hard whacks without even considering giving her the safeword. Yellow. He never used the word because he hated the color, and he hated being reminded of his old man's incessant carping about what it meant to be a man.

"Go, on, Kyle, be a man and do it. Don't be

yellow, now. No one likes a coward. You have to be tough, take charge, be a man!"

The memory of his father's voice soured Kyle's stomach, and because that was not the kind of father he was going to be ever with two daughters and no sons, he put the memory of the old man and of Regan Malloy out of his mind.

Returning to his grilling fish, Kyle turned off the heat and moved the food to a plate while he finished his conversation. "We'll have fun, I promise, Em."

The security intercom at the front door buzzed, surprising him. He wasn't expecting anyone. "Look, honey, I have to go. Someone's at the door. I'll talk to you soon, okay? And don't forget to do your homework."

There was a groan over the line. "Yes, Dad. Bye."

"Bye, sweetheart."

Hanging up, Kyle went to the intercom and pushed the button. "Yes?"

"Mr. Ramsey, it's Sergeant Malloy."

His dick greeted the news with alacrity, straining even more to burst from its confines. This time, Kyle didn't try to disabuse it. What would be the point? Even if his T-shirt wasn't long enough to cover the evidence, the sexy cop had already seen it in action. She knew he wanted her.

Instead, he said, "I'll be right there," and went out to the foyer.

Through the frosted glass of the front door he shared with the other condo, he could see the outline of the tall, lanky woman. When he opened the door, there she stood, hip cocked and wearing jeans, a collarless shirt, and a black leather bomber jacket. Other than her hair still being slicked back, Mistress Regan was gone, including the red nails.

Funny, despite the sexless clothes, Kyle still had to fight the urge to grab the woman by the waist, shove her against the wall, and grind his aching cock against her while he buried his face between her luscious breasts. But, no, that would hardly be dignified out here. Besides, he would bet the bulge under her arm was her service revolver and that she might very well shoot him if he dared to assault her even in the friendliest of ways. So he tried to act nonchalant.

"Sergeant Malloy, or should I say Mistress Regan, I'm surprised to see you."

"May I come in?" Butter wouldn't melt in her mouth, and the saucy look she had sported as a Dominatrix was replaced by a detached professionalism.

"Of course." He stepped aside to let her in and led the way back into his unit. When they were both inside his place, he gestured toward the kitchen. "If you don't mind, Sergeant, I was just getting dinner."

She stopped her unabashed perusal of his living room and turned to look at him with wide eyes. "Oh, I'm sorry. I guess I assumed you would have eaten by now."

"I rarely manage to eat earlier than this on week nights." He eyed her speculatively. "I bet you don't, either."

She shrugged. "As it happens, you're right."

"Then please join me." Oh, man where had that invitation come from? Hadn't he had enough of this woman for one day? He should only want for her to get the ass-reaming out of the way quickly and leave. And he had no doubt he was in for one. She had to be furious about his going to the club. Still, his mother had taught him manners.

She shook her head. "No, thanks. I don't want to take your dinner away from you."

The smile she gave him this time was entirely genuine...and tired. The poor woman looked like she'd been up even longer than he had. And, unlike him, she had worked up a sweat probably most of the day. Desire took a back seat to plain compassion.

"You won't. I made plenty. Please have a seat." He motioned toward the bar chairs on the other side of the kitchen counter.

She pleased him by giving a nod and doing as he suggested. He entered the kitchen and started dishing out a salmon fillet for each of them along with a helping of warm spinach salad with walnuts and goat cheese. He put the plate with a place setting and napkin in front of her before holding up the bottle of chilled Chablis he'd already opened.

"Wine?"

She cocked her eyebrows. "Sure, why not? I'll be off duty in a few minutes anyway."

"A few minutes?" he prodded as he poured the wine.

"After we've had a little chat."

"Ah." He put the glass in front of her, noticing that she was waiting for him to begin eating. Apparently the Sergeant's mother had taught her manners, too. Picking up his plate, he leaned one hip against the counter and began eating. His guest did the same.

Her eyelids drooped down with the first mouthful, and she moaned in appreciation. The sound did nothing to ease his arousal. He abandoned his fork for his glass of wine and downed a healthy swallow. The cool liquid didn't help, either. If anything it stoked the heat.

"This is excellent," the sergeant said after chasing her mouthful of fish with some wine. A drop glistened on her upper lip.

Kyle tried not to stare at that bit of wine, especially when the tip of her tongue flicked out to lick it. Instead, he cleared his throat and focused on his plate of food.

"Thank you," he replied. "I like to eat well, and I put a high premium on self-sufficiency."

"This is more than merely taking care of yourself. My mother taught me how to do basic meals, but this is gourmet."

He shrugged off the compliment, although he was more pleased by it than he should be. What did it matter what this woman thought of him? Her only function in his life was to find his friend's killer, and because he knew she was seconds away from putting down her fork and picking up her verbal cudgel, he decided to go on the offensive, as he would with any adversary.

"So, did you have a productive day as Mistress Regan?"

Over a forkful of salad, she gave him a hard stare. She didn't react further to his question or answer it until she had eaten the bite. "I'm not at liberty to discuss my activities during an ongoing investigation."

"Bullshit!" Putting his plate down on the counter, Kyle braced himself against it with his hands and glared back at the cop. "Need I remind you that I'm the one who found his best friend lying in blood-soaked sheets? I have a vested interest in having his killer found."

"Hmm," she replied with infuriating calm, still

enjoying the meal he had given her. "If you were really serious about finding justice for your friend, you wouldn't have lied to me when I asked you about his sex life."

"I didn't lie."

"Then why did I find you at Club Nemesis?"

It was a fair question, and one he'd known he'd have to answer eventually. With a sigh, he broke eye contact, guilt making him want to squirm like a school boy hauled in front of the principal. He didn't, however, because his father had drilled a sense of responsibility into him. Always own up to your actions.

"I didn't lie. When you first asked, I didn't know about the club. It was later that I remembered he had given me a card for the place, and I went to see what it was like."

"It didn't occur to you to call me with the information?"

He looked at her again. She was finishing her meal, licking the tines of her fork to get the last bit of salmon into her mouth. Thoughts flew from his head as he watched her tongue flick over the metal. It was a quick movement, not meant to be sensual, and yet all he could picture was that moist pinkness sliding up the outside of his cock before her full lips enveloped his glans and sucked it inside the warm cavern of her mouth. He leaned further into the counter to press against his erection.

Despite the closeness he created, the cop didn't try to distance herself. "Did it?" she demanded instead.

"Did it what?" he repeated in a low voice pitched to seduce.

"Did it occur to you to call me and tell me about

Club Nemesis?"

Right, the murder, Jazz's murder. *Focus, moron.* "Ah, yes, it did actually." He kept his gaze steady on her eyes, though, unable to tear away no matter what the topic. "But I wasn't sure until I got there what it was, and to be honest, I'm not the type of guy to stand around and let other people solve my problems."

She picked up her glass of wine and slowly drained it, not flinching from his stare. If he meant to intimidate her, it obviously wasn't working. He bet nothing and no one got the better of this woman, and her strength only served to interest and excite him more.

"I studied criminology in college before going to the police academy, from which I graduated third in my class," she said, placing her glass on the counter with exaggerated care. "I spent years working the streets as a beat cop before being promoted to detective and now sergeant. I worked robbery and vice before homicide, and I've never had an unsolved case. In short, Mr. Ramsey, this is my *job*."

Sliding off her stool, she leaned over the counter much as he was so that they were even closer. "How dare you interfere with my investigation?"

"Interfere?" he sneered, unable to contain his anger. It was a safer way to vent his building emotions than to give free rein to his passion. "You call prancing around in leather slut-wear and getting your jollies beating on guys an investigation?"

"I was working undercover, as you damn well know, not playing games. It was you who was acting like a ten-year old, pretending to be a detective working a case. And I'll tell you something else, boy-o. I wasn't the one in that room with a raging hard-on the whole time."

He narrowed his eyes at her. "I could have cut diamonds with your nipples, they were so hard, and where'd you come up with a name like Mistress Regan anyway? Can you make your head spin?"

He saw the first flash of real anger in her eyes with that question. "It happens to be my actual name," she replied through gritted teeth.

"Born to be a Dominatrix, heh?" He couldn't resist teasing her and was rewarded with seeing her fury mount.

"Born to be a royal pain in the ass, were you, *Kyle*?" Her face came closer to his. Her hot breath, tinged with the Chablis, wafted over to him. "You've got two seconds to come completely clean with me about what you know of Bennington's murder, or I swear to God, I'll haul that painful ass of yours—pun intended—down to the station."

"I've told you what I know. My visit to the club was my way of digging into Jazz's life to help find his killer."

"Not. Your. Job!"

"He was my friend. No, he was like a brother to me, and I can't just sit around while his killer runs free."

His chest heaved, and it wasn't with desire, it was with the sudden grief that welled up and threatened to swamp him. What he said was true. He couldn't do simply nothing. It wasn't in his nature. He was always the one to take charge, to solve problems. Now, when it counted most, was not the time to shy away from duty and let others do the work.

Regan, not the Dominatrix but the woman and the

cop, dropped her gaze and nodded her head. "I understand your sense of frustration and your desire to do something." Shaking her head this time, she looked him in the eye again. "But this is not a legal case. It's a murder. And it's happening not in a court room, but in the world of a serial killer. This woman has already butchered at least two men. If you don't stay out of it, you could be the next victim."

"I can take care of myself."

"I bet your friend, Jazz, could, too," she replied in a low voice laced with empathy.

Now it was his turn to look away. "He could, and he would have if he had known the danger he was in."

He didn't see the hand reaching out to him until it touched his face. Warm, soft fingers caressed his jaw. "I'm sorry, and I'm sick over what happened to him. You have to trust me. I'm going to find his killer."

Kyle closed his eyes, enjoying Regan's touch before he gave her the hard truth. "I can't trust you. I don't trust anyone except myself to do a job right." The soothing touch stopped abruptly. When he opened his eyes again, she was walking away, toward the front door. Kyle hustled from his kitchen to intercept her. "You're leaving?"

She gave him a baleful look. "There doesn't seem to be any point to staying. While I believe you when you say you haven't kept any information from me, it's also clear you intend to stick your nose into my investigation no matter what I say. You'll either end up in protective custody or dead."

She shrugged, as if to say she didn't care which, but he could tell she did. Her cheeks were flushed, and her pupils were big. It could have been simply anger.

He was betting it was something else entirely.

"Are you off duty, now?" he asked with deceptive mildness.

The question seemed to surprise her. "Ah, yes, I guess so. I asked my questions and delivered my warning, so—"

He didn't give her a chance to say more.

The cop part of Regan's mind registered the attack in time to stop it, but the woman part of her brain didn't let her. Kyle's hands gripped her upper arms in a painful hold and propelled her against the wall before his mouth slammed down onto hers. His hard body pressed against her, letting her feel his rigid cock straining against his jeans. When she wouldn't open to the soft entreaty of his tongue, he nipped her lower lip until she welcomed him in.

She remained passive, though, letting him explore her mouth with stark passion and blatant need. She would not let him see how aroused she was, other than her nipples having peaked to hard points. She couldn't help that reaction, nor could she keep her juices from flowing from her cunt and soaking her panties. Her clit burned to be touched, and the muscles around it spasmed with the same need. These things he could not see, could not feel, and if she let him know the effect he was having on her, he would gain the upper hand. She didn't want that to happen.

When his hands loosened their hold in order to roam up her neck and cradle her face, she made her move. Reaching with one hand, she grabbed him by the wrist and twisted it around to his back as she slipped out from under him. In the next instant, their positions were reversed, only she had Kyle face-forward against the wall. She pulled his arm up high on his back to keep him from struggling.

"Hey!" he barked. "What are you doing?"

"I didn't give you permission to kiss me," she replied in a cool tone.

Kyle twitched a little, as if to gauge the strength of her hold on him. "We're not having a session, Mistress Regan." He sounded annoyed but not too annoyed. His obvious ambivalence egged her on.

"Aren't we? I make the rules, remember?" With that warning, Regan decided she needed better leverage. She grabbed a fistful of his hair with her free hand and pulling him away from the wall, frog-marched him into the kitchen.

"Now what?" he demanded through gritted teeth.

She shoved him against the countertop over the dining space and made him lay the side of his face on the cool, granite surface. "I didn't give you permission to speak, either," she admonished before letting go of his hair.

Tellingly, he didn't struggle or try to lift his head or throw her off. With her body wedging him in tight to the counter, there wasn't much room for him to maneuver. But he hadn't made any effort to get away during the short trip from the hall, and he still had a hand free to try something. Even with her expert training, she knew a man with at least fifty pounds on her could give her a run for her money. He wasn't fighting her because he didn't want to. He wanted her to control him and to dominate him.

The knowledge sent her pussy into overdrive. "You're a very disobedient boy, Kyle."

"Yes, ma'am," he agreed in a cheerful voice that

grated on her last fucking nerve.

"And you're enjoying this entirely too much."

She slid to one side so she could deliver a punishing smack to his ass with the palm of her free hand. Although his grunt of pain should have brought a satisfied smile to her face, the sting of the contact on her own flesh took a lot of the fun out of it. She needed some help, so she reached across him and pulled open a drawer. She hit pay-dirt with the first try.

The wooden spoon she wielded elicited a string of curses from its target. "Son-of-a-god-damn-bitch!" he roared, and far worse came stuttering from his mouth with each of the ten quick whacks she gave him.

Still, he didn't try to evade the blows or wrench out of her grasp, which only lightly held his arm back. And most importantly, he didn't use the safeword to stop. When she was finished, they were both puffing out harsh breaths. Sweat trickled down her back and front, pooling between her aching breasts. But because she couldn't take off her jacket without letting go of Kyle, she ignored the discomfort.

Regan tossed the spoon on the counter and ran her open hand across Kyle's bottom cheeks in a soothing motion. "I hope you learned your lesson."

"In your dreams." He flashed her a defiant grin over his shoulder.

"No, in yours." She squeezed his tight flesh once before sliding her hand around his hip and to his fly. She positioned herself directly behind so that she could fit her pelvis against his.

Finding the bulge in his pants was easy, as was unsnapping his jeans with one hand. Regan slowly lowered his zipper, the rasping sound of metal on metal loud in the otherwise quiet room. Kyle still did nothing, made no attempt to stop her. Instead, he remained leaning over the counter, only now he was braced by his free arm. His gaze was focused straight ahead into the living room.

"You know what to say if you don't want this," she reminded him and waited a few seconds for him to respond. Her fingers were poised above the waistband of his boxers. When he said nothing, she slipped her fingers between the cotton and his smooth skin. She played with the stiff, curly hair she encountered for a while before clasping her hand around his hard, pulsing cock.

"Unh." His head dropped down to rest on his arm.

Regan smiled. "Like that do you?" She squeezed her fingers while flicking her thumb over the velvety tip. A drop or two of moisture met her, and she spread it around.

Kyle hissed and thrust his hips forward so that her hand was trapped between the counter and his body.

"Don't," she commanded, jerking up on his captured arm. "Don't move. I set the pace. I decide how aroused you become and when you get off. Understand?"

He hesitated before nodding. "Yes, ma'am." His voice was little more than a growl.

"Good, now relax." She tugged him back toward her with the hand still gripping his erection. When he complied, she rewarded him. "Good boy." And her hand enhanced her words with a slow stroke up and down. At the bottom of the caress, she let go long enough to wedge her fingers underneath his tightly tucked balls.

She spent long seconds rolling them between her fingers and thumb, squeezing and tugging. She knew she was driving Kyle crazy by the quickening of his breath and the occasional moan. When he bucked his hips once more, she dug her nails into the tender flesh in admonishment. He kept himself under control after that. It was amazingly gratifying the way he let her control the dance and set the pace. She was incredibly aroused and had to fight the urge to straddle one of his legs and hump her way to satisfaction.

But that wouldn't do. It wouldn't do at all. If she was in control, she couldn't lose control herself. This was all about the effect she was having on him and how he had to trust her to do what was right for him. She went back to stroking him, picking up the pace.

"I'm going to make you come, Kyle, when I'm ready. I'm in charge, so you just relax and let me do all the work." She quickened her movements even more and could tell he was getting close. "Not yet."

Her fingers pulled his flesh up and squeezed the underneath of his glans before pulling down again. His cock was hot and alive in her palm, begging her to bring it to climax. He started to pant, and his whole body quivered under the strain of not moving. He wasn't going to last much longer.

"Okay. Now!" she said in a loud, commanding voice. Kyle jerked with the last word, and his head reared up and back on a shout. Warm semen spurted from his cock and over her hand, easing her movements and soothing the strain in her fingers.

At last, he was finished, and so was Regan, although she had not allowed herself to come. Pulling her hand out of his shorts and letting the other arm go, she went to the kitchen sink and washed up. She felt exhausted, yet strangely satisfied. She wasn't sure what had gotten into her, but she wasn't going to allow herself regrets, not now anyway. Tomorrow would be soon enough to analyze and feel guilty.

As she finished drying her hands on a towel, she turned to look at Kyle. He was still leaning against the counter, although he was braced on both hands. He hadn't bothered to close his pants, and he stared at her with an unreadable expression. All she could tell by it was that he didn't seem to be mad.

"Are you all right?" She tossed the towel on the counter. She ran slightly shaky hands through her hair. "I didn't hurt your arm, did I?"

He shook his head slowly. "No, I'm fine. Very relaxed," he added with a wry grin.

"Good. I should be going." When she went to pass him, he straightened and blocked her way. He didn't try to touch her, however.

"Wait a minute." His expression was one of confusion.

"Why?"

"What about you?"

"What about me?" Regan shoved her hands in the pockets of her jacket and stared at him.

"You haven't gotten off."

She smiled. "Oh, that. Don't worry about it." She maneuvered around him and headed for the front door.

Kyle chased after her and leaned against the door before she could reach it. "What do you mean 'don't worry about it?' No woman leaves my bed unsatisfied."

"We were never in your bed," she reminded him.

"You know what I mean," he replied in an

exasperated voice.

"Yes, I do know what you mean, and what I'm saying is that it's not your concern." She stepped closer to him. "I make the rules and the decisions here. I decide who comes and when and under what circumstances. You don't have to worry about any of it, because it's not your job. Just like it's not your job to find the killer."

He lowered his gaze. "I'm not sure I can live with things being that way. I never have before."

"With respect to us, to the extent there is an *us,* you can make whatever decision you want. The investigation, however, is another matter. Stay out of it, Kyle. I'll—I'll try to keep you apprised of my progress to the extent that I'm allowed to talk about it without compromising anything. That's all I can promise."

He looked at her and nodded, although whether he was agreeing to obey her order to stay out of the investigation, she couldn't say. Standing to one side, he opened the door for her.

"Good night, and thank you, Mistress Regan, for your company this evening." She acknowledged his thanks with a nod of her head and moved to pass him. His arm shot out to block her way again. "And there is an *us,* just so you know."

"We'll see." She ducked under his arm and left.

Chapter Five

Weird. Regan's life had definitely become weird within the last forty-eight hours, and hunting down her first serial killer wasn't even the biggest part of the weirdness. Kyle Ramsey was. No, that wasn't completely true. Her reaction to him and the way she had suddenly embraced this bizarre Femdom lifestyle was what was throwing her for a loop.

The way she had slipped into what was supposed to be an undercover role so easily at his condo last night was disturbing. Part of it had been temper. His insistence on chasing down his friend's killer still made her blood boil. How much arrogance could one man have? Didn't he see the stupidity of an average citizen trying to do a cop's job? She had wanted to make him listen to her, and the only way she had been able to gain his attention so far was with a beating.

So, teaching him a lesson was part of it, but she didn't have to go to such lengths to deliver her professional message. A stern lecture and threats of arrest should have sufficed. That route wouldn't have satisfied the other emotion welling up inside her, however. Desire, that was the fuel stoking her high-handedness and enticing her to play the role of a Domme. And, Kyle, damn him to hell, hadn't told her to piss off. Instead, he had let her do what she wanted to him and liked it.

Weird was too mild a word for it all. It was frightening, this new wish to control a man. Sure, she liked to be in charge at work, but she had always thought she was an egalitarian in her love life, such as it was. Maybe she had been fooling herself all these years. Maybe she was a domineering bitch from birth. The thought made her squirm in her chair, although she checked the movement quickly. She didn't want to invite any lewd comments from the cops around her. They would see it as a sign of horniness, and they would be right. She hadn't gotten herself off last night when she arrived home, because she had told Kyle the truth. She wanted him to do it when she decided it was time.

She was sinking in deep with this guy, fast, and she wasn't even sure it was ethical given that he was a witness in a murder investigation.

"Hey, partner, how come you're not out beating men?" JoJo plopped herself down on the corner of Regan's desk, a plastic bottle of diet Coke in her hand.

Regan looked up from under her eyelashes. "Please, respectable men don't like being dominated before lunch time. I have to be there by noon."

"I hope you get more customers today," JoJo teased.

Regan rolled her eyes. Besides Kyle, she'd had two other sessions with much older men, both of whom really reveled in her dominance of them, as if they were putting on some kind of tacky play. Because they'd been overacting, she had as well and had worked hard not to laugh herself silly. Needless to say, there was no repeat of the aroused state she achieved with Kyle.

"I'll be happy if I have a chance to speak with

some of the other women who work there. They were too busy yesterday for more than a quick hello, and none of them struck me as the chatty type, either. I'd better get there a little early and see what I can learn while we're all getting dressed."

JoJo took a long drink from her bottle. "Do you think one of them is the killer?"

"It's possible, but my gut is telling me it would be too easy. Hopefully, I can at least pick their brains and understand better what our killer is thinking. What makes these women want to hurt men?" *What makes me want to hurt Kyle?* Regan thought it, then put it aside. She couldn't afford to become engrossed in her own issues while on duty.

"Well, I have somewhere for us to go this morning that may help us understand what motivates the men and the women," her partner said.

"Where?"

"I found a doctor right here in town who specializes in sexual fetishes. Her name's Greta Molvado."

"Greta?" Regan repeated skeptically before reaching over and snatching her partner's Coke out of her hand. She slurped down some of the drink, making a face at the bitter taste of artificial sweetener.

JoJo tossed her a mock-peeved look. "Dr. Molvado is a psychologist with a private practice. She has graciously agreed to fit us into her schedule this morning."

Regan handed the bottle back. "When?"

"In about twenty minutes."

"Let's go then." Regan stood up and unhooked her jacket from the back of her chair. "This ought to be interesting. Five bucks says this Greta looks like Frau Blucher."

****

The doctor's office was located in a downtown building dedicated to medical professionals of all kinds. Other than the woman's name, there was no indication that a psychologist for the sexually adventurous practiced inside. When Regan and JoJo entered, they were greeted by a young woman with large, Bambi-like eyes. She stood up from behind her receptionist's desk and tucked her frizzy blonde hair behind her ears in a nervous gesture.

"Good morning," she said in a squeaky voice. "You must be Sergeant Malloy and Detective Mathers."

"Yes, we are," Regan replied. "Dr. Molvado is expecting us."

"Of course. I'll let her know you're here."

The young woman—Mindy, according to her desk plate—walked around her work station to knock on an inner door. The plain and timid creature was wearing a high-necked paisley dress that made her look flat-chested and almost boyishly slender. It was as if she had stepped off the prairie only moments ago, and while her movements were graceful, her flat shoes barely left the carpet as she walked across it.

JoJo looked at Regan and crossed her eyes. Her expression implied she, like Regan, was wondering how this kid had ended up working for a sex therapist.

There was a delicate throat clearing. "The doctor will see you now."

Regan and JoJo turned toward the receptionist and headed for the open door beside her. "Thank you," Regan said to the young woman and gave her a smile.

Mindy offered back the same gesture. She stood stock still while the two cops passed her, however, her hands clasped in front. Regan noticed they were the only part of the receptionist that seemed the least bit substantial. They would certainly be good for spanking a man, she mused, and then she turned her attention to the woman she had come to speak with.

"Good morning, Sergeant, Detective."

Doctor Molvado greeted them with a broad smile and a hint of excitement. She strode toward them with her hand outstretched for a shake. Unlike her receptionist, Molvado was neither timid nor mousy. Her black hair was cut very short, and the make-up on her beautiful face was bold. She looked like a runway model both with the chic suit she was wearing and the body it encased. Normally, Regan didn't spend a second envying other women, but Dr. Molvado was too stunning to ignore.

"I'm Sergeant Malloy," Regan said, shaking hands and admiring the other woman's firm grip as well. "This is my partner, Detective Mathers."

"Yes, we spoke on the phone." The doctor turned her attention to JoJo. "Shall we sit down?" She led them to a part of her office that was furnished with comfy chairs and a coffee table.

On the way over, Regan pulled a five dollar bill out of her pocket and handed it off to JoJo, who took it with a restrained grin. They both sank into a plush seat and waited for the doctor to take her own before Regan began the interview.

"I know my partner has told you we're interested in learning about Femdom, both from the woman's perspective and the man's."

The doctor spent a few seconds giving them an appraising look before answering. "Yes, Detective Mathers and I spoke a bit about your areas of interest, although she didn't mention why you're interested."

Regan gave the standard reply. "I'm afraid we're not at liberty to discuss exactly why we're seeking this information, because it would compromise an investigation."

The doctor's eyes flashed with humor. "I feel like I'm on TV or in the movies. But I do understand the seriousness of your position. And, because I keep up with the local news and have been adding two and two together now for quite some time, I assume this has something to do with the horrific murder of Joseph Bennington."

There was something about Molvado's expression and the way she did her math so quickly and accurately that caused Regan's suspicions to rise. "Possibly. Did you know Mr. Bennington?"

"Now, I'm afraid I'm the one who is going to have to demure, Sergeant, although I suppose there is no harm in confirming that the man was a patient of mine at one time."

In unison, Regan and JoJo leaned forward.

"He was?" Regan asked. This was not something they had known. Nothing in Bennington's personal papers had kicked out a connection to Molvado, so that must mean he was either paying in cash or—

"He hasn't been in over a year," the doctor confirmed before Regan could ask, which explained why evidence of the relationship wasn't immediately available. There hadn't been time to dig further into the man's background.

"He came here because he was into Femdom, though," Regan pressed.

The doctor sighed and gave a tight smile. "I really can't comment on why he was here unless you get a court order." She shrugged. "Of course, I only specialize in sexual issues, so you can draw your own conclusions."

Yes, they could. The trip to the doctor's office had just become more interesting. She asked the logical next question. "What about a man named Eugene Morales? Was he your patient, too?"

"Yes, very briefly," Molvado admitted with obvious reluctance.

"How briefly?"

"He came to see me only once. I probably wouldn't have even remembered it, except that when I heard about his murder, the name sounded familiar, and I looked it up in my files." The woman shifted her legs, crossing one over the other.

In that brief moment, Regan was able to see that the good doctor wore thigh-highs stockings as Regan was forced to do with her Dominatrix outfit. And, like Regan as well, there was nothing else under the skirt. Regan registered the detail with interest before focusing on the doctor's next words.

"And, that's all I'm prepared to say about it. Again, if you want to see the files, you'll have to get a court order, although I warn you I'll fight the idea based on physician/patient confidentiality."

"Why?" JoJo asked. "These men are dead, and we're trying to find their killer."

"I understand, Detective, however this is an important point for doctors, and I honestly can say that there's nothing in those files about a possible killer. Neither of these men mentioned being threatened in any way."

Probably not, and yet here was another connection to the two men besides Club Nemesis. Molvado would have to be looked into as a possible suspect. She certainly fit the part of a Domme, at least in Regan's mind. So she'd interview the woman with that in mind but make it seem like they were after generic information about the practice of female domination.

"We appreciate your giving us that much information," Regan assured the doctor to ease the mounting tension. "Although it is interesting that both of these men came to you for therapy, I guess it's also true that given their predilections and the fact that you are one of the few doctors around dealing with sexual fetishes, I suppose we shouldn't be surprised at the connection."

"No, you shouldn't," Molvado replied with obvious relief. "I really do wish to help you, of course. What can I tell you generically about the people I treat?"

Regan forced herself to sit back again and adopt a relaxed air. JoJo, being quick on her feet and well used to her partner's signals, did the same. "Tell us why men like Bennington and Morales seek out women to hurt them. What makes them want to lead a Femdom lifestyle?"

"There really isn't an answer to that question, at least not one that covers all men into the lifestyle. Why don't we back up a second and talk about the various ways in which this type of behavior comes out and the possible labels. For example, you keep asking about

Femdom, which means female dominance, but there's also bondage and discipline and sadomasochism."

Regan grimaced. "If a guy likes to be tied up and beaten by a woman, what are we talking about?"

"To a certain degree, all three. It depends on the person involved, and actually the label doesn't matter so much to me as a doctor. I'm concerned with helping those people who either want to become comfortable with their lifestyle, live it without guilt, or put it behind them and adopt a more conventional sex life."

"I'm confused," JoJo confessed, and Regan was glad because she was confused, too.

Molvado shifted again in her seat. "Okay, there are different levels of sexuality that involve pain, or simply humiliation, and dominance. For most of these people, it's part of a rich fantasy sex life that they practice under tight controls and with people they trust. It's a form of role-playing that spices things up for them in the bedroom. Sometimes a couple will switch off with each being dominant and submissive in turn. And it has nothing to do with their ordinary lives."

"Like playing the cheerleader and the gym teacher," Regan offered up with a smirk.

The doctor, however, was completely serious when she replied, "Exactly, or like playing headmistress and naughty student. It's something lots of couples do without ever considering themselves to be sadomasochists or dominant or submissive. For others, though, it is a more pervasive part of their emotional being, and they incorporate the need to hurt or be hurt, or dominate or submit, into every aspect of their lives. They live the role, if you will."

"Like the men who frequent places like Club

Nemesis," Regan interjected. "For those men, it's more than a casual thing, if only because it's expensive as hell."

"Yes, I know of the club, of course. It's a very reputable place, and the men who go there are not looking for sex. They're looking for discipline. It's one of the reasons why we can't use the various terms completely interchangeably. Some men are so stressed about the lives they lead, the decisions they have to make, the authority they wield, that they need the release of letting someone else control their lives even for a little while. The punishment aspect is a form of absolution so they can live with any guilt or worry over the consequences of their decisions and actions."

"They do get aroused, though," Regan pointed out because she had seen as much with her own eyes, and except for Kyle, she had found the reaction to her punishment unsettling and frankly, gross.

"Naturally," Molvado agreed with a shrug. "This frequently comes down to sex. Heterosexual men who crave domination don't want to be dominated by other men. That would be threatening to their sexuality and their primate sense of hierarchy. If they want to be dominated by other men, they can achieve that through professional choices. They need women to do this for them. Some men need a woman to be in charge of their entire personal life, not simply once in a while. In those cases, what happens in the bedroom spills over into their daily lives."

"Bennington was reputedly domineering with women, to the point of breaking up his marriage," Regan said.

"It's often like that. These men know deep down

what they want, but they fight it and can't acknowledge it to the women in their lives even when they can admit it to themselves. Being naturally strong, dominating men in general society, they attract passive women without meaning to. It takes a particularly strong woman to break through the façade and take charge, exactly as the man wants her to."

"This makes no sense to me, Doctor Molvado," JoJo exclaimed. "How can an otherwise alpha-type male want to be dominated by a woman in his private life?"

"It's a dichotomy that's hard to fathom, I agree," Molvado replied.

A sick feeling crept into Regan's stomach as she thought of a reason why. "It's because they were abused as children, isn't it?" Guilt over what she had done to Kyle and why he had let her put a hard edge to her voice.

Molvado blinked at her in surprise. "Possibly. Many of my patients are dealing with childhood issues of abuse, as well as abusive relationships they became trapped in as adults. But just because a man likes to be dominated and punished by women, doesn't necessarily mean that he was abused by his mother or another adult female in his childhood."

"It can, though, right?" Regan persisted. It made sense to her. It made a hell of a lot more sense than the idea that a strong man like Kyle Ramsey would like having her hurt him.

"Yes, it can. There are plenty of men into Femdom, though, who simply crave the lifestyle for no discernable reason and live perfectly healthy psychological lives."

Regan heard the words but didn't believe them. They still made no sense. And there was a flip side that was even harder to face. She did, though, because the investigation hinged on it. "What about the women? Why do they do it?"

Molvado shrugged. "Some women are naturally dominating, and I mean that in a good way. You strike me as a strong woman, Sergeant."

JoJo stifled a chuckle that died with the withering look Regan shot her. "I don't take crap from anyone if that's what you mean." Misery swamped her for a moment. *Plus, I do like beating on guys, at least one guy.*

"That's what I meant," the doctor replied. "I bet you're comfortable in the role of being the boss, and while you might not expect to be in charge of the man in your life, many women enjoy the power, the same way many men enjoy being the head of the household."

Regan raised her eyebrows. "That's not the same as tying up your guy and beating him with a riding crop."

"No, it's not," Molvado conceded. "Now, we're back to the fact that some people are wired that way. They get off on it, although you must understand that for women who work in a place like Club Nemesis, they may be doing it only as a job, a vocation, not an avocation."

"So, they might not be turned on by it?" Regan pressed.

"No more than strippers usually are."

Point taken. Regan had been in plenty of strip clubs, both for men and women, on the job and for the occasional bachelorette party. The dancers were never turned on that she could see. "But for those women who do it at home?" She needed to know. Was she a sadistic cunt? "People who get off on hurting other people can't be normal."

"The definition of normal is a matter of societal perception, Sergeant. All I can tell you is that if we're talking about consenting adults, I consider them normal. If one person is taking advantage of another, tearing down their self-esteem, controlling the other person's life because of their own lack of confidence or hurting them in anger, that's when I step in and say it's not normal or at least not healthy."

Regan didn't respond right away. Rubbing her lower lip with her forefinger, she pictured the reason why they were there talking about all of this to begin with. She pictured two men butchered in their own beds. "And when the dominant person takes the discipline into the realm of murder?"

Doctor Molvado closed her eyes briefly and shuddered. "Now, we're definitely talking about the abnormal, Sergeant Malloy. There are sadomasochists who take their fetish to an extreme, both the killers and sometimes, unbelievably, the victims. We're talking about psychopaths and sociopaths and suicidal depression." She pierced Regan with a knowing gaze. "We're talking about serial killers. You'll have to go somewhere else for insight into those types of people, I'm afraid. Sexual gratification based on death is one fetish I don't handle."

****

"What part of 'no fucking way are we yielding on this point' didn't you understand when I said it the first time five minutes ago, Bill?" Kyle kept his tone deceptively mild, although he knew neither Bill

Schwartzkopf nor his young associate was fooled by it.

He was doing some hard bargaining today, and because his client held the stronger position in the dispute, he knew he was going to prevail. It was merely a matter of how much posturing his opponent wanted to do before capitulating. Given that the associate watching it all was very pretty, he bet Schwartzkopf was going to play macho for a while longer yet.

Kyle didn't care. He was feeling remarkably relaxed today. He had slept long and soundly the previous night, which was unusual for him. The stress of his job tended to make it hard to fall asleep and invaded his dreams once he did. Last night had been different, though. Once the delectable and disturbing Regan Malloy left his condo, he had drifted off with the bone-deep relaxation that comes from a powerful orgasm. Sleeping on his stomach to ease the sting of his abused ass hadn't bothered him, either.

As he waited for his opponent to consider his response, Kyle shifted in his seat ever so slightly so that it wouldn't seem as if he were nervous. His backside was still sore, not surprising after the two beatings he had received the day before. The first one had been understandable, he was looking into Jazz's murder. He had to pretend to be one of those guys who liked being dominated by a woman. That had been acceptable even though he became aroused during the experience. He attributed it to the presence of a woman he desired.

What happened in his condo, however, was tougher to explain or accept. He had wanted Regan, that much was clear and not surprising given how attractive and sexy she was. Grabbing her and kissing her had been perfectly like him. Allowing her to get the upper hand

and keep it had not. Why had he done it? Why had he let her bend him over his kitchen counter and strike him with a wooden spoon? How humiliating and how arousing. The orgasm she gave him afterward had been the most satisfying he'd had outside of a woman.

The thing that bothered him most was the way the pain inflicted by Regan made him hard. It still did as he sat in a conference room, negotiating a settlement with strangers. He kept his chair shoved under the table so his erection wouldn't be noticed. He wouldn't have ever thought he was the kind of man who enjoyed feeling pain, yet there was no denying it aroused him. There was no denying, either, that the pain also had a calming effect on him. He felt more confident and more centered today than he typically did.

It was almost frightening. Perhaps he and Jazz had more in common than he would ever have imagined.

"I need to confer with my client, Ramsey," Schwartzkopf finally said gruffly.

"Feel free." Kyle gestured toward a phone at the far end of the conference room. "I'll give you some privacy."

He waited until the two other lawyers stood up to go to the phone before he pushed back his chair and got up. With their backs turned, they couldn't see how his pants tented, and he quickly slipped out and into the men's room nearby. He had to do something about his hard-on, so he went into one of the stalls.

Although he was alone, he felt perverted unzipping his pants and freeing his straining cock. He clasped the hard flesh and pulled up, sending a satisfying jolt of pleasure through his body. It was tempting, very tempting, to stroke himself to orgasm. He didn't do it, though. Something stopped him, something more than mere propriety. It was hardly mature or classy to jerk-off at work. No, it was a feeling of guilt that staid his hand. He wasn't supposed to control his body. That was Regan's job.

"Fuck that," he muttered under his breath. He was his own man, in charge of his life, including when he came and when he didn't. Still, he turned and sat on the toilet, intending not to jerk off, but to piss his erection away. As he pushed down on the rod, he heard the door to the bathroom open.

"Kyle, are you in here?" a familiar male voice called out.

"Yeah, Dan," he replied, feeling self-conscious. Men weren't supposed to talk to each other in the bathroom, especially when one of them had his hand wrapped around his dick.

"Your secretary asked me to look for you because you have a visitor. Some cop named Malloy."

Kyle's body shuddered violently as the climax ripped through him. His cock pulsed in his hand as hot cum spurted out. Surprised at his body's instant reaction, he struggled to suppress the moan of pure pleasure begging to pass his lips.

"Kyle?" His colleague was still waiting for a reply, damn it.

"Yeah, okay. Be right there." Kyle's voice sounded strangled, although given that he was sitting in a stall, he hoped the other guy would attribute it to something else.

"I'll let your secretary know."

Kyle waited until his body had emptied itself before he stood up on shaky legs. He cleaned himself off both in the stall and at the sink, glad to see he hadn't actually stained his clothing. The look in his eye, however, as he splashed cold water on his face, didn't please him. He looked like a guy who had just had a good fuck. Maybe it was all in his mind, but it bothered him how out of control he was, so he left the men's room with a scowl on his face and loaded for bear.

What the hell was Regan Malloy doing coming to his office anyway, and what kind of hold did she have over him to make him react so strongly to simply hearing her name? This wasn't like him. He had to get a grip on himself and her.

He was a take-charge kind of guy, after all. Sure, he liked it when a woman was a bit aggressive in bed. What guy didn't? Most porn fantasies were based on the idea of a woman who was enthusiastic about sex. That didn't mean he was going to be some woman's lap dog or punching bag.

Chapter Six

Kyle's full head of steam dissipated in an instant when he rounded the hall corner and saw Regan standing by the window of the reception area. She had her back to him, but he knew it was her, of course. She was unmistakable to him even in a blazer and dark slacks. Because she hadn't heard or seen him, he stopped to let himself stare and want. God, how he wanted. His body stirred to life, as if he hadn't come only moments earlier.

"Sorry to stop by without warning," she said, still looking out the window.

He stepped closer to her with his brows knitted. "How did you know I was standing here?"

She turned guileless eyes on him and shrugged. "I'm a cop. Do you have time to talk?"

"Sure." He didn't really, but he also didn't care if he left Schwartzkopf waiting. "Let's go into my office."

Leading the way, he stepped aside to let her pass and enter the spacious corner room he had earned for himself. Regan looked around curiously as she had at his condo, taking in her surroundings, and he took a measure of pride in having an impressive space to show her. In this regard, he was clearly the kind of man he intended to be. As for the type of man he was with Regan...

"Please have a seat," he said, pushing aside his

sexual concerns.

"Thanks, but I'm a little keyed up. I'm in a pacing kind of mood, if you don't mind."

Kyle leaned against the closed door and folded his arms across his chest, deciding it would look silly if he tried to cover his growing erection. "As you wish."

She glanced at him. "As I wish." She ran an obviously agitated hand through her hair and walked the width of the room. "I wish I hadn't been the one assigned to your friend's murder."

Kyle stood away from the door. His focus shifted from the woman he craved to his grief. "Have you made progress on the case?"

She stopped and looked at him. "No, shit, sorry. I didn't mean to get your hopes up."

"Oh, that's okay." He let out a loud breath he hadn't realized he was holding. In a perverse way, he was glad to hear it. When Regan solved the case, would she stop seeing him? He didn't think he wanted that even as he didn't think he wanted to become more involved with her. He needed time, and the murder was a link to this woman that bought him that time. "May I ask why you're here, then?"

"Yeah, that's a fair question." She nodded but didn't answer right away. For a few seconds, she stared back at him with a pensive thought.

"And?" he prodded.

"And I'm trying to find the right way to say it." With hands clasped behind her back, she rocked on her feet in an uncertain way that wasn't like the woman he was coming to know. "I'm sorry, I guess is what I've come to say."

"Sorry about what?"

She looked down at her feet and grimaced. "About last night."

Ah. So, he wasn't the only one who was feeling conflicted about what they had done. "Which part exactly are you apologizing for?" He needed to know if she felt bad about being intimate with him or the way in which it happened. He wanted her, and he hoped she wanted him back, however they might decide to run their relationship.

Her gaze popped up, and her spine visibly straightened, as if she were forcing herself to tackle a difficulty with courage. "The part where I abused you. The part where I took advantage of your grief over your friend's death, and," she licked her lips, "and any vulnerability you might have in addition to that."

"I see."

Kyle mulled over her choice of words for a moment, trying to understand what she was saying. There was some odd subtext to the apology that confused him. He closed the gap between them and stopped in front of her. With her only two feet from him, the pull of her was strong and distracting. His hands itched with the desire to grab her by the waist and pull her against his newly throbbing erection.

He didn't give into the impulse, however. He knew he shouldn't. Hadn't she said she was in control and that he could only do what she said he could and when she said he could do it? Why he should allow her such control over him, he couldn't say. He only knew that in showing the restraint, he felt strong and strangely proud of himself.

"Actually," he confessed, "I don't see. What happened last night was not abuse, at least not from my perspective."

Regan gave him what he perceived as a pitying smile. "I can imagine that it wasn't. The problem is that I took advantage of your perspective."

He shook his head. "You're really confusing me now."

"Yeah, okay, I know I'm making a hash of this, but I'm trying to be sensitive to your feelings, and well, to be honest, sensitive is not my strong suit."

Kyle smiled at the admission. He couldn't help himself. He hadn't known Regan Malloy long, but what he knew told him she wasn't big on the touchy-feely stuff. It was fine by him because her aggressiveness was a big part of what he found attractive about her, perverse as that might be. Still, she seemed uncomfortable, and he didn't want her feeling bad, so he pushed her to be more blunt. "Don't worry about my feelings. I'm a big boy, Regan. You can tell me straight out what's bothering you."

She studied him and gauged his sincerity, he supposed. "Fine. The thing is, I just came from talking to a Doctor Molvadc. Does her name mean anything to you?"

He frowned. "No, why?"

"Because Mr. Bennington used her as a therapist. She specializes in fetishes. I thought maybe he'd mentioned her to you, but then, that's pretty stupid of me to think given how you knew nothing about his predilections."

"No, he never mentioned it to me. Did you learn anything helpful?"

"Only generally with respect to what might lead men and women into the Femdom lifestyle."

"Is that why you're apologizing?" he asked with sudden clarity.

"Yes," she admitted on a puff of breath. Her green eyes bore into his, and he could see the guilt in them. He wanted to kiss it away, yet dared not. He knew she would rebuff him. "She said it's possible that men who seek out punishment from women are reliving an abusive childhood."

"Ah, and you think I let you bend me over a counter and paddle my ass until my cock nearly burst through my pants because I was abused as a child."

Regan's gaze dropped. "Listening to the doctor, I realized I may have taken an unconscionable advantage over you. It certainly explained why an otherwise strong, assertive man would allow himself to be dominated by a woman."

He moved closer, just enough to satisfy his growing urge to be pressed against her. "Maybe it's a simple matter of your being physically stronger than I am."

She still didn't look at him, although her eyes shifted to the far end of his office. "Well, I'm pretty sure I could take you in a fight, but that's training." Her gaze shot to his, and the look was like a sucker punch to his gut. His cock pulled and strained like a stallion desperate to jump a fence and cover a mare. God, how he wanted this woman. "The problem is that you didn't put up a fight at all. You didn't even say the safeword."

"I came up with that word to satisfy your concerns. I warned you I would never use it."

This time, she was the one who moved closer to him. Her expression was intense, agitated. "You should have. You should have told me to fuck off and leave you alone. I had no right to hurt you like that, to control you as if you were a toy for my perverse pleasure."

He leaned in and basked in the feel of her heat. "I was the one who felt pleasure last night, Regan. I might not like the idea—hell, I know I don't like it—but the plain truth is that I let you do what you did because it made me hot and hard, and when you jerked me off, it was the first time I understood the expression 'little death' because, lady, you killed me."

He had to stop and catch his breath. His feelings over this Femdom stuff and his behavior were coalescing in his mind even as he spoke. "This is all new to me, too. Believe me when I say I'm not reliving some childhood trauma. As self-absorbed and vain as my mother may be, she never crawled into bed with me or beat me. I've always had a pretty conventional sex life, and if you'd asked me a mere two days ago if I wanted a woman to dominate me sexually or in any other aspect of my life, I'd have said no fucking way."

It was impossible to stop his need to touch her at this point. He framed her face with his hands. "You're different, though, Regan. I don't know why. I wanted you from the start even though I was in shock over finding Jazz murdered. I wanted you even when you pissed me off over the Femdom angle of his life, and I wanted you even when you had me at your mercy and punished me, as if I were some recalcitrant child."

He rubbed his thumbs along her fine cheekbones. "I know it makes no sense, but not only does your domination over me excite me sexually, it also makes me feel stronger as a man. I can take what you dish out, Regan, and there's a sense of empowerment in submitting to another. I'm giving myself to you. You're not taking me. By letting you control me and punish me, I feel good today. A little confused," he admitted. "But good."

"Is that the truth?" she asked skeptically, although he noted with satisfaction that she wasn't trying to avoid his touch.

"Why in the hell would I lie about a thing like this?" he replied with a little chuckle. "You think it's easy for a man like me, someone who dominates others for a living, to admit he's putty in your hands?"

"No." She sighed, her eyes closed, and she angled her head to press into one of his hands. The obvious sign of comfort she was showing to his touch caused his body to tighten, not in his groin, but in a place much higher. This thing with Regan was becoming more complicated than he had expected and in a quicker pace than he was used to.

When she opened her eyes again, she wore a confused expression. "I don't understand any of this, either. You're not the only one acting out of character. Up until now, the most I've done to dominate a man in my social life is insist on anchovies on a pizza we're sharing."

"You like anchovies?"

"Is that a problem?"

Kyle grinned. "No, I like them, too. You're the first woman I've been involved with who shares my taste buds."

"We're not involved," she corrected him primly.

His smile vanished. "Yes, we are. I have my hands on your face, if nothing else."

"You shouldn't." She made to pull back.

He tightened his grip to stop her. "Don't. Please,

don't. I like touching you."

She sighed again but stopped her retreat. "Okay, although I can't see why. You should find me annoying at the very least."

"Part of me does." He liked the way she took the information on the chin and didn't display hurt feelings the way most women would. "Maybe I should consult this Doctor Molvado to figure out what's going on with me."

"No!" The command was sharp, and Regan's face went hard and serious. "Stay away from her, Kyle."

"O-okay," he agreed. Why, though, he wondered. What was going on with this doctor that had Regan concerned? He would look into it later. Agreeing not to contact the woman didn't mean he couldn't do some research on her. Right now, he had other ideas. "How about we find something more enjoyable to do than analyze our fetishes?"

He gave her a look that he knew left no doubt as to his thoughts and intentions, then let his hands talk for him. Sliding them down from her face, he caressed her neck, shoulders, and arms. He admired briefly the hard bulge of her biceps. No wonder she could manipulate his body so easily and deliver potent slaps. It was merely a passing thought, however. He was more interested in the soft parts of her. His hands moved to cup her breasts, the hard tips of which pressed into his palms.

"We shouldn't be doing this." Somehow Regan found the strength to state the obvious, but she knew the effect of the admonishment was diminished by the way her breath hitched. From the moment she'd realized Kyle was standing behind her in the reception area to the way he was now circling his palms around her erect nipples, her body had reacted with sexual glee. Every nerve ending stood at attention, straining to wrap itself around his hard body and rub until it was satisfied.

This encounter was not going the way she had planned. After leaving Molvado's office, she had sent JoJo on a fishing expedition back at the precinct with regard to the doctor's private life and possible connection with the murders. Two dead patients was not a good track record, and the woman gave off funny vibes. Maybe it was a stretch to suspect her of being the killer. Nevertheless, this was one thing in which Kyle better obey her.

In any event, this trip to his office was supposed to put an end to their personal involvement, not advance it. He said he wasn't reliving some childhood abuse, and maybe he was telling the truth. Maybe he was one of those men the doctor had said are simply wired to want a woman to dominate them. She wasn't sure, but she did know there was no way she could think clearly with his hands roaming all over and his lips leaving a trail of kisses along her throat, fulfilling her desire.

"Kyle, stop," she ordered.

"Why?" he murmured against her skin.

"Isn't it enough that I said so?" She deliberately made her voice authoritative and was pleased when his actions stilled.

Lifting his head to look at her, he said, "Yes, it is." He dropped his hands, and she immediately missed the touch, although she didn't let him see how she felt. "You're not being very fair."

"I don't have to be. When it comes to my body, I

call the shots, and that is not a Femdom issue."

"Point taken," he acknowledged. "Although you could have used the safeword."

She narrowed her eyes. "That's for you, not me."

He chuckled in a self-deprecating tone. "Yeah, right, I forgot." A few seconds went by before he continued. "You can see what you do to me."

Regan glanced down at his obvious erection. "I must confess it's flattering."

"Lady, you have no idea," he replied enigmatically. But before she could make him clarify his statement, he said, "Look, I've had my fun and then some. It's time I took care of you." Leaning in close, yet not trying to touch her again, he whispered in her ear seductively. "Let me make you come, Regan, right here and now. I know you want it."

Her eyes drooped to half-mast at the suggestion. Yes, she did. She wanted him to lavish her body with attention until it screamed in orgasm. She had been tightly wound since she'd met him, and pretty soon she needed to be back at Club Nemesis, beating on strange men and trying to find a killer. The release Kyle offered would relax and rejuvenate her. Still, she resisted. As much as she wanted it, a bigger part of her thrived on the idea that she could control her needs along with him. She was fooling herself by continuing to believe she could walk away from any involvement.

"No, not this time," she said in a clear voice. Holding him back with one hand on his shoulder, she reached down with the other and cupped his balls through the thin fabric of his slacks. His quick gasp made her smile. "I'd say yours is the greater need."

"Regan, let me do this for you," he growled. "I

don't like leaving you unsatisfied."

"You won't." She squeezed up the length of his cock.

He groaned with pleasure. "Regan, don't."

She stopped her movement. "I don't recognize that word. Is there another one you want to use?"

"No." He grit his teeth and scowled down at her, but he was still hard as steel in her fingers, and in addition to not using the safeword, he wasn't trying to escape her grasp.

"All right, then. Do you need to get back to work?"

"They'll wait for me. They don't have a choice because I'm in charge."

"Not here and now you're not." She steered him by pressing on his bulging cock until he was leaning against one of his visitor chairs. "Sit down."

A burst of pleasure centered in her clit and radiated throughout her body when he obeyed. It was thrilling to dominate this man, but only because he was such a potent and powerful person. Bossing around a wimpy guy wouldn't have the same effect on her. There was no challenge in dominating the weak, no sense of accomplishment. Knowing that, when he left her, Kyle would charge through the rest of his day taking no quarter from anyone else made her feel like a goddess.

Because she was calling the shots, she didn't feel diminished by kneeling in front of him. She knew that with a simple command, she could have him on his knees instead. That wasn't what she wanted. Not yet, anyway. If this really was the beginning of a relationship and one based on Femdom dynamics, then she needed to bring him to heel completely before she could be sure he would pleasure her exactly the way she wanted. The best way to control any man was through his cock. She slowly undid Kyle's belt and lowered the zipper of his pants.

"Regan," he began.

"Shut up," she ordered without looking at him. He did as she commanded with an audible click of his teeth. Ignoring his face, she concentrated on freeing his erection and admired once more its length and width. When and if she actually let him slide into her, it would fill her to a very satisfying degree indeed.

"I like this. I like this very much." She stroked the smooth skin up and down. "I want to taste it."

She hadn't had a plan when she took hold of him, but now that she was staring at his rod, sucking it struck her as the perfect thing to do. Lowering her head, she took it inside her mouth. He groaned, and she smiled around the rigid flesh. Yup, nothing like a blowjob to blow a guy's mind. She licked the underside of his cock as she sucked more of it in. One of her hands rested on his thigh for leverage while the other clasped his erection and moved up and down in rhythm with her mouth.

"Oh, God." Kyle moaned, and his fingers tangled in her hair, pressing her head gently down.

Regan lifted her head, popping his slick cock out. "Don't touch me," she commanded. "Keep your hands on the arms of the chair and don't move."

He muttered a curse under his breath but did as she said. His eyes were closed, and his head tipped back. She nodded to herself. If she was going to control the show, he couldn't be allowed to be anything other than completely passive. She rewarded his obedience by returning to her task and was delighted to be met with the salty tang of pre-cum. The guy was so hot for her, he wasn't going to last much longer. His balls were pulled in tight to his body, which quivered with arousal and restraint. She could tell he wanted to jerk his hips up to meet her sucking, yet he didn't do it. He was being a good boy.

She slanted her eyes to one side and watched as his grip tightened to white knuckles on the chair. His breath came out in harsh pants. Picking up the speed of her mouth and hand, Regan sucked hard on his flesh, willing the orgasm to erupt. A muted bark shot from his mouth right before he jerked and hot semen spurted out. Her tongue pushed against the roof of her mouth to catch the salty stream while she pushed down on his thigh to keep him from shoving too deep into her.

When Kyle was finally still, Regan let him go and stood up. Turning to his desk, she found a mug and spit out his juice. She wiped her lips with the side of her hand. "Sorry," she said with a quirk of her lips. "I don't like to swallow."

He lay bonelessly in his chair, staring at her with a hooded gaze. He looked absolutely poleaxed, and she felt enormous pride at having been the woman to do that to him.

"It's okay," he replied. "I wouldn't swallow, either, if I were you."

His admission gave her an idea. She smirked at him and sauntered back to where he sat. "How do you feel, Kyle?"

He mimicked her look. "Very relaxed, Mistress Regan."

"Excellent." She straddled his lap with one leg and, leaning over, hovered her lips over his. "Open up for me, Kyle."

After a second's delay, he complied, and she slipped her tongue inside his mouth. She kissed him long and hard, sharing the taste of his cum with him. Far from shying away in disgust, he wrapped his arms around her and pressed her body into his. She allowed him that bit of liberty, happy with the way her visit had ended, after all. But it couldn't last. She had work to do. Reluctantly, she ended the kiss with a little nip of his tongue and stood up again.

Kyle licked his lips seductively while gazing at her. "So that's what I taste like. Interesting. I think I'll stick to pussy."

"Glad to hear it," she answered with a quirk of her brows.

He sprang to his feet, zipping himself up as he did. "How about right now?"

She clucked her tongue and shook her head. "No. I'm due at the club, and you undoubtedly have work, as well."

"True." He clasped her arm when she started to move toward the door. "When? I'm up on you by two. I want to reciprocate."

"You men are so goal oriented," she chided.

Still, he was right about her not being satisfied. She enjoyed bringing him to orgasm, in exercising control over him, but it was not yet enough. She wondered if anything ever would be with this man. She wanted to forget about the investigation, trip him to the floor and ride him like a bronco. Duty called, however, and she wanted to take it slow with him in any event. The moment she let him into her body would be that much sweeter if she allowed the tension to build.

"Guilty as charged," he agreed. "Regan, I want—no, I need to see you again."

"Friday, your place." There was already a germ of an idea forming about what she might pick up at Veronica's store to play with.

"What time?"

"I'm not sure. I want you waiting by eight. I'll get there when I get there." She walked to the door and turned with her hand on the knob. More thoughts about what they could do were popping up in her mind. "I'll be hungry, so have dinner ready, and I want you in your underwear."

"My underwear?" he repeated on a laugh.

She gave him a stern look. "Just your underwear. Understand?"

He sobered up. "Yes, ma'am."

"Good boy." She opened the door and stepped through. Turning on her heel, she reminded him of one more thing. "And Kyle? Stay away from Doctor Molvado."

"Yes, ma'am," he repeated, but it didn't sound quite so sincere this time.

Regan strode to the elevator. Damn him. He had better obey her about this and about the rest of the investigation. She didn't want another dead man on her hands, and more than that, she didn't want Kyle to be the killer's next victim. He was beginning to be more to her than a weird kind of lover. He was starting to really matter.

****

An hour later, Regan smoothed the lines of her leather dress and stared at herself in the dressing room mirror of the club. She hadn't quite managed to recreate

104

the look Veronica forced on her the previous day, but she supposed it was good enough. She wasn't trying to impress anyone. Kyle wouldn't be among her customers this afternoon.

The thought of the man added a layer of moistness to her already twitchy, wet pussy. Her hips swayed of their own accord. She was dying to get the guy inside her, and Friday seemed a long way off. Looking forward to the end of her work week wasn't like her. Usually she was the last one out the door, reluctant to leave any portion of her job undone even for one night, let alone an entire weekend.

This change in her nature disturbed her. Kyle Ramsey disturbed her. And, yet, there were only two choices. She could either shut down her growing interest in him with ruthlessness or pursue the relationship with her typical aggressive enthusiasm. Given that she had made a quick stop at Veronica's shop and a bag full of sexual goodies was now stuffed in her locker at the club, it was clear which way she was going.

"So, you're the new girl," a female voice said.

Shifting her gaze from her own image, Regan regarded a large, African-American woman through her reflection. "I'm Regan."

The other woman sat down at the make-up counter and started picking up various tubes and brushes. "I'm Cleo."

"Nice to meet you."

Regan watched as her companion liberally applied eye-shadow. Cleo's outfit was equally dramatic, a strapless, leather Playboy Bunny kind of suit from which her ample breasts and muscular ass popped out.

Her boots went all the way up her thighs, stopping just short of her crotch. While Cleo appeared to be about Regan's age, her face had a tired, worn look. Regan imagined the woman had worked in places like Nemesis for some time. She would undoubtedly have a lot of information to give about the lifestyle.

Adopting a nonchalant stance against the wall, she began subtle questioning. "I've been hoping to have a chance to talk to some of you others working here. This is all new to me, and to be honest, I need some tips." She gave the other woman a look, as if she were annoyed with herself for being so helpless.

Cleo batted her eyelashes to gauge her efforts before slanting a look Regan's way. "Sure, honey, I don't mind helping out a new girl." She opened a compact and began brushing blush on her wide cheeks. "But don't think there's anything to this job. These guys are all pathetic. They want their mommy substitute to paddle their asses so they can go out and fuck others over without feeling guilty. It's a game to them. Give them what they want, pick up your paycheck, and go home."

Regan shifted her stance as she contemplated Cleo's answer. She was beginning to think she was wasting her time at the club. The killer was certainly someone who viewed Femdom as more than a job or a game.

"I'm afraid I'm going to hurt them," she prodded.

Cleo barked out a laugh. "Hurt them? Please." She dismissed the idea with a wave of a tube of lipstick and applied a large swath of color to her lips. "With the toys we have here, no one's going to get hurt. No matter how much these dicks carry on crying and screaming, believe me it's all an act. They don't known real pain. They couldn't handle real pain."

Apparently satisfied with her make-up, she stood up and tugged her one-piece down over her ass cheeks a bit. She turned to Regan and looked her up and down. "You got a good look going for a newbie."

Regan smiled at the compliment. "Thanks, Veronica picked it all out."

Cleo nodded. "She knows her business. You look strong enough to pack quite a wallop, too."

"I like to lift weights," Regan admitted.

"Well, if you ever want to put those muscles to use in a legit Femdom setting, let me know. I'm into the real scene."

"What scene is that?" Regan frowned. This conversation was starting to be more interesting.

Cleo shrugged. "People who are serious about pain, both inflicting it and receiving it, know how to find each other. You can't have an open business for it, because the cops would shut it down. They don't like adults making decisions about their own bodies, but they let little girls get the shit kicked out of them by grown men without doing a thing." The woman's eyes went hard and dark as coal with this last statement, and Regan knew Cleo was talking about herself and not a hypothetical.

"This is a way to even the score, isn't it?" she said in a soft, conspiratorial tone.

Cleo's smile in response was bitter. "Yeah, it is. Don't let it get out of hand, here, though," she warned. "Remember, this is a game. You want to make a guy scream in true pain, have him thank you for it afterward and actually mean it, let me know. I'll hook you up."

"Thanks, I'll think about it." Before Regan could form a follow-up question to pursue this developing lead, Cleo turned away.

"Showtime. I've got a regular coming in five minutes. He likes to pretend he's a plantation owner, and I'm a slave who's getting revenge for all the times he's raped me." She stopped and tossed another hard look over her shoulder at Regan. "As if he could ever understand what it's liked to be raped and imagine what a woman would do to the man if the tables were reversed. See you around, honey."

With that parting shot, Cleo was gone, and Regan was left wondering whether she had a new suspect in the murders.

Chapter Seven

Kyle turned the filets over on the broiler and checked the time. It was eight-thirty and still no sign of Regan. Although she had said she didn't know when she would get there, he hoped it would be soon. He was taking a chance with the meat and the potatoes and asparagus he had roasting in the oven. If she took much longer, the food would be either cold or overdone, but he took pride in everything he did, including cooking. He felt it was beneath his dignity to serve something cold or simple for dinner for his date.

It didn't matter anyway. If Regan was pleased with the meal, he would be pleased as well. If she weren't, he might be punished, and he could no longer deny that the idea of it excited him. His cock, which had been neglected at his own volition for the last few days, stood at attention at the mere thought.

"Down boy," he muttered under his breath. He was wearing his boxers as ordered, and even though being single and having cooked in only his underwear before, he still felt weird because he knew a fully-clothed Regan was going to walk in on him. He couldn't help wondering what, if anything, she had planned for him this evening. He hoped that whatever else it involved, she'd let him finally put his dick inside her. Blowjobs were damn good, but nothing was better than seating his cock in the tight, soft warmth of a woman's body.

As he took the tray of vegetables out of the wall oven, the intercom buzzed. His heart and cock jerked simultaneously at the sound and what it meant. He forced his breath to steady and pressed the intercom button. "Regan?"

"Yes," came the cool reply and just the sound of the woman's voice was enough to harden his erection even more.

"Come on in." Undressed as he was, he pushed the button to release the inner security door. Then he opened his unit's door and stood aside as the woman who perversely held sway over him breezed into his home.

"Hi," she said in an easy tone. "I won't ask if you still want to see me tonight." She gave his cock a quick squeeze. "It's obvious you do, and you get points for enthusiasm."

He wanted to kiss her, just a little peck in greeting, but he didn't. Waiting for permission was already becoming ingrained in him. "Thanks. Although I can't take credit for my erection. That's your doing. My own personal dose of Viagra."

She smiled at his remark, and moving farther into the condo, she tossed a large, plastic bag on the floor. "I brought along some things for later," she said when he scrutinized the bag, and his heart picked up speed in anticipation of what it contained. Regan sniffed toward the kitchen. "What are you fixing for dinner?"

"Steak. Shit." He hustled back to the oven. The filets were done, and he hoped not overcooked. He pulled the broiler out and placed it on a trivet.

"Looks like you went to a lot of trouble," Regan leaned against the doorjamb, arms crossed in front of her chest.

Kyle shrugged as he plated the food. "Not really."

"Maybe not for the women you're used to having up here, but I'm more of a burger and pizza kind of date."

He heard the note of insecurity in her voice, and it touched his heart. This cop and he were from very different backgrounds, and yet it mattered not one wit to him. "You're worth the effort, Regan," he assured her over his shoulder and was rewarded by an appreciative grin.

The expression lasted only a millisecond before it was replaced by the hard-nosed Domme he was getting used to. "I see you were a good boy about your underwear."

"Yes, ma'am," he replied. "Does it please you?"

"Yes. I'm hungry, though. We eat first, then we play." The way she said the word play sent tingles up his spine in anticipation. His cock twitched.

"As you wish. I thought we'd eat at the dining table. If you'd like to be seated, I'll bring the plates of food over."

She nodded and did as he suggested. When he joined her moments later with the food in hand, he was pleased to see she had taken the seat at the head of the table as he intended. Her jacket was slung over another chair as was her gun holster. He put her plate down in front of her and sat in the place set to her right.

"Would you like some wine?" he asked.

He'd opened a bottle of Borolo earlier to breath. Although he wasn't sure a woman like Regan would recognize the label or even appreciate the sophistication of its taste, it didn't matter. He wanted to give her the best he could. It was a matter of pride, yes, but more, he felt affection for this woman. She was becoming important to him on more than a sexual level.

"Sure." She took a sip after he poured some in her glass. "It's very nice. As I'm sure you can imagine, wine is not my thing, either, but I like the taste."

"That's all that matters with wine," he assured her.

He watched as she tucked into her meal and was delighted by how much she was obviously enjoying it. He allowed himself time to savor some of his own meal before trying for conversation. If their relationship was to be founded on more than bed games, they needed to get to know each other better.

"How was your week? I mean after you left me the other day?" he clarified teasingly.

Regan swallowed her mouthful. "Not as productive as I would have liked."

"I'm sorry to hear that. The club's not panning out for you?"

She hesitated, as if pondering how much to tell him, then shook her head. "Not really."

"You must at least enjoy playing Mistress Regan," he teased again.

She rolled her eyes at him. "No, I don't. It's boring and hard work, and the men are less than appealing for the most part. They're not like you." She scraped her forefinger up his thigh.

His breath burst out as if he'd been punched in the gut, and he had to take a gulp of wine to ease his suddenly dry mouth. "Christ, I never would have thought I'd get off on this kind of thing."

"What kind of thing?" she baited him.

"Letting a woman dominate me, humiliate me, hurt

me, as you well know. It's like a drug, one hit and I'm hooked."

Regan looked at him thoughtfully over the rim of her wine glass. "You've really never done this before with another woman?"

"Never," he confirmed. "I've always been the one to take charge in bed. My ex-wife expected it."

"Is that what led to the divorce?"

"No, I was raised to be a take charge kind of guy, professionally and in my personal relationships." He gave her a wry smile. "I went into my marriage knowing it was my responsibility to protect and provide for my family. As the man of the house, it was my duty to shoulder all the burden so my wife wouldn't have to worry about anything, including when and how we would make love. I was comfortable with the role in all its aspects. At least, I thought I was up until now."

He took another bite of food and considered how quickly his expectations in a personal relationship had shifted dramatically. "Anyway, Julie wanted out of the marriage, because she said I worked too much and was never home. Funny thing was she never complained about the money I brought home for her to spend."

He shook his head and toyed with his own glass. "She also said she felt neglected, and yet she didn't seem too interested in my attention. I can't imagine what I would have done if she had greeted me at the door one day with a whip in hand, barking orders."

"You wouldn't have accepted her authority, because she wouldn't have been strong enough for you," Regan observed.

"You may be right," he agreed. "I can't say the divorce was a bad thing. Even my relationship with my daughters is better, because I get them every other weekend and make sure my schedule is clear to spend time with them. When I was living at home, I rarely saw them. It took the divorce to make me see how much I was missing."

He took another bite of his steak, although he wasn't really hungry anymore, at least not for food. He wanted Regan. His erection still strained at the fabric of his underwear. But it wasn't his call as to when they began to play, and Regan was still eating. "How about you? You seem rather good at all this for being a novice."

"I'm a quick learner. Besides, I haven't had much time with any one man to do anything really interesting."

"Married to your job?"

"Something like that, and I take care of my father."

"What's wrong with him?"

"A perp pushed him down a flight of stairs and put him in a wheelchair." She said the words with little rancor, just reciting the facts.

"I'm sorry," he murmured. "You take care of him?"

"He takes care of himself, mostly, but my mother died a few years after that from an aneurism, and well, I'm it. I don't mind, although with us sharing a duplex, it does put a crimp in my style."

"Well, we can always meet here, and the walls are thick," he added meaningfully.

Regan drained her glass. "Good." Standing up, she said, "I'm done, and I want you."

Kyle stood, too. He loved her direct manner, the fact that she seemed to be devoid of coyness. It was so much the way he, himself, was, and she was right about his needing to submit to someone he could respect for her strength. He stared hard into her eyes, letting her see how much he wanted her, how much his blood churned with the need to be touched by her.

Her eyes flashed with understanding, and she tossed him a bone, a small one, but it tested the limits of his self-control. Leaning over the corner of the table, she clasped the back of his head and dug her nails into his scalp. He winced in pain but didn't resist when she tugged him to her. She devoured his mouth with her luscious lips that tasted of the rich wine. He gripped the edge of the table to stop his hands from grabbing her and pulling her close. Instead, he was content to let his tongue chase hers and wrestle with it.

She allowed him this bit of liberty until they were both so breathless they parted with a gasp. "Leave the dishes and get into your bedroom," she ordered in a husky tone. She might not be as obvious as he, but she was definitely aroused. The knowledge satisfied some primitive part of him.

"Yes, Mistress Regan," he agreed smugly. With a fast-beating heart, though, he started toward his bedroom, making the effort to keep his gait slow and steady. This was it, what he had asked for, if not begged for. The question was, was he ready? Was he worthy of her? Could he stand up to whatever she had planned for him?

He'd find out soon enough.

Regan willed her breathing to steady as Kyle did as she had commanded. He was actually doing it. He was going to his bedroom to wait for her, his tight ass marching enticingly away. She wondered where she got the guts to order him around like that and realized she got it from him, of course. She was in control because he allowed her to be, and he allowed it because he trusted her to be forceful enough to take command of him. It was humbling.

When he was out of sight, she went to retrieve her bag of goodies, hoping she had made the right choices and that they would both enjoy the effect of them. She picked up the sack and, with a last deep breath for courage, followed him into the bedroom. He was standing to the side of a large sleigh bed, waiting for her to tell him what to do, she supposed. The bed would prove a challenge because she had hoped for a four-poster to tie him to easily, but she had also anticipated this possibility.

"Lie face down," she told him and again marveled at her own audacity. The look of excitement in Kyle's eyes before he complied told her she was doing the right thing.

When he was down, she dropped her bag and pulled out a pair of handcuffs. These were not like her official ones. They were covered in padded silk so as not to bruise the wearer. Still, she knew how to use them well, and seconds later, Kyle's hands were secured behind his back.

The legs, however, were going to prove more troublesome. She wanted them bound, and the only way to do that was to encase the ankles in shackles, which she did quickly. She hooked a bungee cord to one shackle, tossed the other end under the bed, and hauled it up on the other side. When she pulled on the cord, Kyle had to stretch his leg toward the edge, and after she attached a second cord's end to the other shackle, his legs were spread-eagle.

He was now pretty helpless, and there was only one more thing to do to keep him that way. Reaching into her bag of tricks, Regan extracted a ball gag. She had deliberately picked this type over the kind with a plug so as not to be reminded of the serial killer. She held the gag up for her lover to see. He was watching her with sharp eyes.

She made sure to keep the gag in his line of sight as she approached the bed and sat beside him. "Everything all right so far? I mean I assume it is, because I haven't heard the safeword."

"You won't." His voice was thick with passion, and the sound sent her juices flowing.

"I certainly won't if I use this thing. Perhaps it's too early in our relationship to use it given how it will keep you from telling me if I go too far." This was an important issue to resolve before they got started. Although the idea of gagging Kyle, making him completely helpless, caused her insides to quiver with excitement, she didn't want to scare him.

"I trust you, Regan," was the man's simple reply.

He did. She could see the trust in his eyes, and part of her wanted to run from the sight. It was scary to have another human being put his life in your hands. She wanted to prove to them both that he wasn't making a mistake, so she stuck the gag against his mouth. "Open up." When he did, she wedged the ball between his teeth and left the strap hanging down.

"I'm not going to secure the gag. If you need to safeword, you'll be able to spit the ball out."

Sliding off the bed, she stood and took in the length of him. His hard body was spread out for her pleasure, the muscles twitching with his confinement, his sides expanding rapidly with quick breaths that told her he was as excited and stimulated as she. Well, he was about to become more so, at least she hoped he was.

"I picked up a little something of my own to wear," she informed him in a low voice. She didn't make a big show of taking off her clothes because she felt self-conscious trying to be sexy and seductive. Instead, she rid herself of her outer layers as if she were getting lazily ready for bed.

Kyle's gaze never left her body, and his eyes went wide when he saw what she was wearing under her ordinary shirt. It was a simple silk camisole of deep purple trimmed in black lace. In Veronica's store, she had liked the contrast of the delicate material and her hard, muscled arms. The slippery softness of the silk clung erotically to her breasts, making her nipples peak to hard buds. She bet Kyle was thinking of fastening his lips to them right then, and he wasn't going to have too long to wait.

When she slipped off her pants, however, his eyes wandered down and away from her breasts. An explosion of air and noise came past his gag, and Regan gave him a knowing grin. She was wearing panties that matched the camisole, and they were crotchless. It had been weird to wear only her pants against her pussy, especially when she was so wet, but the effect the sight was having on Kyle was well worth it. His body strained against his bonds.

"Like what you see?" she purred.

It was so unlike her to be kittenish and teasing in the bedroom, but she couldn't help it. The outfit alone made her feel unbelievably sexy and feminine. She sauntered back to the head of the bed and stood near his face to give him a close look at her pussy. She waxed regularly, not out of vanity, but because she liked the clean look and feel of having only a thin line of pubic hair. The curly strands, a shade of red darker than her hair, peeked out provocatively from between the silk, and Kyle's nostrils flared as his eyes feasted on her cunt.

Regan spread her legs and braced them apart. "Like what you smell, Kyle? That's me wanting you." He made that grunting sound around the confines of his gag again, and she knew she was driving him wild. "Soon, I'll let you have a taste. Right now, I want to play with your body."

She left him and moved to her bag of toys. She pulled out a peacock feather and a riding crop. Soft and hard, they were contrasting weapons to use on a man. "What do you think?" She held them up for Kyle to see. Then, on impulse, she dragged the length of the feather through the folds between her legs to see what it felt like and to tease him. It tickled and caused her to give a little shiver. Kyle, however, jerked hard against his restraints, as if he were trying to free himself to get to her.

"Uh, uh," she admonished, delighted with his response. She was dying, too, to try out the toys on him directly. Kneeling on the bed, she sat on her haunches and ran her palm down his back. His skin was smoothness stretched over hard muscles. His ass was a perfectly shaped bubble that bunched under her touch as she dragged his boxers off it as much as she could. Damn, she should have made him strip before tying him.

In contrast to his movements, she squeezed and kneaded and finally sank her short fingernails into his flesh. He hissed in response.

"Does that hurt?" she asked. "How about something soothing?" With the feather, she caressed the place she had just dug and watched him react to the gentle touch. He was passive to the sensation, which disappointed her, so she made the feather more threatening by dragging it between his cheeks. *That* made him move. There was a grunt of protest, and he twisted his body to avoid her.

"Don't move!" She delivered a sharp slap across the rump in emphasis. "You're mine. I can touch you any way I want, and you will accept it, unless you safeword."

She waited for him to say something. When he remained silent, she drew the feather again between the cheeks. She moved it back and forth slowly. "I know how sensitive straight men can be about this, Kyle, but the idea of pegging you turns me on. If we continue our relationship, we'll discuss whether you can agree to that kind of play."

She meant it, too, even though she hadn't thought about it at all until this moment. The idea of fucking a man had crossed her fantasies from time to time. She hadn't thought she'd ever be in a position to act on it. Now, she realized the possibility was real. Not tonight, but soon if they kept up this relationship. And she had a feeling they would. Kyle was doing an excellent job of tamping down his aversion to this kind of play. His buttocks clenched off and on, yet he wasn't trying to avoid her anymore.

"Good boy," she praised with a pat on his ass and

removed the feather. Time to get down to business.

Without warning, she tossed aside the feather and picked up the crop. She brought down the first stinging blow without a word. Kyle howled through his gag, and his whole body jerked upward. Regan got up on her knees for leverage and delivered the second blow. She kept on raining blows down until his ass was bright red, and both she and Kyle were breathing harshly. The sound of his muted yells rang in her ears. Her blood raced through her veins, and her skin felt as hot as Kyle's looked. Her arousal was painful, and she wanted to straddle her lover and rub herself to orgasm.

Not yet. There was a better way. She unhooked the bungee cord from Kyle's ankles. "Turn over."

She helped him onto his back. The tip of his cock, wet and angry, poked out from his partially removed underwear. She reached up and pulled the material all the way down until it was caught under his tight balls. He grunted and bucked his hips upward.

"Lie still," she commanded. "It's almost time."

She slid off the bed and dug her way through the plastic bag until she retrieved the packet of condoms she'd bought. She fumbled with the plastic to open it, her fingers clumsy with her passion, and pulled free the black roll. She had picked the color to add additional atmosphere. With the protection safe in her hand, she returned to Kyle and straddled him. She inched up to his chest, careful not to send herself over the edge through touching him alone, and snatched the gag with her free hand.

"How are we doing, Kyle?" She meant it as a serious question given how she had just wailed on his ass. Although she didn't know him very well, she suspected he might be too stubborn to use his safeword. His answer was a feral growl, and his eyes were hard with want and need.

"I'll take that as a good sign." She wiggled closer so that her crotch hovered over his mouth. "Want a taste?"

His head reared up in answer, and he tried to fasten his lips to her clit. She was too quick for him. Her palm slammed down on his forehead and forced him back, as she pulled her body away from his reach.

"Naughty boy," she chided. "I didn't say you could. You wait for permission. Understand?"

He growled again. "Regan, please," he bit out through gritted teeth and pushed against her grip.

Her leverage was too great, and it was easy to keep him back. "Do you understand?" she repeated in a harsh voice. "If you're not going to play by the rules, I'll leave."

He fought for control, his breath coming out in short pants, his eyes flashed with banked fury. But, finally, he proved how strong a man he truly was.

"Yes, Mistress," he said in a strained voice.

"Very good." She released his head, moved back into position, and stayed there for a full minute. She made herself actually count—one Mississippi, two Mississippi. It was agony. She wanted to slam her cunt down on his face and make him lick and suck until she screamed with her climax. Kyle wasn't the only one who was strong, though. She waited, and then slowly squatted until she was almost touching his lips. "Now, you may lick my clit five times. Only five times, Kyle. No more, and do it slowly."

He gazed into her face while his tongue flicked out

and lapped up the full length of her folds, soft moistness against soft moistness. He was as slow and deliberate in his movements as she had demanded, proving that she was the one in control and that he could be trusted to follow her orders. It cost him, she could tell by the look in his eyes. It was hard, but he was doing it to please her. And, oh, how it pleased her. She wanted to close her eyes and let go to the sensation, but she didn't. It still wasn't time.

At lick five, he stopped and waited for her instructions.

"Excellent." She pulled back and read the disappointment on his face. "Don't look so sad. We're both going to get what we've been waiting for." She slid down to his groin and carefully rolled the condom on his raging hard-on. He hissed and bucked in her hand until she slapped his thigh. "Easy, now. I'm going to put you inside me, Kyle. You'd like that, wouldn't you?"

"Yes, please, Mistress," he begged.

"All right." She rose up over him and held his cock in position. "Remember, you don't come until I tell you to. If you fail me on this, it will be a very long time before I'll let you inside me again, if ever."

He nodded mutely, and sure that her message was clear, sure that neither of them could stand to wait any longer, she placed the tip of his cock inside her cunt.

Once again, she stopped and waited to see if he would be able to contain himself. She wanted to laugh with glee when he stayed stock still, waiting for her to make the move. He was so frigging fantastic. Only a strong man could do what he was doing, and he was giving himself to her. The emotional high she felt from the power was almost enough to satisfy her. Almost. She sat down on him hard, seating him to the hilt within her, and to her unexpected delight, the tip of his cock hit her G-spot dead on. Her body shuddered, and she strained to hold back the orgasm.

"Not yet," she muttered to herself, looking at Kyle through the slits of her lowered eyelids. He wore a similar expression, the effort of holding back evident on his face. "Suck me," she commanded as she began pumping up and down on his hard length.

To make herself clear, she leaned over to offer him access to her breasts. She was relatively well-endowed, but still, he had to raise his head for his mouth to meet her nipples. Clever boy, he used his teeth to tug down the thin material of her camisole and expose her aching flesh. He fastened his lips on one puckered bud and began to suck at it greedily.

"Oh, oh God!" She groaned as the tension mounted unbearably within her.

She had to let go; she had to let go. A scream of pleasure burst out as her insides exploded. Her hands gripped the bedcovers, and the walls of her cunt gripped Kyle's cock. She panted and mewed as waves of her climax built and crashed, over and over. And still, he sucked at her nipple, pushing the next wave higher and higher. How was he holding on? Where did he find the strength to do it? It must be killing him. She had to let him go, some part of her mind told her.

"Come now!" she cried out, and her eyes opened just enough to see his head drop back, and his mouth open. He bellowed and bucked, sending her over once more, and he didn't stop until she went blind from the pleasure and collapsed on top of him.

Chapter Eight

This final scream was more of a mewl, a pitiful sound that told her he had given up and would welcome death. Well, that was fine, because she would give it to him soon. Blood gushed over her fingers. The feel of it, the smell of it made her wet, and she wanted to come while it remained coating her skin. But, no, that would be weak, and she wasn't weak. Her victims were weak, unable to control themselves. She was stronger than they were and could wait for her pleasure.

She walked around the wooden frame—so convenient of him to have a dungeon to play in—and stuffed the offending mass of flesh inside the man. He barely twitched at the invasion, telling her that he was close to gone already. She would help him along, of course, a way of thanking him for playing so well with her this night. It had been more than he had been expecting, yet no more than he deserved.

Picking up her knife, she placed it against his throat.

****

The theme song from Hawaii Five-O blasted Kyle out of a sound sleep. Instinctively, he sought to tighten his grip on Regan, not sure yet what was happening, but she tore out of his arms and dove for the floor. He sat up in bed, wincing at the soreness of his ass, and watched her dig into the pocket of her pants for her phone.

"Hello?" She was down on her knees, leaning on her elbows, one hand propped up her head while the other held the phone. Her ass wiggled at him enticingly, allowing him a view of her pussy through those wicked crotchless panties she still wore. His cock amazingly stirred at the unintended invitation. Christ, was there no pleasing him these days? Apparently not where Regan Malloy was concerned.

Although she said little, he could hear the strain in her responses and knew, just knew, there had been another murder. His gut tightened with sympathy for this new man who had joined Jazz as a victim and with concern for Regan, who would undoubtedly leave the comfort and safety of his bed to investigate it.

What time was it anyway? Tearing his eyes from the delectable sight of Regan's backside, he glanced at his bedside clock. Four in the morning.

After their incredible sexual adventure the previous evening, he had cajoled her into staying the night with him. Once she had admitted her father wouldn't find anything unusual in his cop daughter not coming home, he knew he had her. There was no reason not to stay, and with his arms finally free, he was able to wrap them around her and hug her tight to him. Such simple joy in holding a woman. His woman. Sleep had come as quickly as falling off a cliff.

Now, though, his brief fantasy of waking up with Regan the next morning and having breakfast with her was over. She signed off the call and, standing up, turned to give him a grave look.

"She's struck again, hasn't she?" he asked before Regan could say anything.

"Yes." Her mouth flattened into a straight, grim line. "I have to go." She grabbed up her pants and shirt from the floor and rummaged around in the bag of tricks. She pulled out a sports bra and cotton underwear. Mistress Regan was turning back into Sergeant Malloy. "I need to use your bathroom if you don't mind."

"Of course, take a shower," he replied.

"No time, I'm afraid." She disappeared into the bathroom.

He heard the water running and wished she were in the shower and he could join her. Another part of his fantasy that wasn't going to come true any time soon. Instead, he got up gingerly from bed, testing the various aches and pains of his body by stretching his muscles. Damn, but she had worked him over good, and the weight of his body lying on his cuffed hands and arms had added a sweet agony to the ecstasy of being inside Regan's pussy, of coming within her. The lingering discomfort, however, was much like the kind he felt after playing a rough sport. It made him feel strong and vital somehow.

He picked up the hand cuffs Regan had left on the nightstand and ran a finger along the silk border. It left no mark to evidence his captivity, and he supposed it was a good thing. Hard to explain bruised wrists to colleagues and clients. His ass, however, was a different story. Those hard blows that had sent him yelling into his gag and the sting of which he felt even now had to have left something on his flesh.

Moving to his closet doors, he opened the one with the mirror attached and turned to look over his shoulder. Yes, they were there, angry red welts that would torment him for days. He could take it. He smiled. It was like sporting a badge of honor, proof of his fortitude.

"Jesus!" Regan hurried over to him from the bathroom and bent down to inspect the damage. "I didn't mean for it to be that bad. I'm sorry." She looked at him with concerned eyes. "I got carried away."

Leaning into her, he planted a soft kiss on her lips and smiled. "I like the fact that you got carried away." When he saw that she was going to argue the point with him, he spoke quickly to override her. "Regan, last night was incredible, as if everything in my sex life up until then was merely a warm-up for what I really crave. You didn't hurt me any more than I wanted to be hurt. You were magnificent, the perfect combination of sex kitten and authoritative woman. I've never been so relaxed in the bedroom. I didn't have to plan or worry about performing adequately. I only had to obey and endure. It was liberating."

He dared to run his thumb down her cheek and over her lips in a loving caress. It was important that he get this right, so she didn't shy away from him out of a sense of guilt. "I want more. I want to see you again and not just for the sex." This point was important, too. She had to understand she wasn't merely a means of getting his rocks off. "I'd like to take you out for dinner and a movie if you'd like, or a show in the theater district. Whatever you want."

Whatever you desire. Pleasing Regan had become very important to him.

She narrowed her eyes at him. "Really? You're all right?" When he held her gaze and nodded, she visibly relaxed. "Okay, I want to see you again, too. I don't know when, though. This case is escalating. I'll call you when I can."

With that, she closed the gap between them and grabbing his head with both hands, pulled him in for a punishing kiss. Her tongue invaded his mouth, swept every corner and pulled out again. Her teeth nipped and tugged his lower lip before she let him go.

Without another word, she turned and walked out of the bedroom. He followed her, naked and proud of how he was once more erect. He watched her strap on her gun, and a sick feeling wormed its way into his stomach. Her profession was a dangerous one, and she was about to go out in the middle of the night to view another mutilated body. The worry for her came fast and painfully but couldn't be helped. He was sinking in deep with her, sexually and emotionally. She mattered to him, and he wasn't sure exactly how he felt about this new attachment.

One thing was certain, though. He wanted her safe. "Be careful," he admonished as he held the door open for her.

"Always," she assured him, and then she was gone. But the ache of his body stayed with him, and oddly enough, he found that comforting.

****

Regan blinked her eyelids to clear the blur from lack of sleep. The crime scene was hours old and had been invaded by dozens of cops and CSI types. The victim was still there, however, hanging from a wooden frame designed to torture a person. He had been left specifically for her to see once the local police had realized it might be connected to the Boston murders.

It was a grotesque sight. David Foster, a forty-two

year old investment banker—single, no children—had been tortured to within an inch of his life before being castrated and nearly decapitated. All this was done in the privacy of his own dungeon in the basement of his beautiful home in the city of Newton, west of Boston. Apparently, Mr. Foster had been in the Femdom lifestyle for some time and had accumulated all manner of tools for punishment, some of which had been used on him. The room was sound-proofed, so unlike the other victims, no gag was stuffed into his mouth.

"She had the pleasure of hearing this one scream and beg," Regan observed, and her stomach churned at the thought. Poor bastard. "She really went to town on him, too. She's escalating, both in frequency and activities."

"Had the time and the perfect location to satisfy her craving," JoJo chimed in. The other woman had managed to beat Regan to the scene and had gotten the low-down from the local police.

"The roommate, Ben Cohen, was supposed to be gone all night, so she could have still been at it when the guy got home. As it was, he said he knew something was wrong right away because the alarm wasn't set. He said Foster never went to bed without turning it on."

"He knew to look for him down here?" Regan asked.

JoJo shrugged. "I didn't get all the details yet."

"Well, let's go interview him." Leading the way up the stairs, Regan left the pitiful remains of David Foster for the coroner's office to bag and cart off. In the elegant living room, she found a much younger man with weepy red eyes sitting on the couch. She jerked her head to the uniformed officer standing nearby and waited until that woman had left the room before approaching the witness.

"Excuse me, Mr. Cohen. I'm Sergeant Regan Malloy of the Boston Police Department, and this is my partner, Detective Mathers. We'd like to ask you a few questions."

Cohen turned those red eyes on her and blinked as if confused. "I don't understand," he said in a wobbly voice. "Why are the Boston police here?"

"Because we think there's a connection between Mr. Foster's death and two other murders in the city. May I sit down?" She sat on the couch about two feet away from him before he could respond to her rhetorical question.

He angled his body to see her better and probed her with sharp eyes. "Are you talking about those two men I heard about in the news?"

"Yes. We haven't released details to protect our investigation, but the manner of death is similar to how Mr. Foster died."

A violent shudder ran through Cohen, and he looked as if he might gag. "He was tortured, butchered, mutilated!"

"I know." Regan kept her voice low and soothing to help stay the mounting panic she heard in her witness's voice. "I know, and I'm very sorry, but we need your help to catch his killer."

The young man looked away and took a visible breath. When he turned to her again, he appeared calmer. "What do you need to know?"

"First of all, can you tell me if you knew who he was seeing tonight?"

Cohen shook his head. "No, he was going to try to hook up with someone, of course. He tried to several nights a week. It keeps him on an even keel, he says—said."

"Hook up with someone? Like a Dominatrix?" Regan probed gently. For all she knew the dungeon might have been something Cohen knew nothing about.

She needn't have bothered with delicacy. "Sure, that was his thing, you know. David liked strong women. He liked to be tied up and played with. He liked pain." Another shudder ripped through him. "Not that much pain, though. No way he agreed to that."

"I'm sure he didn't," Regan said. "He did have the set up for it, however."

"Yes, he showed it to me the first day I arrived. He wanted to make sure I understood what he was about, so I wouldn't freak out over it."

"How long have you lived here, Mr. Cohen?" It struck her as odd that a wealthy investment banker would need a roommate.

"Only a few months. David's my cousin, distantly. When he heard I was relocating to the Boston area, he offered me a place to stay. He knew I was leaving a bad relationship and was a bit unsteady financially."

"Are you into the Femdom scene, too, Mr. Cohen?" JoJo interjected.

Cohen gave them a crooked smile. "No, I'm gay, actually. Such a scandal it is in our conservative family. David didn't care, though. He understood what it was like to be different."

"Okay," Regan replied. "Let's go back to Mr. Foster 'hooking up' with a woman. How did he find women who suited his needs? Did he belong to a club?"

"No, he told me once that clubs were too bush-league. He wanted the real thing, so he had these connections through the internet."

Regan cocked an eyebrow at her partner, who immediately nodded to confirm that she was in the process of securing a warrant to impound Foster's computer. "Go on, please?"

Cohen lifted and dropped one shoulder. "That's all I know. I met one or two, but I didn't catch more than a first name. They're all pretty careful not to reveal themselves. People don't understand them, you know? They have to worry about their reputations, because they get labeled as freaks and weirdos and perverts."

Freaks and weirdos and perverts? Oh, my, that was about right. Regan, herself, was seriously questioning her own freaky nature. Had she really whaled on Kyle like some sadistic bitch hours ago? Yes, she had, and her cunt still ached sweetly from the multiple orgasms the experience had led to. She wasn't certain she had the right to distinguish herself from the killer she hunted, except that while Kyle was red and achy, he wasn't bleeding. And he was pleased with her actions, not dead like Foster or the others. Those differences had to mean something, didn't they?

In the meantime, she needed to concentrate on finding the killer, not obsess about her sex life. "You don't know who he was going to hook up with tonight, but you weren't supposed to be back here yourself?"

"No, I was going to spend the night with my new boyfriend, only he turned out to be an asshole, so I packed up and came home." His face scrunched up in obvious grief, and his eyes became wet with unshed tears. "At first, when I saw the alarm was off, I thought maybe he had someone over still, even though it was kind of late for him. David likes a good night's sleep. I almost went straight up to my room, except I didn't want to scare him by suddenly popping out this morning. I checked around the first floor and his bedroom, instead, and when I didn't find him, I decided to check the dungeon."

Cohen rubbed his arms as if cold. "Because I was afraid I'd be interrupting something, I opened the door just a tad and listened. When I didn't hear anything, I called down for him, and when that didn't work, I made myself walk down the steps."

The tears started to fall now. "I smelled it before I saw him. Oh, God, it was awful!" He hugged his waist and bent over his knees. "Who could do such a thing? They must be crazy."

Yes, crazy, and dangerous and out of control. Time was running out.

****

"Shit!" Regan grabbed a handful of napkins and swiped at the dollop of salad dressing that had dripped on her pants. She was tired and stressed, and the gallons of coffee she had consumed since waking at four that morning weren't helping in the least. Little wonder she was having trouble getting a fork to meet her mouth. Oh, well, at least she was wearing her clothes from the previous day, so the overall grunginess of her appearance was not harmed by the addition of a food stain. Given it was Saturday, there were also fewer detectives running around the place to rag her over it.

A familiar pair of legs came into view as she tossed the greasy wad of paper into her waste basket. "I have something that might cheer you up a bit," JoJo said when Regan looked at her.

Interest peaked, Regan sat forward in her chair. "What?"

JoJo sat in the visitor's chair beside the desk and held out a piece of paper. "This is a copy of an e-mail to Foster from a month ago. There's nothing about anyone he was going to meet last night, and the cousin was right about his not being a member of Nemesis, but this looks like a connection." She shrugged. "Then again, it's not exactly a rare name. It could be someone else."

In response, Regan slowly shook her head, her eyes peeled to the e-mail address of the sender. She felt that kick in her gut she got when she sensed a case was about to crack wide open. She lifted her gaze to her partner. "Pick her up."

An hour later, Regan stood in an interrogation room, arms folded across her chest and legs braced as JoJo led in an angry Pamela Williams, a/k/a Mistress Cleo. The Domme wore a raincoat belted around her waist, undoubtedly because she was dressed for work underneath it.

"I should have known you were a cop," the woman spat out.

"I was working undercover," Regan replied in a mild voice. "We're trying to catch a killer."

"Huh! You won't find one by dragging me down here like this. You're making me stand up good clients, regulars."

"I'm sure Veronica will take care of them. Have a seat." Regan tossed her head toward one of the chairs. She made it clear by the tone of her voice that it wasn't a suggestion.

Cleo curled her lip in response, but yanking out

one of the chairs, she did as she was told. She crossed her legs, causing the coat to drop open and confirming that she was indeed dressed for play.

"Who's going to make up the money I'm losing?" Cleo demanded, her voice still hard and pissed. If she was involved with the murders, she didn't sound guilty or afraid.

Regan had become quite adept at reading suspects over the years, and Cleo was giving her the wrong vibes for a guilty person. She found her building excitement over cracking the case start to falter. Nevertheless, there seemed to be a connection between this woman and the latest victim. She had to pursue the possibility that the killer was in the room with her. She tossed the copy of the e-mail onto the table.

"Did you send this message, Mistress Cleo?"

Cleo hesitated for a second before picking up the paper and reading it. For the first time since entering the room, she looked uncertain. "Yes, I did." She bit her lip. "Why?"

Regan placed her palms on the table and leaned on them. "Because the man you sent this to is the third man to be tortured and mutilated and killed in the last few weeks by a woman who likes to play the game a little too well."

Cleo's eyes went wide, and the piece of paper slipped from her fingers. "Dead! David's dead?" Regan could hear the horror and disbelief in the woman's voice. If it was an act, it was a damn good one. Then, again, play-acting was part of Cleo's profession.

"You knew him?" Regan prodded.

"Hell, yes, I knew him. He and I got together a couple of times. He has this killer set-up in his home."

Her gaze left Regan's, and she looked off into a corner of the room. "We had a fine time. The man knew how to take pain."

"Apparently too well," JoJo replied in a cold voice.

"What?" Cleo turned to look at the detective. "Now wait just a minute. Am I here because you think I killed him?"

"David is the third man killed by a woman who is obviously a devoted and experienced Domme with a lot more than consensual fun and games on her mind."

Regan picked up a file from one of the other chairs and slapped it on the table for dramatic effect. It wasn't Cleo's criminal record, but the record of the man who'd featured in her childhood.

"You told me in the dressing room, yesterday, that the law doesn't help little girls as well as it should," she reminded the suspect. "I did some reading while I was waiting for you to come in. Your stepfather did some vicious things to you, didn't he, Pamela, before your mother found the courage to go to the police?"

In Cleo's eyes, Regan saw fear and hurt creep past the anger for a moment before the woman put her emotional shields back in place. "Why bother to ask me? It's all in there, and the asshole got his while serving in Walpole, so what does it matter anymore?"

"It matters if you're taking your revenge on other men."

Cleo laughed, a harsh, dismissive noise. "I get my revenge every day at the club and on my own time with guys I meet on the internet like David. It helps me deal with the memories, I don't deny that, and the guys are begging me to do it. It works out real nice that way. But if you think I've gone crazy and am killing people, think again. I've got two babies to take care of. No way I'm going to let some man goad me into prison for the rest of my life." She leaned toward Regan and locked eyes with her. "If that happened, then my asshole stepfather wins, doesn't he, because he'll have ruined my life for sure."

Damn it! Regan hated how much sense the woman made, and worse, she hated how much she believed her. Still, Cleo, through Club Nemesis, was the only known connection to all three victims. "Okay, Cleo." She pulled away from the table and paced thoughtfully. "I can see your point. Tell me, though, how well did you know David Foster?"

Cleo sat back in her chair. "Not well enough to know his last name. We only met a couple of times at his place, and that was it. I'm not looking for a relationship, and neither was he. I haven't seen him in three weeks, at least," she added in anticipation of Regan's next question.

"What about Eugene Morales and Joseph Bennington?"

Cleo blinked at her and didn't answer for several seconds. "I know those are the two men who were killed recently if that's what you mean. I listen to the news like everyone else."

"They were club members."

Cleo shrugged. "Not my clients, but I heard a couple of the girls talking about it. You know, after the murders."

"What did they say?"

"They were freaked out, weren't they? A couple of nice regular clients who tipped well. The kind of guys you like dealing with, because they're into the scene but not in a self-indulgent way. That gets old real quick even when the money's good."

Regan stopped her pacing and leaned against a wall. "I don't understand what you mean." She really didn't, and she wanted to know, to understand this lifestyle, even though her question wasn't necessarily being driven by the investigation. It was more personal than that.

Cleo made a face. "See, some clients go way over the top during the scene, wailing and crying and begging forgiveness. Like they're in some bad morality play or something. It's hard to take them seriously, and for sure, you don't respect them."

"You respect others who don't carry on so much."

"Uh-huh," Cleo confirmed with a nod as if the point were obvious. "A real submissive is strong and has pride. There aren't many people who can acknowledge they need domination and discipline, demand the pain, take it and draw strength from the experience. You have to admire people like that."

"You admire these men even as you torture them?" It sounded like a huge rationalization to Regan, and yet, didn't she feel the same way about Kyle? Was she trying to justify her perversion?

Cleo bristled at the question. "I don't torture. When I finished with David, he walked me to his door and kissed me good night."

"If you kick a puppy, it will whimper at your feet and lick your hand."

"It's not like that!" Cleo slammed her palm on the table as she rose to her feet.

Regan straightened, alert for possible trouble. On the other side of the suspect, JoJo showed the same posture. "How do you know?" Regan demanded. How did Regan? After all, Kyle had done the same to her not so long ago. Guilt gnawed at her belly once more.

"You wouldn't understand," Cleo answered after a few moments of silence. She looked at the floor and rubbed at her forehead with her fingertips. Her head angled toward the e-mail still lying on the table.

"The person who did that to David is not a Domme. The Dominant respects the submissive and is humbled by the trust placed in them. Such trust is not to be abused." Cleo's eyes met Regan's. "You're searching for a killer among the wrong people. The person who did these horrible things is a psycho who has no respect or empathy for her victims." Her gazed dropped. "I may have issues to work out. I won't deny I entered the lifestyle and my profession for that very reason. But the people I've met, like Veronica and David, have taught me how to do it right."

"Perhaps," Regan conceded because what this emotionally scarred woman said made a lot of sense. She also was fading rapidly as a viable suspect in the killings.

Placing her palms on the table, she leaned forward. "I can't ignore how the killer was able to access the victims through the Femdom connection. Whatever she may be psychologically, the victims saw her as a Domme. Can you think of anyone in your world who may have, shall we say, gone over to the dark side?"

Cleo shook her head. "No, but I'll try."

Try. That was all any of them could do, and Regan hoped to hell the killer didn't strike again in the meantime.

Chapter Nine

Kyle stared at the phone number he had found on the internet over the weekend and debated with himself. Regan had been more than clear about his staying away from the sex therapist. The woman was a possible suspect in the murders, and his Domme didn't want him interfering with the investigation or getting into harm's way. He had his orders.

The problem was Kyle didn't take orders. Not since becoming an adult male had he allowed another to control his personal life and not since making senior partner had he knuckled under in his professional life.

Except, he was voluntarily submitting to someone else now. He had handed Regan the reins of his sex life. Even sitting in his office, he thought of her constantly, at least at a low level, because his body ached. And so did his cock. It strained against his pants, egged on by the raw flesh of his ass rubbing against the relative softness of his boxers. More than once throughout the day, he had been tempted to relieve the pressure in the men's room. He hadn't, of course, because his body belonged to Regan.

The question was how far did her control extend to the rest of his life? Obviously, she had no say over his work life. Being one of the top litigators in the country was a source of tremendous pride and fulfillment he would never relinquish, and he would never expect

Regan or any other woman to demand he do so. No, the gray area was those aspects of his personal life that didn't involve sex. Was he willing to do Regan's bidding outside of bed?

There was no easy answer to that question. If it were a matter of where they lived, what he wore, or how they generally spent the money he earned, he supposed he would do whatever made her happy as he had with Julie. It was easy to cede such decisions because those things simply didn't matter to him. Jazz's murder did. And while he could trust Regan to make good choices about damn near anything and he could trust her with his body, he couldn't trust her when it came to finding the killer. He wasn't being fair to her, but it wasn't only her that he didn't trust. It was everyone. Kyle fundamentally trusted himself, and only himself, when it came to certain matters.

Besides, Kyle reasoned as he picked up his phone, if Regan found out about his efforts, she would punish him for it. The thought of what she might do pumped more blood to his cock, and he had to bite back a moan just as his call was being answered. The female voice on the other end sounded timid, yet professional. He covered the receiver as he cleared the passion from his throat.

"Yes, I'd like to make an appointment with Dr. Molvado please. As soon as possible." He paused for effect. "I'm in a bit of a crisis."

"I see." The voice developed a concerned edge to it. "As it happens, the doctor had a cancellation, and a spot has opened up at ten o'clock on Wednesday." As Kyle checked his calendar to see whether the time was free, the woman added, "Of course, if you need immediate help, we urge you to go to the hospital."

Kyle smiled at the implication he was about to hurt himself over sex. Hurting him over sex, after all, was Regan's job. "No, no, nothing like that," he assured the woman. Damn, he had a meeting that conflicted with the opening. He'd have to reschedule. Jazz was more important to him than work. "That date and time work for me."

"Good. If I could have your name please?" The timidity was back.

He hesitated only a second before replying. "Kyle Ramsey."

"Very well, Mr. Ramsey. Please try to arrive fifteen minutes before your appointment to fill out some forms." If his name meant anything to the woman, she hid it well.

"I will, thank you."

He hung up and, sitting back in his chair, contemplated his ceiling. He had done it, and he would live with the consequences. If nothing else, maybe this Doctor Molvado could help him understand better what was happening to him. Why had he suddenly developed a passion for being dominated by a woman? The obvious answer was that the inclination had been in him all along, and he had ignored it, beaten it back. Perhaps the common desire had drawn him to Jazz as a friend without them even realizing it. Hadn't they spent countless hours as young men watching Mrs. Peele kick ass in The Avengers and hooted and drooled in equal measure over cheesy sci-fi amazons in B-grade movies?

Regan was different, however. She was the real deal, although she struggled to accept her desire to dominate as much as he struggled with his desire to submit. But she was so good at it, and they were so good together. The memories of Friday night flooded in, and he pressed his hand against his dick as it swelled and hardened once more. The weak voice of the doctor's receptionist had softened him. Now the thought of a commanding female voice tightened his balls and sent his heart pounding in anticipation. He needed the domination.

He needed Regan.

Sitting forward, he punched in another phone number, one he'd memorized already without even using it. The call was answered on the third ring by an impatient-sounding voice. "Sergeant Malloy."

This time, Kyle couldn't keep the groan from escaping his lips.

"Hello?" There was more bite now to the tone.

"Sorry," he breathed into the phone. "It's Kyle. Just the sound of your voice almost made me come."

"Don't." She barked the order in a low voice that did nothing to diminish the strength behind her command.

With effort, Kyle brought himself under control and was pleased with how steady he sounded when he answered. "I won't. You haven't given me permission to."

"That's right, I haven't." Her tone was playful now. "What's up?"

"Aside from my cock, nothing much. I called because I miss you, and I wanted to see how you're doing."

There was a stifled yawn over the phone. "Sorry, I'm beat. I guess that about says it all."

Kyle felt concerned and frustrated. He wanted to

take her home, his home, and tuck her into bed so she could get the sleep she so obviously needed. "It's almost five. When does your shift end?"

"It doesn't. Not when I'm tracking down a serial killer. I worked all weekend, too."

"You have to rest, Regan."

"I will later. Much later."

Not the words he wanted to hear, yet he was also buried in work and wouldn't normally contemplate leaving so early in the day. An alternative thought came to him. "You have to eat, though, right?"

"More or less," she agreed.

"How about meeting me for dinner?" When they parted in the wee hours of Saturday morning, he had spoken of dating, and he had meant it. This thing with Regan was more than sex. He wanted to get to know her.

She groaned over the phone. Not a sexy sound, but a weary one. "I don't have time. Sorry."

"I'm talking about an hour, Regan. You can spare an hour, can't you?"

"I suppose."

"Good, I know a great Thai restaurant right around the corner from your precinct. We can meet there so no one will know you're taking a break for yourself," he teased.

"Okay," she agreed, but he sensed reluctance.

"What? Don't you like Thai? We can go somewhere else. Whatever you want." And he was serious. He would clog his arteries with a fast food burger and fries if it would please her.

"Thai sounds fine. It's just that I've never had it."

"Do you like Chinese?"

"Sure."

"Then, you'll love Thai." He gave her the name and address of the restaurant. "I'll see you at six."

****

Kyle checked his watch again before taking another sip of his water. Regan was almost ten minutes late, hardly something to worry about, yet he couldn't stop fidgeting. It was nerves, plain and simple. The kind of nerves a young man has on a first date, which was odd because he was neither young nor on a first date. Unless one didn't count having sex as any kind of date. He shifted his body to agitate his sensitive skin and immediately felt the confidence and calm the discomfort gave him. He was a submissive. If his mistress was making him wait, then he would wait patiently, because he was strong enough to handle anything she dished out.

When he saw her walk inside the restaurant moments later, however, he knew she wasn't playing any game. No one who looked that exhausted was up for anything more than a good meal and some down time. He intended to give her both.

Spotting him, she gave a quick smile as she walked over. That one bit of affirmation sent a bolt of desire through his body. It also warmed him in a way that was purely emotional. He knew then he was infatuated with this woman, if not falling in love with her.

"Hi," she said, running a hand through unkempt hair. "Sorry I'm late."

"I don't mind waiting for you." He held out a chair for her. He could tell by her brief hesitation the move surprised her. It pleased him to know he was doing something for her that no other man had. Even better was the look on her face when he planted a quick kiss on her lips. It was a gesture of affection, not lust, and he grinned knowingly at her as he sat down.

She gave him a look he suspected was one usually reserved for people she thought might be suspects before settling in her own chair. She took a look around. "This looks like a pretty popular place. I'm glad it's not fancy, though, given how I'm wearing clothes that look like they came from a dumpster. I didn't have time to do laundry this weekend."

He heard the insecurity underlying her comment and said simply, "You're beautiful and sexy."

She narrowed her eyes and gave him that suspicious look again. This time, he kept his expression serious, because he meant what he said. "Thank you," she finally replied and opened up her menu. "What would you recommend?"

"Thai iced tea, for starters." He followed her lead and switched away from personal comments. "As for food, I guess it depends on whether you like noodles."

She looked at him from over the menu. "Who doesn't?"

"Everyone who's on a low carb diet."

Regan shrugged and scanned the menu again. "I never diet."

"Really?" He was truly surprised to hear her say it.

"Why? Do I look like I need to diet?"

It was the first time he had ever heard Regan say anything he considered typically female, and like a typical male, he back-peddled as fast as he could. "No. Absolutely not."

She grinned at his obvious discomfort. "Men are so easy to tease. I know you didn't mean I was fat. I'm sure you've never met a woman who wasn't on a diet, which is pathetic. I control my weight with exercise. So, back to my question. What do you recommend?"

Kyle felt himself relax, really relax. Not merely because he hadn't insulted her, but because he was enjoying her company. Other than Jazz, he couldn't remember the last person who made him feel that way.

Thinking of his dead friend reminded him that he was keeping a big secret from the woman across from him. Not wanting to spoil his good mood, he pushed the thought aside. He would deal with the consequences of his decision later. Feeding Regan was the most important thing on his list right now. "Do you like spicy food?"

"Not so much," she confessed.

"May I order for you?"

Closing her menu decisively, Regan replied, "Yes, I trust you."

There was a quick squeeze to his heart, and he held her gaze for a second before turning to the server who'd arrived. He ordered the tea, steamed shrimp shumai, Siam rolls, and pad Thai for them both. When they were alone again, he tried to think of something to ask her that didn't involve the serial murders. He was on the verge of asking her a standard question about what she liked to do off duty when she blurted out what he hadn't dared ask her.

"The killer struck again Friday night, as you've undoubtedly heard on the news. I confirmed it when I arrived at the crime scene." Her voice was quiet so as not to be heard by other diners. "It..." She took a sip from her water glass. "It was really bad. The poor bastard had his own sound-proofed dungeon and our girl took full advantage of the opportunity."

She was looking down, so she didn't see his hand reaching toward her until he clasped hers. "I'm sorry, sweetheart."

She still didn't look up at him, and whatever response she was going to make, it was delayed by the arrival of their tea. Kyle was happy when she didn't pull her hand away from his. Instead, she tried the tea with her other one.

"This is great," she exclaimed and treated him to a bright smile. "And I'm not going to think about the details of this latest murder, or it'll put me off my dinner. I do need to ask, though, did you know David Foster?"

Kyle caressed her fingers while he thought. Finally, he had to shake his head. "No, sorry. I didn't know him, and I don't remember Jazz ever mentioning him, either."

"Damn, too much to hope for, I guess."

The appetizers came, and he reluctantly let go of her so they could eat. He missed the contact but enjoyed the way she dug into her food. They talked about more pleasant things than murder. He found out that she liked to play softball, and he resolved to find a coed team so they could play together. He told her more about his daughters and felt that strong emotional tug again when she said she'd like to have children of her own. It was a comfortable, if hurried meal, and while the sexual tension was there, it was simply a low humming in the background.

At least, until Regan leaned over and remarked, "So, how does your ass feel?"

Just like that, he got stiff. He wiggled his body to

gauge how he felt. "Decidedly tender still." When a concerned look crept across her face, he did a preemptive strike. "Don't you dare start on the mea culpas. I like having a sore ass."

"Do you?" The skepticism in her voice was clear.

"Yes." He held her gaze for long seconds so she could see the honesty in his eyes.

"Hmm." Leaning back, she picked up a few stray noodles and sucked them into her mouth. She let the fork linger for a few seconds between her lips and sucked as she pulled them it again.

Kyle closed his eyes to the sight. His body ached enough as it was. "You're not making me any more comfortable." He popped his eyes open again at the sound of her throaty laughter. Seeing her relaxed and well-fed was worth a case of blue balls.

She waited until their dishes were cleared before she let out a long, slow breath. "Don't move." He cocked his head at her in confusion. "Not a muscle."

He did as she commanded, instinctively responding to the authority in her voice, although not understanding why she wanted him to do it. Then he felt toes sliding up against his bulging package and understood very well indeed. The pressure against his burgeoning hard-on was like an electric shock, yet no one around them would have ever guessed Regan was playing footsie with him, such was his restraint. He kept his gaze fixed on hers, daring her to do more.

And she did. With lazy circles, her big toe teased his aching flesh, lightly at first, then with increasing firmness. His cock hardened, lengthened, and pressed back painfully against her foot. She used her sole to rub up and down from tip to balls, using a rhythm guaranteed to make him shoot his load.

"Regan," he hissed out a low warning.

Still she kept up the stroking, a look of challenge and demand on her face. Kyle remained motionless as she had commanded, except his hands curled into fists and his breath became more labored. It wasn't possible she was going to make him come right here in the restaurant, was it? Surely, she would stop and leave him in agony. The tension built, however, all the faster because of the day he had spent yearning for her. He could almost feel the cum pumping up his dick, desperate to erupt.

He opened his mouth to give her one final warning to stop, and the climax hit him with shocking intensity. His eyes widened, and he forced his lips closed so that he wouldn't cry out. His fists tightened so hard, he thought his fingers would crack with the strain. His body shook with fine tremors as he worked to keep still. It was like a sunburst going off inside him, the pleasure dispersing to the far corners of his body. And all the while, his gaze remained locked with Regan's, her mouth formed into a small smile while she gently milked his orgasm.

When she finally moved her foot from his crotch, the fog lifted from his mind. He slowly became aware of the noise of the restaurant, the people nearby. With a quick glance around, he tried to gauge whether anyone had known what they were doing. No one seemed to be staring at them or smirking. Apparently, he had managed to hide what had happened, and knowing he had, he felt another measure of pride.

Taking a sip of water, he noticed his hands shook a bit. "That was a dirty trick," he observed in a thick voice. He took another swallow to clear his throat and steady his breath.

"I know," Regan admitted with a sly smile. "Sorry, I couldn't resist. Are you mad?"

He gave her a well-satisfied smile. "With you? Never. It's a good thing, though, that I'm wearing a suit coat to hide the evidence of your control over me."

The bill was placed in front of him before she could respond, and he paid it quickly, wanting to get out of the place and have a chance to show his appreciation for Regan's attention. He did have to adjust his jacket to hide the wet spot on his pants, and the naughtiness of it all caused his cock to stir once more. Damn, if he wasn't a goner where Regan was concerned.

Escorting her out of the restaurant, he led her into a remote corner of the building. He used his body to press her up against the worn brick, knowing she complied because she wanted to, not because he could make her do anything.

Bracing his arm above her head, he bowed his face over hers. "I've been thinking about you pretty much since you left my bed. Every time my ass stung or a muscle ached, I thought of you, and I wanted more. You saw how easy it was to make me hard with your touch and make me come. Christ, I'm getting stiff again already just having you near and talking about it." He watched as her gaze slid down to where his pants bulged. "Please tell me when I can see you again."

She shifted her gaze to his, and there was a bright gleam there that told him she wanted him, too. Seeing it, his control broke, and he dropped his lips to hers. He wrapped her in his arms and slanted his mouth so that he could invade her with his tongue. The sweet and salty taste of peanuts met him as he assaulted her with quick, hard strokes. Only a couple of bites from her teeth made him slow down and draw back.

He didn't go far, however. He kept his forehead pressed against hers, panting from his effort and restraint. But he wasn't the only one affected by the kiss. Regan breathed hard, too. Her hands clasped his waist with her fingers digging into his flesh. "You're getting ahead of yourself, boy-o."

"I'm sorry, Mistress. I want you too much, and by my estimation, I'm being very restrained."

"Ah, but it's my opinion that counts," she corrected him.

"Yes, ma'am," he agreed with a short laugh. "Please, Regan, when can I see you again?" He didn't even care that he practically begged.

She didn't answer right away. She kept him waiting, wondering, until she finally put him out of his misery. "Tomorrow night I have something to do. Maybe we can meet Wednesday night, depending on how the investigation goes. Frankly," she blew out a breath, "if we don't get a lead soon, there won't be anything for me to do about the case at that point." She gave him a hard look. "I wonder, though, if either of us really appreciates what we're getting into."

Kyle slowly moved his head back and forth. "I don't know. Honestly, I don't. I do know that I want you, and I'm willing to do whatever you want in bed."

"Whatever?" she asked in a low voice. "I'm not so sure."

"I'm serious, Regan."

"Maybe it's time for both of us to find out if we're

serious about this lifestyle."

"Try me," he challenged.

"Move away from me," she ordered in a matter-of-fact tone.

He complied instantly and was rewarded with soft, sweet kiss. "I'll call you," she promised and walked away.

He felt suddenly unsteady, whether it was from the controlled orgasm in the restaurant or with new unspent need he couldn't tell. He leaned against the building. What was he doing? What had he promised? What would she do?

It didn't matter. He pulled himself upright again. He could take whatever she did to him, and he would enjoy it. To pretend otherwise would be weak, and Kyle Ramsey was not a weak man.

****

Tuesday night, Regan jogged up the front steps of the house that was a second home to her. The Gallagher sisters, Sheila and Maeve, had been as close as twins, and had made sure they lived within a block of each other after they both married cops and started their families. Daire had come first, but Regan had been only a few months behind, then came Ronan and Finn. Maeve hadn't been able to have more kids, but the Callaghan boys had been more like Regan's brothers than cousins. They had treated her like another brother as well, always including her in their plans and assuming that she was, like they were, going to be a cop. Nobody had ever laughed at the idea or told her she couldn't do something because she was a girl.

Her Callaghan cousins meant the world to her and as tired as she was from long frustrating days in her investigation, not to mention her intense encounters with Kyle, she'd promised to come over and help with the side project they all tackled from time-to-time.

Aunt Sheila and Uncle Rory had been murdered, gunned down on the streets of Boston, some eight years back, and so far no one had been charged with the crime, much less convicted of it. It was a cold case, and the only people who still investigated it were their sons and Regan.

As much as she would have loved to go home and gets some sleep, or visit Kyle, Ronan had asked her to come over and look at some new evidence. She wasn't going to let them down by begging off. Besides, there was no clear lead in the serial killings, and she was afraid she had jumped too fast into the deep end with Kyle. A night off from seeing him was a good thing. She couldn't even keep her hands—or foot—off him in a restaurant, for Christ's sake.

She rang the bell and offered up a smile to Daire when he opened the door.

He narrowed his eyes at her even as he stepped to one side. "You look exhausted."

"It's nothing. I've caught a difficult case, is all."

"I heard. A serial killer?"

"Looks like. The FBI has been called, and they're a major pain in my ass. I spent most of the day going over the evidence we have with their profiler, who by the way, is convinced we're looking for a man. Says women are too rare."

She shrugged off her bomber jacket and slung it over the back of the couch. When Aunt Sheila had been alive, she wouldn't have tolerated it, but the boys were more casual about their home. Or rather Daire's home.

Finn and Ronan had moved out. Speaking of whom, they were both sitting at the old dining table. Pieces of paper and photographs were laid out all over the surface.

"Virtually all serial killers are men," Ronan stated without looking up from what he was staring at.

"I am aware. This one is a woman. I'm sure of it."

"Want a beer?" Daire asked.

"No, thanks. It'll put me under given how tired I am. I'll take a Coke if you have it, though."

"Yup, be right back."

Finn glanced up at her with a frown. God, the guy still looked like he was in high school. No wonder he'd been picked to go undercover a few months ago as a homeless teenager. "You should go home and get some sleep."

"Naw." She brushed off the concern and sat down across from him. "I'm good for a few hours yet. What have we got here? None of this looks familiar. Where did it come from?"

Every once in a while, she and the boys poured over documents, pictures, and anything else they could find from Uncle Rory's personal belongings, as well as poked at the official file. They hoped against hope that something new would jump out at them to make sense of the murders. This stuff on the table, however, was not anything she'd seen before.

Daire put a tall glass of soda with ice in front of her before taking his seat at the end of the table. He looked down the length at Ronan. "You want to field this question?" His tone told her something was up.

She looked at her middle cousin, the one who could charm the birds out of the trees and had an angle for everything. He gave a very un-Ronan-like sheepish grin.

"It's a box of stuff we took out of Mahurin's house. Diego found it. The CSI folks missed it, but not so Diego. The man has mad skills at finding people's hidey-holes of stuff."

Regan turned her gaze to Daire. "Are we talking about something that never made it to the evidence locker?"

Her cousin grimaced. "Yes." He took a swig of his beer. "Ronan and Diego knew if they turned it in, chances were it would disappear before they had an opportunity to go through it."

Regan frowned back. Fuck, yes, she knew it. Her uncle had known there were bad cops back in his day, and she was as sure as she could be that it was those same bad cops who killed her aunt and uncle to keep him from exposing them all. They were still there, more than one, as near as she and her cousins could tell. Someone had tipped off the head of the prostitution ring that Finn had infiltrated and nearly gotten him killed. There were people in high places that had been in the guy's pocket according to what he'd bragged to Finn, thinking he was going to kill the young cop before he could tell anyone.

Ronan and his partner, Diego, had found evidence that their father's old partner, Mahurin, had been one of the dirty cops. The guy had been tipped off by someone at the station and had died trying to escape them. They were pretty sure Mahurin had killed or orchestrated the killing of a snitch named O'Malley. It was the video O'Malley had imbedded in his computer that led them to Mahurin and now Mahurin's stash of information could lead to others.

Her tiredness fled with the excitement of the find.

She leaned over to peruse a picture near her. It was oldish-looking, and one of a guy handing a package off to another. "Hard to see faces in these," she observed with a squint of her eyes. She looked over at Ronan. "Mahurin died weeks ago. Why didn't you call me over to look at this stuff before?"

Her cousin looked away guiltily. "Didn't want anyone else to get into trouble."

Daire snorted. "Don't feel bad, Regan. He didn't tell me or Finn until last week."

"I didn't want to get anyone else in trouble," Ronan repeated through gritted teeth.

"Fuck that," Regan said without heat, although she was pissed that he'd kept her out of the loop. "We sink or swim together on this. It takes more than one set of eyes to see things. You know that."

"I had Diego helping me," he muttered around his bottle of beer.

"Oh, yeah? Where is he, then?"

"Cassidy has to work late tonight. We make a point of at least one of us picking her up to drive her home whenever that happens."

Regan grunted in response. Overprotective men could be a pain in the ass. Sweet, of course, but annoying. Cassidy Barnes, the new ME in town, had two men to hover over her. It was weird, but her middle cousin was in a three-way relationship. She picked up another picture and stared at it.

"Where's Michael?" she asked of Finn. Michael was Finn's partner, and while the man worked vice, he had a keen pair of eyes and good cop sense.

"Craig's started school, and Michael's making sure he does his homework and gets to bed on time."

Craig was Finn and Michael's foster son, one of the boys they'd rescued from the prostitution ring. "How's he getting along?"

Finn's eyes brightened, and he smiled. "He's doing really well. He's made new friends, quirky kids. Michael and I refer to them privately as the Breakfast Club. They're good kids, though. Craig's really worried everyone will find out what happened to him. Hard enough to be a gay teen, but one who was forced to sell his body to strange men?" Finn shook his head. "I think even if by some chance kids do find out, his friends will stick by him."

"That's good. High school is hell on Earth. I'm glad he's fitting in okay."

Regan had known for years before Finn dared to come out that her baby cousin was gay. She was glad he was secure in who he was, although she worried he'd jumped in too deep with his boyfriend, moving in and raising a troubled teen. Still, he looked happy whenever she saw him, and there was no denying that Michael was not only a good cop, but a good man for Finn as well.

Looking at her two younger cousins and thinking about their somewhat unconventional relationships, she thought of her own with Kyle. What they had together was outside the vanilla world she'd been raised in. She wasn't comfortable with it, and yet it made her happy and satisfied. Who was to say what was normal, anyway? Perhaps she was overthinking the whole thing and, worse, worrying about what people might think. Maybe Ronan and Finn had some insight she could benefit from. Did she dare bring it up with them?

Too unsure of the reception she'd get, she sucked on her drink and pushed pictures and papers around. She wasn't really seeing anything, because she was too distracted with her thoughts. Finally she decided to "man up" and broach the topic of her new-found Domme side. She waited until Daire left to use the bathroom. As the oldest, he was more straight-laced than the other two. She supposed so much responsibility at a young age would do that to a person.

She drained her glass and took a deep breath. "So, um, I'm hoping for some advice."

Ronan and Finn both stopped what they were doing and stared at her as if she had two heads. Well, no surprise. She rarely asked anything of them or from them. She tried not to squirm under their scrutiny.

"The thing is," she fiddled with her glass, not meeting their gazes. "I've met this guy while on assignment. He's not a suspect or anything, although he did find one of the bodies." She cleared her throat. "Anyway, I won't bore you with the details about how we hooked up, but he and I have been doing this BDSM thing." She sneaked a peek at them. Their eyes were wide, and Finn's mouth was open.

"You let him tie you up?" her little cousin asked, his voice almost a squeak.

"You let him beat you?" Ronan's tone was harsher, more menacing, as if planning out Kyle's murder.

Rolling her eyes, she said, "No. I tie *him* up, and I beat *him*."

There was silence for two seconds. Then both men said, "Oh," and went back to what they'd been doing.

Regan blew out a breath in frustration. "That's all

you have to say? Don't you find my relationship a little weird?"

"Not really," Ronan said. "The idea of your going all medieval on some guy's ass makes perfect sense to me."

"Yeah, Regan, you're a scary woman," Finn chimed in, then flashed her a smile. "And I mean that in the nicest sense of the word."

"What I'd miss?" Daire asked as he came back.

Oh, great. Now she'd get an earful from this cousin and maybe that was a good thing. The other two were being way too casual about her announcement.

"Regan likes to tie up and beat on her new boyfriend," Ronan supplied unhelpfully.

"It's not exactly like that," she protested. Except it was exactly like that when all was said and done. "And, he's not my boyfriend." Except he kind of was. Christ, bringing it up had been a mistake.

Daire stared at her unblinkingly for a few seconds. "He likes this too, I assume?"

"Of course, or I wouldn't do it."

Daire shrugged. "To each their own, I guess."

"Yeah, Regan, what's the problem?" Finn asked. "Are you afraid that what you do isn't normal or that people will judge you badly for it?"

"Both of those things," she admitted.

Ronan snorted. "Fuck what other people think. As long as it's consensual, that's all that matters. Look at me. I go to bed every night with a woman and another man. Not exactly Leave it to Beaver."

"Didn't you meet Cassidy's parents recently?" Regan asked.

Ronan heaved a sigh. "Yeah, and it didn't go very

well. I'm not sure what freaks them out more, the fact that their daughter lives with two men or the fact that one of those men is Irish and the other is Puerto Rican. I bet if we were both old Yankee WASPs, they'd adjust better."

"I'm sorry to hear that." She was, too. Ronan was so obviously happy, just like Finn, and Diego and Cassidy were both great people.

"We're spending Thanksgiving with Diego's family down in New York. Wish us luck on that one. He's explained everything over the phone to his mother, and he says she's trying to understand, but..." He shook his head.

"Lots of people are still freaked out over gay couples, let alone two men raising a gay teen," Finn pointed out.

Regan blew a raspberry. "That's just stupid."

"I agree. I'm just saying not everyone sees it that way yet, and maybe never will. Cut yourself some slack, Regan. You've been alone for a long time. If this guy makes you happy, what difference does it make how you get your rocks off?"

Such wise words from such a young man. She smiled in appreciation and nodded. Talking about her sex life with three men who meant the world to her had helped. She was there to work, though, so she turned her attention to the scraps of paper with dates and dollar amounts on them, bribes maybe, with locations and the occasional name. She picked up one and looked at the name, B. Smith, then grabbed the picture she'd seen earlier.

"This guy." She shook the picture at her cousins. "He looks familiar. And this name, B. Smith. Wasn't there a guy about your father's age named Brendan Smith who committed suicide a couple of years ago?"

Daire snatched at the picture and studied it. "Yeah, there was. This guy is much younger, but then the picture is at least twenty years old given their clothes and the car in the frame. I think it's him."

"There was something about a corruptions charge, wasn't there?" Ronan chimed in. "He hung himself before it went anywhere, though."

"That's right." Regan's memory flashed on a man hanging from his shower rod with a belt around his neck. "I caught that case. ME said suicide, but there was some bruising on his arms and the tox screen said he was drunk. It always sat wrong with me. There was pressure to close it down, keep the stain away from the force, I guess. Fuller said to wrap up the case. ME said suicide, so that was that."

She raised an eyebrow at Daire. "I wonder how many of these old pictures can be matched to cops from your father's era."

Pushing back in his chair, Daire said, "We need to see these faces more clearly. I'll get a magnifying glass."

Regan got up to refill her glass. She paused on her way to the kitchen and turned back to her younger cousins. "Thanks, guys. I appreciate your helping me feel like I'm not a freak."

They both grinned back at her. The unconditional love and support clearly written on their faces gave her hope and courage.

Chapter Ten

It was almost midnight before Daire finally shooed his brothers and Regan out of the house. It had been a good night's work. They'd identified a few other cops, although none of them was actively working in Boston, being either dead or just gone from the area. Not surprisingly, her father was up, the soft glow of his television showing around his window blinds and the sound coming through his doorway into the hall they shared. On impulse, she let herself in.

Her father turned his head to look at her as soon as she walked in. "Regan, my girl, the hours you keep." He shook his head in mild disapproval and went back to watching his show.

"Like father, like daughter," she retorted in a teasing tone. She went over to an easy chair next to him and sat on the fat and worn arm.

"I'm retired. I can stay up all night if I want." His eyes stayed glued to the screen.

"I was referring to when you used to get home as an active duty cop, Pops."

"Pissed your mother off no end," he admitted. "It's the job."

"It is that." She didn't get into the fact that part of her extended absences over the last few days had nothing to do with the job and everything to do with the exquisite pleasure she found in Kyle's bed. She didn't mention the work she'd done at Daire's, either. The Callaghan murders infuriated her father, and there was nothing new to report anyway.

Rubbing a tired hand over a more tired face, she added, "I've got three corpses and no leads."

"Ah, I'm sorry to hear that, honey." Her father muted the television and turned his wheelchair slightly toward her so he could look at her without twisting his neck. "Driving yourself into the ground won't help you find him, you know."

"Her," she corrected. "And I know. It's just that I hate doing nothing, waiting for her to strike again in order to gather more evidence. I want to find her now." Regan pounded the back of the chair in frustration.

"You need a good shot of whisky and some sleep," her father advised. "A husband and some kids to come home to wouldn't hurt, either. Gives a person perspective to have a family. Something to focus on instead of the damn job all the time."

Regan chuckled ruefully at the suggestion. "Oh, Pops, what guy would have a woman like me?"

"Like you, what?"

"Domineering with a demanding job as a lover." Kyle flashed through her mind, but she banished the idea quickly. Kyle liked the sex with her. It was novel and satisfied a part of him he was only now aware of. Playing with a Domme was one thing, but he would never want to live with one, especially one from the working class.

"Your mother put up with me, didn't she?" was her father's reply.

Regan slid down until she was slumped in the big chair. "That was different, Pops. Mom was a traditional woman who was content to stay at home and let her man earn the money and make the rules."

Her father didn't respond right away. His gaze slid back to the TV, and he shifted around in his chair in his limited fashion. "Well, now," he finally said, "you're about half right."

Regan furrowed her brows. "What do you mean?"

"Your mom did like to stay home and care for you and the house. She had her clubs and charities, too. She knew I could earn my keep. At least I did until the injury," he added with a small amount of bitterness. "As for the rest, though." He shrugged.

Leaning forward, Regan prompted. "As for the rest, what?"

Her father looked her in the eye once more. "I wouldn't have thought it was something we should talk about. After all, what happens between a married couple is private even from their children. But I hear something in what you're saying about yourself that makes me think you need to know you're not so unusual and destined to remain single."

He took in and let out a deep breath. "Your mother was not such a traditional woman when it came to submitting to me. You heard me plenty of times refer to her as the boss."

"A joke," she replied.

"The truth disguised as a joke," he corrected. "Your mother was the boss of me. We learned early in our relationship that taking charge was natural to her as taking orders was for me. You know I never got beyond the level of patrolman."

Regan looked away. "You got hurt."

"I did, but I had been a cop plenty long enough to

buck for detective and sergeant. Look at you, how far you've come in less time than I was on active duty. The truth is, I was never going to get promoted because I never wanted to be. I liked the freedom that came from following orders and not having the responsibility of making sure those orders were right. It was no different in my personal life. I handed my paycheck over to your mother and let her make all the decisions."

Regan was silent for long minutes while she digested the news. To a large degree, she wasn't surprised by what her father said. She had known in her heart her father wasn't an ambitious man. But learning that her mother had been the one in actual charge of their marriage and their lives was stunning. Her parents had done a great job of hiding it, and perhaps that was because her mother had ruled with subtle confidence instead of heavy-handed dictatorship. It was similar to what Cleo had said about sexual dominants. One had a duty to wield such power carefully. And, speaking of sex, an unsettling thought about her parents flashed through her mind before she could stop it. No, she wouldn't go there.

"So, you see, honey," he father continued, yanking her from her thoughts. "I don't want you thinking that, just because you're a strong woman, there's no man out there for you. You have to find one that's suited to your personality. One that appreciates your strength and is even grateful for it."

Regan smiled at her father and, standing up, went to give him a peck on his cheek. "Thanks, Pops. I love you."

"Love you, too, Regan."

Leaving her father's place, Regan dragged herself

upstairs and got ready for bed. Thoughts of what her father had revealed about her parents' marriage swam around her exhausted brain. If her father had been telling the truth, and she had no reason to believe he had made it up to make her feel better, then she was simply carrying on her family tradition.

She wasn't certain the knowledge helped. She was still concerned that her behavior with Kyle was unacceptable and should end. Still, it alleviated some of her concern that her cousins and her father supported the way she was and didn't think it was weird or deviant or any of the other bad things she kept worrying about.

Putting the thoughts aside, she let her exhaustion take over. She still had a killer to catch, and if she didn't do it soon, another man was going to die.

****

Kyle shifted in the waiting room chair, not trying to find a more comfortable position but trying to feel the last vestiges of the beating Regan had given him. Perversely, he missed the pain and hoped Regan would be free tonight to see him. When he stopped to consider it, his view of himself in relation to women had turned upside down in barely a week's time. Given he was already thirty-five, it seemed impossible that he'd been so obtuse about his own needs and desires. He'd wasted so much time chasing after the wrong type of woman and the wrong type of pleasure. No more.

It was all because of Regan, of course. He didn't merely adore her. He worshipped her. Although he didn't consider himself a romantic, he couldn't deny that love had caught him by the short hairs. It might not quite constitute love at first sight, but it was close enough.

Of course, he didn't think she felt the same way about him. He was sure he pleased her sexually. Her cool demeanor left him mystified if she felt as strongly for him, though, on an emotional level. He was pretty sure he was more comfortable in his new role than she was in hers. *More comfortable.* Not entirely.

A man couldn't change a lifetime of behavior and viewpoint without a few doubts, especially given how outside the box his new-found sexuality was. The question on his mind this morning was whether loving Regan was a sickness or a cure. He supposed he was about to find out.

"Mr. Ramsey, Dr. Molvado will see you now."

Kyle looked up at the receptionist and gave her a tight smile as he stood. She was exactly the way he pictured her over the phone, mousy. He found it hard to believe she wanted to work for a sex therapist. Then again, she looked at him with a certain awkward coyness, so he supposed she might find more than a few dates. That was assuming, of course, that she liked kink. Looking at her prim clothes and blandness, he found that hard to believe. On the other hand, few looking at him would believe that he would volunteer for a beating and like it.

The door to the inner office opened before he reached it, and standing there was an entirely different sort of woman. His cock took an instant interest before remembering it belonged to Regan and going back to rest. Stylish, sleek, and exuding palpable power, Dr. Molvado was the kind of woman he had no trouble picturing in leather. She smiled at him and extended a hand.

"Mr. Ramsey? Please come in." She shook his hand, a brisk, professional touch, before releasing him again. He followed her into her office and sat on the couch she motioned toward. She took the opposite seat. "I understand from Mindy that you're going through a crisis."

Kyle hooked his ankle over the opposite knee and tried to get comfortable. When he made the call, his goal was to ferret out the possible killer of Jazz and the other men. Now that he was face-to-face with the doctor, he still thought she was a good candidate, but he was unsure of how to proceed. He supposed the best thing was to do the obvious and talk about himself.

Clearing his throat, he said, "Yes, I am." His gaze flickered downward in genuine embarrassment. "It's hard to talk about this."

"I understand. Please take you time."

She had that standard soothing doctor tone that actually was more grating on his nerves than reassuring. Nevertheless, he appreciated how she approached their talk as if it were perfectly normal. She had to be used to people coming in and talking about all kinds of weird behavior. Surely he wasn't about to confess anything all that strange.

"I recently discovered something about myself that I find disturbing."

When he paused, she probed. "Something sexual?"

He nodded. "Yes. Something about the type of sex I like to have, and the type of woman I like to have that sex with."

"Go on," she encouraged when he paused once more.

He chuckled ruefully. "It's hard for a man of my

170

stature to admit this, but I find I like to be dominated by a strong woman." When the doctor merely looked at him with a detached interest, he rushed on. "To be frank, I like being beaten and teased and ordered about. I like being told what to do in bed and revel in the freedom being controlled by my partner brings." He looked the doctor straight in the eye. "How weird is that, the idea that being controlled makes me freer?"

Molvado shrugged. "Why is it weird? When the rules are bright and rigid, you know exactly what is expected of you, what you must do. There's no indecision, no worry about making the 'right' choice or doing the 'right' thing. It's all spelled out for you. It allows you to relax."

Kyle sighed and tipped his head back in thought. "I suppose so. It's a relief to leave the worrying to someone else, I must admit. But it's also arousing, as is the pain my partner inflicts. Isn't it sick to enjoy being hurt?"

The doctor raised her eyebrows. "Well, let's explore that question, shall we? How badly does your partner hurt you? Is the pain crippling or disabling?"

Kyle shook his head. "No. No, it's nothing like that. It hurts, and sometimes it leaves marks, but it's nothing I can't handle."

"And you feel pride about your ability to handle it."

"Yes, yes, I do. I feel strong."

"But you're still uncomfortable about it all. Do you wonder if it makes you less than a man?"

"I do, yes."

"Why?" The doctor's eyes were wide when she asked the question as if she were truly confused. He knew it was a head-shrinking tactic, although he also had the gut feeling that she was toying with him, getting off on having power over him.

He narrowed his eyes at her and lowered his voice. "Because I'm a man. I'm supposed to be the one in charge."

"Oh." Her tone was mocking.

"I'm not being sexist," he insisted defensively.

"No?"

"No. I have two daughters, for God's sake. I don't for one minute believe they are inferior to any boy or that they're supposed to kowtow to the men in their lives. But those men need to look after them all the same, protect them, support them if that's what my daughters want. Men are supposed to be the pointy end of the spear in the family so that the family can be safe and prosperous."

"So when that man gives himself a break and allows the woman to dominate him in bed or even make the decisions for the family, he isn't fulfilling that destiny?"

"How can he?" Kyle challenged.

Molvado shrugged. "Let's explore how it's possible. For example, do you have the desire now to stop working and lie around all day while your partner works?"

"What?" Kyle furrowed his brows at the absurd idea. "Of course not."

"All right, then," Molvado said with a nod. "You're still willing to support a woman. How about if you're out one night, and she's cold. Would you give her your jacket?"

"Naturally." He could see where she was going

with her questions, and he had to admit the woman made sense.

"And if someone shoots at her, are you willing to take the proverbial bullet?" The doctor smiled when she asked this last question.

"Yes," Kyle sighed. "I get it. Just because I defer to her, doesn't mean I'm abdicating my responsibilities as a man. I can be both submissive and supportive and protective."

"As long as you find the relationship sexually fulfilling, there is no need for you to change your lifestyle based on your preconceived notions of what it means to be a man. On the other hand, if you feel degraded and abused by the activities…"

"No," he was quick to assure her. "I don't. My partner is very careful to make me feel…cherished." Yes, that was the right word to describe Regan's handling of him.

Running his hands through his hair in a sense of relief, he decided to put aside his own issues and get down the real business at hand. "You know, Dr. Molvado, I was reluctant to see you, but my friend, Jazz, was very impressed with you." He lowered his gaze and sadness crept into his expression. He didn't need to playact about his feelings about Jazz's death. "You would have known him as Joseph Bennington."

He shot his gaze up as he said it and caught the way the doctor stiffened at the mention of her dead patient. She caught herself quickly, however, and relaxed almost immediately.

"I'm afraid I can't discuss other patients, Mr. Ramsey." Her voice was professional, yet he detected a hard edge to it.

"I understand. There's nothing to discuss, in any event, although I must say his murder was one of the reasons I've had concern about my lifestyle."

"You're worried you're at risk?"

"Not really. I trust my partner, but when I think about how Jazz was killed, I have to wonder about the healthiness of allowing a woman to hurt me."

"It's not the same." The answer was rather curt. "A woman who likes to dominate is not necessarily a woman who likes to kill. Inflicting punishment on an attractive man is something that appeals to many women." The look she gave him was blatantly sexual for a split second, all traces of professionalism gone. "It's a far cry, however, from torture and mutilation. Your friend's killer is truly beyond the realm of acceptable deviation."

"What would drive a person to become a sadistic murderer?"

"Although we don't have all of the answers yet, we do know that early childhood experiences can warp a mind and drive someone to extreme violence. Sometimes people are simply born with the desire to hurt others."

"Or be hurt."

"Yes, but again, deviation from the norm is not a cause for alarm unless it becomes nonconsensual and/or harmful for one or both partners."

Kyle unhooked his legs and leaned forward with his arms resting on his knees. "How can one know if he's hooked up with someone dangerous?"

Dr. Molvado shifted in response to his change by crossing her legs. Her short, straight skirt rode high up her long leg, giving him a glimpse of a garter belt and a lot of pink flesh. He was certain she was trying to be provocative. The idea of a professional woman sitting in an office without wearing underwear was certainly the type of thing to elicit a response from a man. Kyle was no different from any other man, yet his body's reaction was muted. This doctor was not Regan.

Molvado was answering his question, so he focused on her face, not her crotch. "You can't usually," she said. "Psychopaths are very adept at hiding their proclivities. They can be very charming, attractive, sexy even, or simply blend into the background. They may place themselves in a position of trust, someone you would go to for help. You may have no idea what their true natures are until it's too late."

She was describing herself, Regan, Mistress Veronica, or any number of other women he, Jazz, and the other men may have come in contact with. The idea that he might look a killer in the eye and not recognize her as such was deeply disturbing. Still, he couldn't believe it of Regan. He simply couldn't.

Dr. Molvado, however, was a different story. There was something about her and the way she stared at him, gauging his reaction to her words, that unsettled him. He was not supposed to even be here. Regan's warning ran through his head. He felt in some way as if he were cheating on her. The guilt sent him shooting to his feet.

Eyebrows raised in surprise, the doctor stood as well. "I'm sorry if I said something to upset you." Her tone of voice had changed. The concern sounded genuine.

"No, not at all." It was mostly the truth. It was his duplicity regarding Regan that upset him. "You've given me some things to think about. I appreciate your time." He moved towards the door.

Molvado shadowed him and slipped in front of him before he could open the door to her reception room. "Mr. Ramsey, I can tell that you're agitated by this session. I want to make sure you're all right."

Kyle nodded briefly. "I am, really. I need to think things through."

She licked her lips. "Of course. One moment, though, please." She held up a forefinger.

She hurried to her desk and opened a small case. She returned and held out a business card to him. "This is a card I give out to patients I'm particularly concerned about. It has my private cell phone number on it. I want you to call me at any time you need to talk or if you'd like to meet privately." She licked her bright, full lips again. It was half nervous gesture, half seductive cue.

After a moment's hesitation, Kyle took the card and stuffed it into one of his pants pockets. "Thank you, although I'm not a candidate for suicide or anything if that's what you're worried about."

"No, not really." She gave him a small smile. "I do sense you are a man on the verge of finding himself. It can be a trying time, and you shouldn't have to go it alone or with strangers. The right woman can help you come into your own."

"You mean the right doctor?" he questioned with a frown.

"However you prefer it," was her enigmatic reply.

"Thank you, ma'am." It seemed the proper address, and he could tell by the way her eyes widened, that he had pleased her. A part of him preened at the knowledge, but it wasn't truly important to him. There was only one woman he wanted to please.

As he left the strange doctor, he thought of Regan and wondered where she was and what she was doing. More importantly, he wondered when he would be able to see her next. His whole body began to hum in anticipation.

****

After a fairly decent night's sleep, Regan was back at her desk, mulling over what her next steps should be to catch the killer. A hand waved in front of her face.

"Good morning?" JoJo said in a tentative voice.

Regan blinked and looked up at her partner, sitting beside Regan's desk. "Sorry, the caffeine hasn't kicked in yet."

"I hear you." JoJo held up a piece of paper. "I have the results of the national database search for similar killings."

"And I can tell by the lack of enthusiasm in your voice that it turned up a big, fat goose egg."

"Uh-huh," her partner confirmed. "The closest thing I came across was a single murder in Nebraska about four years ago." She scanned the paper in her hand. "One Thomas Johnstone, an auto mechanic living in a small town outside of Omaha, was found tortured to death in his bed. Like our vics, he had his penis cut off and stuffed up his rear."

Regan took a long swallow of her coffee. "Wife, girlfriend?"

JoJo sighed and slapped the paper on Regan's desk. "Wife had been dead for a few years from cancer, no known girlfriend."

"Daughter?" Regan asked in a desperate voice.

"One son, Thomas Johnstone, Jr., who was at the University of Nebraska at the time."

"Go Big Red," Regan quipped before downing the rest of her coffee. She was hoping for a big jolt of energy so that she could somehow miraculously think her way to the answer of who their serial killer was.

"Crap!" she exclaimed once the liquid was swallowed. "I take it no one was ever charged."

JoJo shook her head. "The case remains open but frigidly cold. It was one of those shocking 'he was such a great guy' kind of killings, and no one could imagine who would do such a thing."

"No witnesses, no evidence," Regan surmised.

"No sign of forced entry, and the only finger prints were his and his son's. Johnstone also lived in an isolated old farm house. He wasn't even gagged because there were no neighbors close enough to hear. He was found after a couple of days when he didn't show up for work. It was such a strange occurrence that his boss went out to check and noticed the flies on the screen of the bedroom window."

"Ew!" Regan exclaimed.

"Yeah, ew," JoJo agreed. "Anyway, that's all I have. It could be the same woman or…

"Or it could be that angry and psychotic women naturally tend to want to cut off a guy's dick and occasionally get the idea to stuff it up their ass as payback for rape and other abuse."

"Johnstone was a pillar of his community."

"The pricks usually are, but I can't see it. It makes no sense to kill once in Nebraska and then wend your way to Boston years later and start killing over and over again."

"Maybe she's been practicing other places and hiding her work."

Regan nodded thoughtfully. "It's possible, although it still doesn't get us any closer to figuring out who it is. Any of our suspects come from Nebraska?"

JoJo pursed her lips. "If by our suspects you mean the women at Club Nemesis and Dr. Molvado, then no, none of them is from Nebraska."

"Run everyone associated with both places, including administrative and janitorial staff. We may be looking for a sheep among the wolves."

JoJo stood up. "Will do. In the meantime, we have nothing else to go on."

Sighing, Regan let her head fall back against her chair. "I know."

She spent the day glued to her chair, surfing the internet for Femdom sites in the vain hope that something would pop. Other than her nipples, nothing did. The images on her computer screen of leather-clad women dominating naked or nearly naked men had her wiggling her butt all day. Although she felt guilty about enjoying once more what was supposed to be work, she couldn't deny the pleasure her search brought. Only the presence of a dozen or more cops and perps kept her libido in anything close to check. Yet, by six o'clock, she was hot and desperate for relief.

Frustrating as it was, there was nothing more for her to do, so she did what she'd been dying to do all day. Picking up the phone, she dialed Kyle's office number. She got his secretary and was pleased when she was told that Mr. Ramsey had left orders to be found if she called.

He came on the line within a couple of minutes.

"Regan, I was hoping you would call. I didn't want to disturb you given the investigation."

His deep, sexy voice gave her stomach a satisfying jolt. "I wish I could say I'm making progress. The sad truth is I'm not." She paused. "Are you up for seeing me tonight?"

"Why Sergeant, what an interesting turn of phrase," Kyle drawled. "I'm always up for seeing you."

"Haha. When will you be home?"

"When do you want me home, Mistress?"

Hearing him call her that upped her squirm-factor. "Eight o'clock." She wasn't sure she could wait so long, yet needed to put in some more hours and she knew his job was as demanding as hers.

"Then that's when I'll be home. Would you like me to fix dinner?"

"No, I'll bring take-out."

"How do you want me, Mistress Regan?"

A myriad of scenarios flashed through her mind. She settled quickly on the mundane. After the intensity of their previous encounters, she wanted to keep it low-keyed. "Stay as you are or get comfortable. Pretend this is a typical date for you."

He chuckled again. "You do ask a lot of me, Mistress."

They said their good-byes, and with effort, Regan made use of the rest of her day in trying to find a clue to their killer.

She arrived at Kyle's condo with a bag of her favorite Chinese food. He greeted her in shirtsleeves and slacks, took the bag, and carried it to his kitchen. Because he had been a good boy and not acted on the obvious desire to kiss her, she rewarded him by grabbing him as he took the cartons out of the bag.

They held the embrace until Regan had to pull up for air. Pushing him away, she said, "Feed me."

He grinned and finished taking out the food and plating it. She was amused by the formality of putting Chinese take-out on platters to be placed on the dining room table. It reminded her of the great difference in their upbringing and social status. If she let it, her insecurity would nag at her existing doubts about them, but she decided she wouldn't allow it. She needed to relax and see where things went.

As he walked back and forth setting up for dinner, she undid the belt to her trench coat. Underneath, she wore her Nemesis dress, complete with fishnet and boots. She wasn't working undercover anymore, but it seemed a shame to let it go to waste. She watched in delight the look on Kyle's face when he turned and saw what she wore. Even across the room, she could see his nostrils flare and his chest start to heave.

"Down, boy," she commanded. "I want to eat first."

"You can be a very cruel mistress," he replied glibly, but he restrained himself. The only change was the speed in which he completed his task.

He offered her wine, and she accepted. They sat down, her at the head of the table, he to her right, and tucked in. The food was good. The way Kyle stared at her while attacking his plate was better. It was as if he were trying to satisfy his need to put something in his mouth, and the food was his only outlet. The thought gave her an idea.

She tortured them both by taking her time to savor each bite of food and each sip of wine. Long since finished with his meal, Kyle sat back, toying with his wine glass and almost panting like a dog. He was devouring her with his eyes. His cock strained against his pants. It was time to relieve them both.

With a last swallow of her wine, Regan pushed back from the table. She leaned close to Kyle, shoving the dishes farther across the table. With a little hop, she perched herself on the edge of the smooth wood and splayed her legs in invitation. She kept her eyes on Kyle the whole time, and he kept his eyes on her as well. He understood immediately what she was offering. His gaze remained locked on hers while he shifted his chair so that he sat directly in front of her. He didn't act on the invitation, though. He waited for permission.

Regan made them both wait long, agonizing seconds before giving him the command they both wanted. "Eat me," she said in a quiet voice and gripped the edge of the table in anticipation.

Kyle said nothing. He wasn't sure he had any spit left in his mouth to speak. He simply moved to comply, his hands reaching slowly and deliberately to first cup her knees under her dress. It was an act to steady himself, to keep him from launching his body into hers, to devour the lusciousness she offered him. It was important that he do it right. He needed to give her more pleasure than she had ever felt before.

His gaze dropped now. He watched his hands roam up her thighs, catching the buttery material of her dress and scrunching it up to her waist. The fishnet stockings she wore were scratchy against his palms, a tingling sensation he wanted to repeat. He did by rubbing her thighs back and forth a few times before continuing his march up her leg. He could tell Regan enjoyed the feeling as well because her head dropped back and her eyelids went to half-mast.

That was nothing compared to his own reaction. Kyle's breath wanted to burst from his lungs in harsh pants, and his cock ached for release as her smooth, pale upper thighs came into view. She wore no underwear, like the creepy doctor Molvado, but on Regan, the nudity was electrifying. Her trim, dark red bush called to him with drops of moisture winking in the light that caught them. He cradled the creases where thigh met hip with his hands, using his thumbs to frame her cunt lips.

A tiny explosion of air erupted from Regan's mouth at his touch. He caught that puff and inhaled deeply to steady his nerves. God, how he wanted to dive in, plant his lips against her lower ones. Hard earned discipline stopped him from acting on the urge. He was better than that. He could do this right, give this woman he loved the time and attention she deserved.

So, instead of using his mouth, he used his thumbs. With little circles, he massaged the pouting flesh. Regan's hips bucked at the motion, and a moan encouraged his pursuit. He pressed down with his hands so that she couldn't wiggle too much. After a few seconds of torturing them both with this, building the anticipation, he leaned in and ran his tongue right up her slit.

"Yes," Regan hissed.

Kyle stole a glance up at her. Her head was back even farther, and her eyes were completely closed. He smiled at the sight and went back to his task.

This time, he slid his tongue between the folds and

licked her clit. He kept his touch light and quick, varying from moment to moment the motion of his tongue—up and down, around and around in small circles—alternating between the tip of his tongue and the long flat of it. The smell and taste of her made his blood boil even hotter. He kept up the pressure from the outside with his thumbs, digging deep inside to reach the parts his tongue could not.

Regan moaned again. Her stomach quivered against his head. One of her hands grabbed him by the hair, and her nails dug deep into his scalp as she pressed his face hard into her crotch. He could tell she was almost there. Increasing his pace, he urged her on and reveled in the effect he was having on her. Her body undulated like a belly dancer. Her breath rasped out, and the moans of pleasure spurred him on even faster. As she reached her peak, she enveloped him in her body. Her thighs overpowered his hands and pressed against his face. He could barely breathe and didn't care. He only wanted to send her into ecstasy.

Kyle worked his tongue with a fury until he felt Regan's climax subsiding. When her frantic motions stopped, so did he. He pulled his head away from her body as it relaxed its grip on him. He looked up at her, keeping his hands lightly on her thighs. Her eyes were still closed, but she was smiling.

Standing up, he wiped his mouth quickly on his sleeve before stealing a kiss. She didn't mind his boldness. Instead of pushing him away, she wrapped her arms around his waist and pulled him closer to her. It was she who parted his lips and let her tongue wander into his mouth. He liked that she didn't mind the taste of her own juices. But it wasn't enough for him. His cock was pressed between his body and the edge of the table. It begged him to rub himself to release. He wouldn't do it, though. It would be an insult to Regan and not what he craved, in any event.

He broke off the kiss and spoke in a whisper, "Please, Mistress, may I come inside you?"

"Yes," was her quick reply, and more, she reached to undo his pants and free his cock herself.

The feel of her hot hand on his hotter flesh was almost too much. "Wait," he pleaded and fumbled for a condom in his pocket. He was clumsy in his desperation, so she took over that chore for him as well.

As soon as he was ready, he dove into her. They both gasped at the joining. She was slick, yet tight, and oh so warm and cozy. He wanted to savor the feeling, but knew he couldn't. He started pumping into her with short, frantic bursts. She grabbed his waist once more and urged him on.

With hands under her ass, he angled her back, so he could go deeper, harder. He could tell she was climbing again and tried to wait for her. He couldn't. The climax ripped through him. He threw back his head in a primeval cry of satisfaction as cum pulsed through his shaft to collect fruitlessly within the condom.

Above his voice, he heard Regan doing the same. He hadn't disappointed her after all. And that made him feel like a god.

Chapter Eleven

Regan stepped into Kyle's living room and winced at the carnage. The remnants of the Chinese food remained on the dining table and articles of hers and Kyle's clothing lay scattered across the floor. She had spent the night. Kyle had begged so appealingly, that she couldn't refuse. The truth was that after another vigorous round of sex on the table, she hadn't felt like getting dressed and driving home. Thank God she kept a gym bag in her car with spare clothes. Kyle had gallantly fetched it for her this morning, and while she was dressed a bit shabbily, at least she didn't look like Mistress Regan.

Kyle had promised her a fabulous breakfast of waffles, but he was still dressing, so she decided to be useful and pick up. Going around the large room, she snatched up stockings, a shirt, a dress, and pants. The pants were upside down when she hauled them into her arms, and a card fluttered from the pocket. Bending over, she picked it up and found herself staring at it with first confusion and then growing anger. By the time Kyle came out of the bedroom, she had dropped the clothes in her arms and was gripping the card with white hot fury.

The smile on his face died in an instant when he spied her standing there. "What's the matter?" He stopped in front of her.

Regan took a couple of deep breaths to try to ward off the yelling and cursing demanding to be unleashed. It didn't help much. She held up the card. "You went to see Molvado."

Kyle didn't answer right away. He dropped his gaze briefly before looking her square in the eye. "Yes, I did." His calm and matter of fact tone fueled her fury.

"I told you not to!" She wasn't quite yelling, but it was the tone she used with subordinates at work when they screwed up. "I very specifically told you to stay the hell away from that woman."

"I know." His tone remained calm. He wasn't cringing at her rebuke, but then she would have been surprised if he had shown such weakness. Yet, his lack of contrition was intolerable.

"Why?" she demanded. "Why did you disobey me?"

He heaved a sigh, the first sign that he was also upset. "Because I had to do what I could to find Jazz's killer, that's why. I told you from the beginning I'm not the kind of man to sit back and let others solve problems for me."

Regan crushed the card in her hand and walked away, trying to put some emotional distance between them, too. She rounded on him after a few futile steps. "You told me that when we were strangers, and I told you that you had no business stepping between the police and an investigation. Once we became personally involved, I thought you had agreed to obey me. Has this all been a lie, Kyle? All this 'Mistress Regan, I'll do whatever you say' is just bullshit?"

He took a step toward her before apparently thinking better of it and stopping. "No. God, no, Regan.

I meant what I've said." There was a pleading in his eyes. "I think I love you, as crazy as that sounds after such a short time. And against all instincts and experience, I'm willing to let you lead me by the cock. You're the one person in the world I'll obey in bed and out, except that there are limits. I can't let you dictate to me about certain things like my job."

"This is not your job!" She was shouting now. "It's mine."

"I know it's your job." His voice was rising, too. "That's why I don't make a fuss when I see you with that gun strapped to your body as you leave this safe place for the dangers out there. But I consider finding my friend's killer my job as well. I can't help it. It's the way I'm made, Regan. You can't change me."

"I don't want to change you. I want to keep you safe. I warned you that Molvado might be dangerous."

"She's creepy, I'll give you that," he replied in a more normal tone. "I think she's a likely suspect."

"Ugh!" Regan groaned in frustration. The man was not getting her point. He was maddening. He said he was willing to let her call the shots for them both, but it was conditional. He would only do what he thought he should do. He wasn't really submitting to her at all. The whole thing was a sham, a sex game, and maybe a way to disarm her about what he did against her wishes. Well, she could accept that what they had been doing was all a big game, but she could not tolerate his using her to play detective.

She forced her voice steady and low. "I'm only going to say this one more time, Kyle. Stay out of this investigation."

"I won't go back to see Molvado. I can promise

you that, and if she tries to contact me, I'll let you know."

Regan grimaced. "It's something. I'm not sure it's enough, but it is something. It doesn't change what you did or how angry I am over it, though."

Kyle gave her a wry smile. "I know I've been bad, and I understand how mad you are. Why not simply give me a good beating and get it out of your system? I understand I deserve it."

Regan stood staring at him, trying to take in his words and have them mean something other than what they did. It was no use. She backed away from him, unable to hide her upset. His expression changed as he looked at her.

"What?" he demanded. "What's the matter?"

"Didn't you hear yourself?" Disgust rang in her voice. "You want me to beat you for your disobedience."

"Yeah, right. Jesus, Regan, that's what we've been doing for the last little while. Why are you shying away from it now?"

"You don't see the difference." Her stomach was churning. Things had spun out of control. Perhaps it wasn't a game to him, after all, but the kind of sick need she had feared from the start. She turned away and headed quickly for the front door. She had to get out of here.

Kyle was on her before she got there. Reaching out, he grabbed her arm and brought her up short. "Talk to me, for God's sake. What did I do wrong?"

Regan wrenched free but didn't race for the door. He genuinely looked confused, so it was up to her to explain and cut this awful relationship off for his sake as much as her own. She spoke in measured tones. "I'm angry with you, Kyle. Furious, and you want me to hit you, hurt you, under these conditions. That's not a sex game. That's abuse. If I let loose on your now, that's abuse, and I arrest people for that kind of thing."

"You'd never hurt me," he protested. "I trust you."

She shook her head and stepped to the door again. This time, he didn't try to stop her. "Letting someone hit you when they're mad isn't trust. It's unhealthy, and I can't be part of that kind of relationship, Kyle."

He took a step forward, hand outstretched. "Regan, please, I'm sorry."

"So am I." She turned and shut the door behind her.

****

Regan sat at her desk chewing over her fight with Kyle, a sick feeling in the pit of her stomach. Had she done the right thing? Was breaking off with Kyle the right choice? Given how he'd assumed her beating him was a way to resolve a fight, she had to believe it was the right decision.

She was miserable, though, and had been since leaving him that morning. The devastated look on his face as he'd pleaded for her to reconsider ate away at her. He'd said he loved her. In the heat of the moment, she'd glossed over that declaration. It was insane to love someone you barely knew. Still, she believed him, because she felt it, too.

What had started out as a disturbing new chapter in her sex life had become an emotional upheaval she could not ignore. Could she really be in love with Kyle? It seemed crazy to think she could feel something so deep and long-lasting for someone she'd known for such a short time. It had been an intense time, though, and maybe that explained the depth of her feeling. Or, maybe it was the sexual intensity masquerading in her mind as something more important. Love.

Christ, Jesus, how could she be in love with a man who said he respected her yet went behind her back on the investigation as if he didn't trust her judgment or competency? She was in love with a man who let her tie him up and strap his ass as foreplay and still didn't understand that she could only play that way as long as it didn't tip into an abusive relationship. There was a fundamental disconnect in their interactions and had been from the start. Of course, she'd done the right thing breaking it off. So why did she want to run to him and take it all back? Take him back.

She didn't have time to dwell on it further when Fuller approached.

"Tell me you have something," the lieutenant commanded in a weary voice as he sat down on the edge of Regan's desk.

"City Hall biting your ass?" Regan ventured in way of an answer.

The lieutenant gave her a hard stare. "That's right, and here I am ready to chomp on yours."

Regan scrunched up her face. "Get out the salt, LT, because we have nothing."

JoJo joined them by rolling her chair over. "Zip."

Fuller grimaced. "What about the woman from the club?"

"The Queen of the Nile has solid alibis for the first two murders," Regan replied. "She had no connection to those vics, either, that we could see." She shrugged. "Anyway, I'm sure we have one woman at work here, so even with the decent link between Cleo and Foster, she's cleared."

"Crap." Fuller's direct manner was one of the things Regan admired about him. "So, you're saying we have no other viable leads." It was more a statement than a question.

Regan nodded her assent and then elaborated. "The only other possible clue here is the Nebraska case. It's a long-shot, though. We haven't placed anyone we have here to there, have we?" She looked at JoJo.

The other woman shook her head. "The best I can give you is that Veronica Pugh was born Veronica Beals."

"Wait a minute," Regan interrupted. "You mean she changed her name to Pugh?"

"Her ex-husband's name. I guess she kept it because she has a couple of kids. Anyway, the Beals are a family from Lincoln, Nebraska, although Veronica, herself, never lived there."

The lieutenant perked up instantly. "Now there's something." Regan and JoJo had filled him in on the Johnstone murder.

"I don't know, LT," Regan replied. "Lincoln and Omaha are pretty far apart."

"The Nebraska vic's kid, the son, went to college there," JoJo reminded her.

"Yeah, but it's a good school and the state university. Virtually every native Nebraskan must want to attend it. Can we place Veronica in the state at the time of the murder?"

"Not yet. We could bring her in for questioning," her partner suggested.

Regan slumped back in her chair and stared at the

ceiling. She pictured the woman who had transformed her into a Domme. "I can't see it. She doesn't give me the right vibes."

"Are we solving murders based on your vibes now?" Fuller's tone was biting.

Regan sighed. "No, but if I had to pick a favorite at this moment, it would be Molvado. She gives off the right vibes," she added, looking at her superior.

JoJo nodded in agreement. "She does."

"Fine." Fuller stood up. "Keep digging into both women and every other line of inquiry you have. I don't have to tell you time is short. Odds are that, in the next couple of days, another man is going to be tortured to death. It would be nice if we could stop it. The mayor and the governor are talking about taking this case out of our hands entirely and handing over to the FBI."

"Shit!" Regan sat up straighter. "It's a purely local case. They have no jurisdiction."

"They do if it's related to a Nebraska case. Besides, the governor has the power to ask them to step in if he wants to. And frankly, if we can't find the killer before we have another victim, who are we to say it's a bad idea?"

Regan watched as the lieutenant left. The guy had a good point, damn it all, except she was sure the FBI would work under their profiler's assumption about the killer being a man, and she still didn't believe that for a moment. They were all scared of another murder, yet they were doing what they could. It wasn't going to be enough. She could feel it deep down in her gut.

Later that afternoon, JoJo stopped by Regan's desk, nursing her undoubtedly umpteenth Coke. She sat heavily in the guest chair and stared at her partner. "It may be that I've had too little sleep and too much caffeine today."

"We both have, but I'm not certain why you're bringing it up."

"I'm anticipating you're telling me that I've lost it and giving you an excuse in advance."

"Okay," Regan nodded in confirmation. "So?"

JoJo put her Coke down on the desk and tapped a manila file she had in her other hand. "I've been trying to track Thomas Johnstone, Jr."

"The son."

"The son. After the murder, he went back to the university and finished up his degree in psychology."

Regan grabbed the Coke and took a long pull. "The major of the undecided. So what, he then went into criminology?"

"No, he went into the Peace Corps."

"Altruistic."

"Weird because he disappeared right after his stint."

Regan's heart sped up with the news. This was something, she was sure of it.

JoJo continued. "I spoke with someone in the organization and according to their records, he was stationed in Haiti and called to let them know he wasn't coming back to the States. That was the last they heard of him."

"Okay," Regan said, her eyes unfocused as she thought. "It could be something, or it could be he was so traumatized by his father's murder he tried to escape the whole thing the best way he knew how. We can't read too much into this yet."

JoJo shook her head. "I think we can. See, it just so

happens that Mindy Fortensky was also with the Peace Corps at the same time."

Regan frowned. "Mindy? You mean Little Mouse on the Prairie?"

"She's from Oregon. I don't think they have prairies out there."

"But she was stationed with the son of our murder victim?"

"Not exactly. She was assigned to an African nation. They may have met during orientation, that's all, and what that says, I can't imagine. We don't even know if there's a connection between that murder and ours."

"It's our best lead, though. Dig deeper into Miss Mindy. She may have learned the details of the Johnstone murder from the son."

"And what? Do you think she's replaying what she heard? She doesn't seem the type."

"I know, she doesn't give out the vibe, but as Fuller pointed out, we can't solve a murder based on vibes. Besides, it may not be her doing anything. Maybe she's hooked up with the son, and he's acting out some weird catharsis using her. Better yet, maybe she told the story to Molvado, and the good doctor is putting the idea into action. It would explain why it's been so long since the original murder."

"You're right." JoJo stood up. "The minute I saw the overlap, I sensed it was a good lead. I'll dig deeper."

"Good." Regan looked at her watch. "With the time difference, there should be no problem contacting people out in Oregon. See if you can find members of her family or friends, classmates, anyone who might

195

shed some light on her background. Who knows, maybe she liked to torture animals or something when she was a kid."

"On it." JoJo hesitated and stepped back again. "You know this is a one person job at the moment. Why don't you go fix whatever it is that's been eating at you all day."

"That obvious, huh?"

"You've got man trouble written all over your face."

"Shit," Regan muttered under her breath. Her partner was right. She couldn't work as effectively with the Kyle issue occupying her thoughts. Might as well see if she could set things straight with him, although it didn't seem possible that they could solve fundamental problems with a simple short discussion. On the other hand, with her anger over his Molvado visit dissipated, maybe they could have a rational discussion. Yeah, right. With a sigh, she grabbed her jacket and headed out the door.

With the end of September looming, the days were getting darker earlier. By the time she reached Kyle's condo, the evening commute was thinning out, but dusk had set in. There were no spots open near his building, so she double-parked, figuring it was worth a ticket. She wasn't the only one, either. A Mercedes was doing the same thing just ahead of her. She left her car and tried, as she had multiple times on the ride over, to come up with what she wanted to say to Kyle. Words still failed her. Oh well, she'd just have to wing it.

As she trotted up the stairs, a woman already stood in front of the intercom to the building, muttering under her breath. Regan saw tall, sleek, and stylish before she hit the top step of the stoop.

"Come on Kyle, you have to be home, damn you."

Regan's step faltered as the woman's words sunk in. She pulled out her badge and held it up. "Excuse me, ma'am, are you looking for Kyle Ramsey?"

The woman whipped her head around. Her eyes went wide when she saw the badge. "Oh, my God, has something happened to Kyle? Was there an accident?"

"No." Regan was quick to a reassure her, although alarm shot through her at the question. "I'm here to ask him a few questions about an investigation." Which was almost the truth.

"Oh, you mean Jazz's murder, I suppose. Such a horrible thing." The woman shuddered theatrically. "But he doesn't have time tonight for questioning, I'm afraid. We have to go to our daughter's back to school night."

Regan slipped the badge back into her pocket. "I see. Is he home? He doesn't seem to be answering."

The woman blew out a frustrated breath. "No, he's not. Not the buzzer here, not his cell phone. The night receptionist at his firm swears he's gone. I'd think the woman was just covering for him, except that isn't like him. He never misses things for the kids." She crossed her arms and snuck a peek down at the street. Her gaze seemed fixed on the double-parked Mercedes.

"I have Emma in the car. Kyle was supposed to pick us both up. I just don't understand what's going on." She turned and jabbed at the intercom again.

Please answer. Please. Regan stared at the door, as if wishing alone would make the man appear. She gave it a full minute before accepting that he simply wasn't home. Or, maybe he was and couldn't respond.

Something was wrong, and her imagination went into overdrive even as the more rational part of her brain told her she was overreacting. He was running late, that was all.

"Do you have a key to his place?" she asked the woman who was clearly Kyle's ex.

"Yes, I do. For emergencies. It's on my key chain." She motioned toward the car.

"Please go get it."

The former Mrs. Ramsey blinked back at Regan for a second before hurrying down the steps. She was back quickly, a fancy key ring in her hand. She showed Regan two keys. "This one opens the front door, and this one is for the condo unit itself."

Regan took them. "Thanks. Please wait in the car."

"You think he's in there and is hurt or something?" The woman bit at her lower lip."

Regan tried to give her a reassuring smile. "No, but it's best to be sure."

She wasted no time in opening the front door and shutting it carefully behind her. Once she was out of sight of Kyle's wife, she pulled out her revolver and put the key in the condo's lock. She went in expecting trouble, gun at the ready, eyes scanning the room quickly. There was no one in the kitchen/living room area. She paused, straining to hear if anyone was in the bedroom. All she heard was the pounding of her own heart and the rasping of her labored breath.

She forced herself to calm down. If Kyle was in trouble, she'd do him no good by letting her fear override her training. Satisfied that no sounds came from the back of the condo, she stepped carefully farther inside. Down the hall she crept, scanning, listening, and sniffing until she popped into the open bedroom. She knew a moment of relief when she didn't find Kyle sprawled dead on his bed. A quick check of the bathroom and the second bedroom confirmed he wasn't home. She holstered her gun and considered her next step.

Where the hell was he? When he talked about his girls, his love and devotion for them was obvious. He wouldn't blow them off. Not even his ex-wife thought that, and exes tended to be critical of one another. Something was wrong, very wrong. And there was only one very wrong thing she could think of at the moment.

Given what that was, she started hoping Kyle had been in some kind of accident. The alternative didn't bear imaging, although the killer's M.O. was to do her dirty work at her victim's home. Because Kyle wasn't here, it made more sense that it was something more mundane, like an accident or work.

Just as she'd managed to talk herself out of the worst case scenario, her phone rang. "What's up, JoJo?"

"I just got off the phone with the head nurse at the facility where Mindy's aunt resides. Mindy's parents died in a crash when she was eleven, and this aunt raised her after that. According to the nurse, the aunt encouraged Mindy to follow her dream of doing global aid work by joining the Peace Corps instead of hanging around Oregon while her aunt slowly and literally lost her mind."

"And?" Regan left Kyle's condo to let his ex know he wasn't there.

"And Mindy was good about checking in via email and phone calls for her entire stint in the Corp until the last few weeks. Then she sent one last message that said she'd met a guy and was staying in Africa and wouldn't be in touch anymore. Said the aunt was too far gone anyway to know if Mindy was there or not, which was mostly true. Still, the nurse was surprised. Mindy had always struck her as a devoted niece, the kind that would at least want updates on her aunt until the end."

"Instead, she what, runs off with the Johnstone kid?" Regan trotted down the stoop and over to the Mercedes.

"The nurse didn't know who Mindy had met, but the timing fits. Of course, now she's here, so obviously she didn't stay in Africa."

Regan held her phone in a death grip. The fear she'd experienced when she first entered the condo was back tenfold. "JoJo, Kyle Ramsey is missing. It may be nothing, but I want you to get hold of Fuller and have him secure a warrant for searching Mindy's place. Then text me her address and meet me over there ASAP."

"Will do, although I don't know if we have enough to get a warrant."

"Fuck that. Everyone wants the killer found, so someone better make sure we get permission to search a suspect's place."

"And if we don't?"

"We go in anyway. There has to be some connection here with our killer. The whole story about Mindy and Johnstone Jr. is too off for it not to be, and if Kyle is in danger, I'm not taking any more chances."

"Roger that." JoJo hung up.

Regan went around to the driver's side to speak to Kyle's ex-wife through the open window. She managed to shoot a reassuring smile to the tween girl in the passenger's seat. "Here's your key. He's not in there. I suggest you head over to your event. I'll track Mr. Ramsey down for you and have him give you a call."

"All right, if you don't mind," the woman said with a forced smile. Obviously the woman was worried, too, and didn't want to upset her daughter.

"It's no trouble at all," Regan said stepping back. "You have a nice night."

She waited until the car pulled out into the traffic before sprinting back to her own. She wanted to believe in the reassurance she'd given, that Kyle was okay. Deep in her gut, she knew she would be lying to herself. Kyle was in trouble, and if she didn't figure out where he was quickly enough, he was going to be the fourth victim.

JoJo's text with Mindy's address came in, and Regan hit her siren to clear a path. The secretary lived in Brighton, not too far from where Ronan used to rent. It didn't take long to arrive, and Regan killed her siren before she reached the last block. If Mindy had Kyle at her place, Regan didn't want to announce her arrival. She pulled up to the building, double-parking once more, and got out. JoJo arrived by the time Regan had reached the front steps.

"Tell me the warrant came through?"

Her partner shook her head. "Fuller's on board with trying, but so far no luck. It's a stretch to say Mindy is our prime suspect."

"And yet she damn well is." With a grimace, Regan backed up a bit and looked at the building's façade. "What number is she?"

"2A."

"I'm going to assume that means it's a front

apartment on the second floor. I don't see any lights on."

"She could be in a back room," JoJo replied as they jogged up the steps.

Torturing Kyle to death. Regan had to keep it together. The front door had a security lock that someone had jammed open, so they got inside without any trouble and trotted up quietly to the second floor. They stood silently in front of Mindy's door for a few seconds, listening for anything that might indicate if anyone was inside. JoJo's phone pinged, and Regan watched expectantly as her partner checked the message.

JoJo frowned. "Still no warrant."

"Fuck it." Regan ran to her car and pulled out her handy dandy and illegal lock picking kit from the glove compartment. It had been a gift from her father, and she always carried it with her, even though she'd never had occasion to use it. It took little effort to open the old door. Sliding the kit in her back pocket, she pulled out her gun and gestured to her partner to go in low.

Regan pushed the door open as quietly as she could and immediately scanned the room as she entered. It was dark and as small as the apartment was, she could clearly see that no other lights were on in the efficiency kitchen at the far end or in the room to the left that she assumed was the bedroom. Still, she took no chances as she quickly crossed through to the back of the apartment. There was no sound in the place other than the relatively harsh breathing of her and her partner. Nothing smelled off, either, so by the time they entered the bedroom, she was sure Mindy wasn't home.

Holstering her gun, Regan switched on the

bedroom light and stared at the frilliest girls room she'd ever scene. That which wasn't pink, was purple, and everything looked to be made from either satin or silk. Fluffy pillows and cutesy stuffed animals adorned the white four-poster bed. It was like a ten year-old's bedroom. The only thing missing was posters of pop stars and actors. JoJo whistled.

Regan glanced her way. "Yeah, I know. Weird. Check the bathroom, will you?"

Regan tackled the bedroom, not sure of what she was looking for. Something, please God, needed to give her a clue. She opened the closet and found a hefty amount of clothing, most of which was like the dress she'd seen the admin wear at Molvado's office. She searched through to see if any of it was more in the Domme theme, but nothing was. Next, she opened the dresser drawers and stared at the predictable amounts of underwear, bras, panties, except...

Pulling out a bra, she held it up and studied it. It was padded, completely, creating breasts in the cups. A quick look confirmed that all of the bras were the same. She tossed the one in her hand down and yanked open the next drawer. It contained a bunch of Spanx, except, no. These were underwear with padded bottoms, creating feminine curves. With dawning fury, Regan realized the import of the clothing.

"Jesus," JoJo exclaimed from the bathroom. "For someone who looked washed out, this girl has a lot of make-up."

Regan rushed into the tiny room and stared at the broad array of tubes and bottles and brushes crammed onto a small wicker table. Everything clicked into place. "I'm a fucking moron!" she spat out. "They were right, the FBI profiler, my father, even Kyle, every fucking person was right all along, and I was so sure I was right, I didn't even consider it."

"What are you talking about?"

Shoving the underpants she was still holding at her partner, she pulled out her phone. "What was Molvado's office number?" she mumbled as she did an internet search.

JoJo held up the underwear. "So, she padded her booty? What am I missing?"

"Mindy's not here," Regan explained without looking up from her phone.

"I can see that."

"She was never here." She shook her head. Finding the number, she dialed it. "I'm going to see if Molvado is still at her office. See if you can find a home number for her."

"Okay, but I still don't get what you're talking about here."

"Mindy's dead. What's left of her is probably moldering somewhere in Africa. She was likely dead when she sent that email to the aunt's nursing home." The phone rang and rang. *Pick up!* When no one did, she reluctantly ended the call. She looked at JoJo expectantly.

"I've got a home number. You want me to call it?"

"Yes. No. I'm going to go to Molvado's office first and see if Mindy left anything there that will tell me where he'd take another victim. You stay here and keep searching."

"He?"

On her way out of the room, Regan stopped and took the seconds needed to bring her partner up to speed. "The person we know as Mindy isn't a woman. The padded bras and underwear, and the heavy foundation and other make-up that looks like stuff you'd see on RuPaul's Drag Race tell me it's a man dressed as a woman."

"Mindy's transgender?"

"No, not the real Mindy. Like I said, she's probably dead. The guy pretending to be her stole her identity after he killed her, I bet. Then he sent the email to the nursing home to keep anyone from wondering what happened to her. The killer has been a man all along, but has a female identity."

"The Johnstone kid." JoJo finally got it.

"Again, that would be my guess. He killed his father, not some woman scorned, and I wonder if the old man had it coming, too. I'm no profiler, but the brutality of it and the sexual component spells abuse to me. Maybe the boy was born transgender or maybe his father fucked with his head so much he took on a female identity. Who the hell knows, but once apparently wasn't enough. He developed a taste for killing and heads for the Peace Corps maybe looking for easier targets or just wants to lose his old self. Then he meets Mindy, an orphan for all intents and purposes, drops off the planet as himself, follows her to Africa, and well..." Regan made a gesture toward the room. "I've got to go."

"Don't worry. I'll let you know if I find anything."

"I hope to God one of us does," she called out as she ran through the living room. She was still putting the pieces to the whole thing together, but she was sure of one thing now.

Kyle was in the hands of a serial killer.

Chapter Twelve

Kyle didn't want to open his eyes. The pounding in his head was enough to make him want to sink back into oblivion. It wasn't the only thing hurting, either. His arms and legs ached, as did his back. He felt stiff all over but couldn't quite remember why. A sharp, acrid smell hit his nostrils, making his eyes pop open.

"Wakey, wakey, little boy. It's time to play."

The cloying sweetness of the voice made him shudder, and as his vision cleared, the woman's face came into focus."

His memory returned with a jolt, making him recoil, except there was nowhere for him to go. He was trussed up on some kind of wooden frame, arms and legs pulled tight with his front and back fully exposed. And he was naked. That was the least of his concerns, although the lascivious look on the woman's face as she gazed at him made his skin crawl.

Mindy, that was her name. Dr. Molvado's mousy assistant. What was he doing with her? Oh, yeah, he'd been leaving his condo when she'd rushed up to him, speaking almost incoherently about how the doctor was crazy. Molvado was the serial killer and Mindy was scared to death, didn't know what to do, begging for help.

What an idiot he'd been, not even stopping to consider that it made no sense for Mindy to come to him for help. And when the woman had mentioned Regan was in danger, well that had killed all of his remaining brain cells. He'd simply reacted, shoving Mindy into his car in order to ride to Regan's rescue.

Then, nothing. His mind was a blank. Obviously, Mindy had done something to incapacitate him, drugs maybe. It would explain his aching head and dry mouth. But how had this wispy woman managed to get him trussed up as he was?

As he pondered that question, he took stock of his surroundings. It was a nicely appointed dungeon, not unlike the room at Nemesis. Mindy stood with a sick smile on her face, dressed to the nines in Domme-wear. From the spider-web silver choker to the black bustier to the thigh-high boots, she looked much like the women at the club, although she lacked a certain something. He stared hard, trying to clear his head and his vision more, until he finally realized what was off about the woman.

"You're not a woman at all," he croaked out.

The open-palm slap made his head spin again. "Shut up! I didn't give you permission to speak." With a toss of her head, Mindy added, "You don't know what you're talking about. I'm the realist woman you'll ever meet and the last real woman you'll ever know." She said the last bit with a twisted smile.

Kyle fought to get himself under control, fear threatening to cloud his judgment. This was the person who'd killed at least three men, including Jazz. He was next unless he held on long enough for Regan to find him. She would, too, he had every faith in her. He swallowed down the lump forming in his throat and steadied his breathing.

"My apologies, Mistress." He dropped his gaze in the most submissive way he knew how. Fingers brushed along his jaw, and he fought the shiver running through him. Up close, he could see those hands clearly and realized they were the give-away if anyone cared to look closely. They were too big for a woman.

"Very prettily said," Mindy cooed. "I could almost believe you mean it." She strutted away. "Of course, by the time I'm done disciplining you, you will mean it. And you'll see what other men have, that I am a woman, and I am in control."

She stopped in front of a low table covered with whips, canes, and paddles. Picking up a paddle about the right size for Ping-Pong, she whirled around and gave Kyle a coquettish look.

"My father was the first man to see me for what I was, even though when I was young, I tried to hide my true nature. I was confused and ashamed because I had these awful boy parts. Papa wasn't fooled, though. When Momma died, he told me he knew exactly what I was, and if I wanted to live under his roof acting like a girl, I could damn well take Momma's place. At home he made me wear her clothes, keep his house, fix his meals, and sleep in his bed. Only when others were around did he treat me like the boy I really wasn't. Nobody noticed how wrong that was."

Mindy's expression morphed into one etched with pain. "Nobody noticed anything."

Knowing that so long as Mindy was talking, she wasn't hurting him, Kyle interjected. "That was their mistake. People should have paid more attention and protected you from him. What he did was wrong." It was easy enough to speak up, because, of course, he believed what he was saying. Kyle sympathized with the transgender child being abused by his father.

Mindy's gaze wandered to a spot beyond Kyle's head. "Yes, they should have. I think maybe some of them did, but no one cared about me." She laughed suddenly and almost maniacally. "I showed him who was boss in the end."

The sympathy didn't help the chill in Kyle when those eyes turned back to him and lit up with sadistic glee. "He made a mistake, you see. Sent me off to college when I got a scholarship. He didn't like people thinking he wasn't doing right by me. Made me come home most weekends so I could do his laundry and suck his cock. He didn't even notice how strong I became, physically and mentally, until it was too late. Oh, how he begged and screamed, just like I used to. And just like he used to, I ignored it all and kept on going."

She sighed deeply. "The power was intoxicating. I tried to resist the temptation to do it again and just move on with the next phase of my life, the one where I could live like the woman I am. I even wanted to do good in world. Then I met that silly girl, Mindy, who didn't deserve the life she had, the life I wanted. So I took it and made much better use of it."

She turned in little circles as she spoke, the paddle bouncing against her leg. "I wanted a doctor to help me make my transition fully. Molvado was supposed to be the best in helping strong women find their true self. She didn't understand me, though. Not really. She was more interested in those weak men who came to her, and honestly, anyone could tell they needed a firmer hand than she was giving them by *talking*. Once I had them in my control, I just couldn't resist feeling the power that comes from ultimate domination." A blissful look crossed Mindy's face that made Kyle sick.

"You father was a bastard who got what he deserved, but you also killed innocent men," he choked out. "My friend, Jazz, never hurt you or anyone. He didn't deserve to be tortured to death."

Mindy scowled back, tapping the paddle against her leg. "Those pathetic creatures were begging for the kind of discipline I meted out." She sauntered closer to Kyle. "They said they wanted pain, that they could handle pain. They knelt before me and kissed my feet before I tied them up and showed them what being dominated really means."

Without warning, Mindy swung the paddle into Kyle's middle. The pain exploded across his skin and deep into his muscles. He doubled over as much as his bindings would allow and bit back the groan trying to get out. When he could catch his breath, he straightened up and glared back at his tormentor. He wanted to spit and snarl at her. It was hard to hold it all in. He had to, though, or the violence might escalate too fast and he'd die before Regan could find him. He lowered his gaze.

A shudder ran through him when Mindy caressed his arm as she walked behind him. "You're just like those other men. I can see it in your eyes. I wanted to take control of you the moment you stepped into the office. I know that you struggle with it. I checked Molvado's notes on you. She didn't realize I accessed her files on her patients until tonight. Stupid cow. She won't be bothering us, though. I made sure of that. You're very good at pretending to be submissive. I intend to test the limits of your act. We'll see if you can handle what I have in store for you."

A puff of air hit the back of his neck before the blows rained down on his ass. Each hit drove him forward, his arms and legs pulling against the straps holding him in place. His eyes watered with the growing agony, and he tried to keep from crying out. He didn't want to give his torturer the satisfaction.

All through it, he kept thinking of Regan, his real mistress. She would come for him. He knew it. He had to hold on.

****

Regan stood over the body of Dr. Molvado, cursing. The poor woman's head had been bashed in with a heavy wooden clock she kept in her office. Mindy, no doubt, although why the killer would have taken out her boss was a mystery. Perhaps Molvado had figured out Mindy's secret. As she called in the murder, she looked around, desperate for some piece of information that would lead her to where Mindy might have taken Kyle. She was convinced the killer had Kyle, because he still didn't answer his mobile and his office was sure he wasn't there.

She spotted a purse open on the carpet not far from the body. Its contents were strewn about as if someone had gone through it. Kneeling down, she poked through the stuff to see what Mindy would have been looking for. She found Molvado's wallet, some make-up, breath mints, tissues and some stray receipts. Nothing stood out...except there were no keys. She stuck her hand inside the purse to see if they were there and came up empty. A thought struck her. It was a long shot, but maybe.

There was no time to wait for the crime scene

people if she was right. She grabbed Molvado's wallet and looked at her license, then bolted from the office. She called JoJo on the way.

"What's up?" her partner asked.

"Molvado is dead, killed by Mindy I'm assuming. I think she took the doctor's keys and went to her place."

"Why?"

"Molvado gave off the Domme vibe, right?" When her partner murmured her assent, she continued. "So, it stands to reason she'd have a play room at her house. I'm betting Mindy took Kyle there so she could do her worst like she did with Foster."

Images of what Kyle might be going through at that moment sent a wave of nausea through her. She fought the rising sense of panic. If she didn't keep her shit together, she'd be no good to Kyle.

"We don't know for sure she has him. I mean the others let her come inside and tie them up. Ramsey was a pretty big guy. How the hell could she get him to go anywhere with her unless they're already involved?"

Regan winced. "They're not, because he and I are. And I don't know how she did it. Maybe she tranqued him or something."

"Okay, I'm going skip the part where you said you're involved with him and assume your gut is on point. What's the address? I'll meet you there."

Regan rattled off the information as she hopped into her car and once again hit the siren. Molvado's house was in neighboring Brookline, and in a fairly upscale part of the town. It was a quick ride from downtown with people getting out of her way. When she was a few blocks from the location, she killed the siren but not the lights. If Mindy was in the house, she didn't want to announce her arrival. There was no telling what the killer would do if cornered.

It was a quiet area as she suspected and easy enough to find a place to park a block away from her destination. Checking her gun out of nervousness more than anything, she trotted down to the Molvado house. There were no lights on that she could see, but there was a car, a sporty BMW, parked in the driveway. She looked at the plate and took a moment to call it in. Her blood froze, and her heart lurched when she got confirmation that it was registered to Kyle. She texted the info to JoJo with the additional message she was going in with or without a warrant.

She scooted around to the back of the house and picked the lock. She said a short prayer about the alarm not being on and opened the door. A quick glance to the side told her there was an alarm system, but it was off. Mindy must have ferreted the code out at some point yet hadn't bothered to reset it. Of course not. She didn't expect to be disturbed by anyone.

Gun at the ready, Regan moved silently through the kitchen, ears straining for sounds. The house was silent, although she sensed she wasn't alone. Foster's playroom had been in the basement, so that is where she looked first. There was nothing in the lower level, though, except the usual crap. Racing back to the kitchen, she continued into the other rooms on the ground floor. Everything was dark and quiet and perfectly normal. Her heart beat painfully as she crept up the stairs to the second floor.

It was equally dark and silent on the upper level until she gazed all the way down the hallway. At the far end, she saw light underneath a door. That was where

Mindy had to have Kyle. Molvado had undoubtedly sound proofed it, and Regan hoped that meant any noise she made wouldn't filter through, either. She wanted to bolt down and kick the door in. As hard as it was, though, she made herself go slowly and as silently as she could. She might only get one chance to bring Mindy down without hurting Kyle. Surprise was her best ally.

The closer she got to the door, the more aware she became that some sound was coming through. Laughter mingled with cries of pain. She clenched her teeth against the rising fury. Her hand shook just a little as she reached for the doorknob. She took a deep, steadying breath to control her movements before slowly twisting the knob. As soon as she felt the latch release, she shoved open the door with her gun up.

The scene before her caused her to freeze. In the middle of the room, Kyle was spread eagled against a wooden frame, his body covered in welts and big red splotches. He'd been beaten within an inch of his life everywhere except his face. Johnstone in his Mindy persona stood in front of Kyle, a knife poised to slash Kyle's chest. The killer's head whipped around at the sound of Regan's entrance.

They stared at each other for a second before Mindy's face twisted in rage. "You've spoiled everything, you cunt!"

"Drop it, Mindy," Regan ordered and stepped farther into the room.

Instead of dropping the knife, Mindy raised it higher and swiveled back to Kyle. Regan didn't hesitate. One shot and the would-be Domme went down, red blossoming under her arm.

Regan raced over and kicked the knife away from the twitching Mindy. She was unconscious, but alive, at least for the moment. Keeping half an eye on her, Regan yanked out her phone and called for a couple of ambulances. She figured JoJo was close to arriving but didn't want to wait on medical help coming for Kyle. When Mindy still didn't stir, she turned her attention to Kyle.

Oh, God, up close it was worse than she'd thought. How he was staying conscious was a mystery. Not only that, somehow he managed to give her a pained smile as she approached.

"Knew you'd come," he said in a hoarse voice. "Just had to…" A shudder racked his body. "Just had to hang on."

"Shh," she admonished gently and reached to free one of his ankles, squatting down to do so. Given the locking mechanism, she had to holster her gun so she could use both hands. She glanced back at Mindy to confirm the perp was still out.

"Of course, I came for you." She moved to the other ankle. A sob almost burst out. She ruthlessly shoved it down. Kyle needed her to be strong right now. She could break down into a puddle of goo later.

Standing, she reached for one of his wrists. "I'm sorry it took me so long to figure out where you were and who had you."

"No, this is all my fault." His breathing was so labored, she wanted to cover his mouth to silence him. "You were right. I shouldn't have played at detective. I was so fucking arrogant, I put us both in danger."

When she freed his other wrist, he sagged against her. She helped him slide to his knees in a controlled fall. "No more talking, now, boyo. When you're all better, we'll set some ground rules." She ran her fingers through his sweaty hair. "I need to put you on a short leash."

"Yes, ma'am," he murmured and smiled wearily at her. His gaze shifted to a point behind her, and his eyes went wide. "Regan!"

Her world tilted suddenly, Kyle's body slamming into hers, sending them both sprawling. Her shoulder clipped the wooden frame, but she ignored the pain. She understood what was happening even before she saw Mindy swaying on unsteady feet, the knife in her hand, slashing clumsily toward them. Regan freed her gun just as Kyle rolled away so as to not block her. The shot she fired hit Mindy square in the chest. This time, when the killer went down, Regan was sure she wouldn't be getting up again.

Regan curled her arms around Kyle's limp body. The effort to move out of range of the knife had sent him over the edge into oblivion, and she didn't think that was such a bad thing. Part of her wished she could join him, but there was work still to be done. It would be a long night. Sirens wailed in the distance, a door banged open somewhere in the house.

"Regan?"

"Up here, JoJo!"

Regan wrapped her arms around Kyle, needing to hold him until she had to let him go. He stirred and mumbled something in an anxious tone. She hugged him tighter.

"Shh, it's okay. I have you." She kissed the top of his head. "We have each other."

Epilogue

"Sorry, I'm a bit early," Regan said as Kyle opened his door.

"You're kidding, right?" He swung the door shut. "Let me get that for you." He grabbed the bag she was carrying.

Regan walked inside Kyle's beautiful home that she felt comfortable in after so many weeks of dating. She recognized the classical music playing softly in the background. Hanging out with Kyle was giving her a great appreciation of culture she would have sneered at not long ago.

"You've had time to eat?" she asked.

Having fully recovered from his ordeal with Mindy, Kyle was back to work full time. Regan encouraged him to eat as soon as he got home at night instead of waiting for her. She may not have another serial killer case, but regular old murder was still unfortunately a frequent occurrence in a big city like Boston. Most nights she was lucky to arrive at his place before nine.

Putting down the bag, Kyle raked her with eyes already burning with passion. "I'm ready for you, make no mistake, Mistress Regan. Can I get you anything?"

Regan had thought about the need for alcohol this night. "What do you have in the way of whisky?"

"I have several different single malt scotches."

Of course, the good stuff. "Pour me about two fingers of whatever one you like best." It was more for him than her anyway.

"Yes, ma'am." She watched him walk to a bar in the corner of his living room. "Is the music to your liking?"

Regan wandered around a bit, nerves making her antsy. "It's fine. Vivaldi's The Four Seasons, isn't it?"

He handed her a squat cut crystal glass of amber liquid. "That's right."

She raised her eyebrows. "I'm learning from you."

"Only fair, given what you've taught me."

They had really been teaching each other, exploring the BDSM lifestyle and trying on the limits of a Domme/sub relationship outside the bedroom. In the aftermath of Kyle's torture, she'd wanted to eliminate the pain aspect of their relationship, but Kyle had insisted on continuing it after he'd healed. He didn't want something so pleasurable between them to be ruined by the twisted mind of Thomas Johnstone, who had, as near as they could tell, murdered not just his father and the three men in Boston, but Mindy Fortensky, Dr. Molvado and perhaps some number of men in Haiti and Africa. They were still trying to piece it all together.

Regan and Kyle had also discussed long and hard the limits of their relationship and the difference between consensual discipline and abuse. They were in a good place now with their relationship. So good in fact that Regan wanted to up their level of play to a place that had always intrigued and aroused her. She hoped Kyle would be willing to explore this new boundary.

She smiled at him over the rim of her glass as she took a long swallow of the fiery drink. "I have a new lesson in mind for tonight. Take my bag, go into your bedroom and strip down."

"Yes, ma'am," he said deliberately, his eyes boring into hers for a second before he did as she commanded.

Watching him walk away and admiring the sight, Regan took another sip of her drink and relished the warm sting of the scotch sliding down her throat. Dutch courage it might be, but by God, it was great stuff. Kyle Ramsey was a man who settled for nothing less than the best. She could see it in his home, his possessions, his career, and his bearing. If he was going to put himself in her care, then she owed it to him to be the best Domme she could be. What she was about to do to him was the ultimate domination. Stopping at any other level of play would be second best, and that wouldn't do.

Regan followed Kyle with a sense of mission. When she arrived at his bedroom, however, her doubts came creeping back. Seeing him sitting naked on the side of his bed, watching her, waiting for her next command, she realized she needed to do this right. He had to be as fulfilled by this experience as she hoped to be. That meant taking it nice and slow and easy.

She sauntered toward him and handed him the glass. "Sit back against the head board and hold this for me."

Kyle did as he was told, resting the glass against his thigh right next to his hard-on. He kept his gaze on her, and she reciprocated while taking off her clothes. She hadn't worn anything special. Underneath her jeans and T-shirt was a lacy bra and panty set. Not her every day wear, yet nothing too provocative. She stopped there, intending to bring him to the brink gradually.

She got up on the bed and swung her legs over his lap. His free hand curled into a fist, and she assumed he did that to resist the urge to touch her. "Good boy, Kyle," she praised. "No touching unless I give you permission."

"I hope you'll give me that permission soon, Mistress."

She shook her head while taking the glass from him. "It's not your job to worry about things like that, Kyle. Remember, what you want is unimportant. We're here to please me. Concentrate on doing what makes me happy."

So saying, she leaned forward and took his lips in a gentle kiss. It was little more than a pressing of soft flesh against soft flesh. She pulled back and saw Kyle struggle not to follow her with his mouth. His lips remained parted, and his breathing became more rapid. She kept her eyes on him while taking another sip of the scotch. Once more, the liquid burned a path down her throat. A warm relaxation was starting to spread throughout her, too.

She took yet another sip and leaned forward again, keeping the scotch in her mouth. When her lips met Kyle's, she used her free hand to clasp the hair on the back of his head and angle him so that her face was over his. He opened his mouth wider to let her in, knowing what she was going to do. It was tricky, but she managed to feed him the drink without spilling it. He swallowed it, and his tongue met hers to play. She allowed this bit of aggressiveness for a few seconds before breaking the kiss.

She repeated the process again and again until there was only one swallow left in the glass. Sitting back on his lap, she studied him and was pleased to see a languid look in his eye that did nothing to diminish the desire he radiated toward her. His cock was still rock-hard, too, proof that he hadn't had so much to drink that he was losing interest. With her forefinger, she slid up the side of his erection and was gratified to see his eyes go even darker with passion.

Regan tossed back the last of the scotch before putting the glass on the side table. As with before, she didn't swallow, only this time, she didn't feed it to Kyle. Instead, she wiggled down his legs until she could bend forward to his cock. She took the hard length in her mouth, letting the liquid dribble out at the same time. She sucked in as much of him as she could and pulled back up again, licking the scotch as she did so.

Kyle grunted and groaned, and his hips flexed up. His hands fisted the bedcovers below him, and his breath hissed in. Regan lavished more attention on his cock, sucking and licking, trying to achieve the perfect balance of arousal and relaxation she could in her lover. When she gauged he had had enough, she sat up and swung her leg over to get off him.

"Slide down and turn over onto your stomach, Kyle, but don't hump the bed," she ordered with a smile.

His mistress' order, issued in a tone that was part seductress, part drill sergeant, shot more blood into Kyle's already straining dick. God, the effect she had on him only grew with time.

For a while, after the night when he'd endured the

killer's grotesque parody of the Domme/sub relationship, he feared he'd been ruined for this. He'd insisted to Regan that he was fine continuing, but he'd known a few moments when panic threatened to swamp him. Stubborn pride and total trust in Regan had given him the strength to suppress the fear and submerge himself in the play. His marvelous mistress had reclaimed him from the horror, and each time they played, she took him soaring to greater heights of pleasure and peace.

Something was different about tonight, however. She was upping the game and a frisson of concern and excitement shot up his spine. Still, he gave no more than a second of thought to what might be coming, complying immediately with the order. He turned his head toward her, watching and waiting for the next order.

Regan ran her hand down to the small of his back and caressed the slope of his ass. He knew instantly it was the part of him she was really after tonight. He drew a quick breath before consciously relaxing again. As terrifying as the thought of her taking him down there was, his desire to please her was far stronger.

She slapped her palm against the globes he worked hard to keep firm. As punishment went, it was a love tap, one she repeated several times on each cheek. In between the slaps, she squeezed the flesh and pushed and pulled. Being spanked was old hat, and he focused on the delicious heat spreading across his backside. When she deemed him sufficiently warmed, his mistress stopped, resting her thumb in the crease of his ass. He tensed immediately despite his resolve not to.

"Easy," she admonished and hummed in

encouragement when he relaxed beneath her fingers again. "Now, Kyle, listen up." She stared at him, and he stared back. "I'm going to start playing with you. Up 'til now, I've been warming you up, keeping you aroused while using the scotch to relax you a bit." She leaned toward his face. "Are you aroused and relaxed, Kyle?"

He nodded, pleased to be able to reassure her.

"Good, because it's going to get intense, and I'm not going to tie you down. I'm going to trust you to keep it together and do what I tell you. Can I count on your doing that?"

"Yes, Mistress." His voice was low and thick with passion. He meant what he said, though. He could do this for her, would do this for her.

"Good. Very good. And remember to use the safeword if you want me to stop what I'm doing, if it gets too intense for you."

"I'll never say that word." He hadn't yet, not even when Mindy had been whaling on him. But no, he wasn't going to go there, not now, not when he was safely under Regan's control.

"We'll see."

Regan let go of him and, gripping the bottom of her bra with crossed hands, she pulled it over her head and tossed it on the floor. He watched her every move, and the reward for his controlled behavior so far, was her pinching her nipples with thumbs and forefingers. She rolled them into hard points. He parted his lips with the desperate and sudden need to latch onto those nipples and suck. She pumped her hips toward his face in obvious pleasure at her own touch. The muscles in Kyle's shoulders twitched, his eyes riveted on her crotch. As a bonus, she released one nipple and slid her hand, palm open, down her front to cup her mons. Now, he wanted his mouth *there*. He fought the urge to lunge at her.

"I want to fuck you very badly, Kyle," she confessed.

He growled a response even as his hole clenched.

She squeezed her folds through her panties and arched her back. Her other hand still tweaked her nipple. "Shall I fuck you now, Kyle?"

"Yes, please," he begged.

Christ, he didn't even know what he was asking for. Instinct warned him to safeword the idea away. A stronger need to please his mistress overrode it. He clamped his lips shut.

Regan stripped off her panties before bending over the side of the bed and retrieving something from her bag. Kyle's eyes widened when he saw that it was lube, yet he said nothing. Regan scooted to his side once more and straddled the nearest leg. Her knee wedged up against his ass cheeks, and she sat back on her heels.

This was where it started getting serious. But this was Regan, and he had to trust that she wouldn't do anything he couldn't handle. Despite the scotch humming in his veins, taking the edge off, his heart raced with excitement, anticipation, and some trepidation. Closing his eyes, he focused on the sounds she made, the snick of the cap of the bottle, a squirt of the lubricant popping past an air bubble.

Something, the lube probably, bounced on the bed beside his hip right before her hand caressed one of his ass cheeks.

"Relax, boy-o." Easy for her to say, he thought as

she pulled at his flesh to expose his hole. The tip of a wet finger pressed against the puckered ring and stayed there, not trying to enter, not yet. Still, he tensed. He couldn't help it. The finger remained in place, undaunted by his reaction, and made small circles. All the while, she murmured encouraging words.

"That's it. You're okay, my brave boy. Breathe, Kyle. Relax and breathe. I won't hurt you."

She kept up a steady stream of soothing words, all the while gently stroking and teasing his hole. He found it easy to obey her and relax into the touch. She released him long enough to put more lubricant on her finger and resumed the caress. Then, just as he got used to that simple touch, she slid the tip of the finger inside. Kyle jerked, again unable to suppress the reaction.

Regan slapped his ass back down, and he was grateful for the correction. She could do nothing about the way his hole squeezed her finger, however, and neither could he. His natural aversion to having anything inside him was too strong to override. He tried to push her out even as he fought to accept the minor invasion.

"Do you have something to say to me, Kyle?"

He understood she was waiting to see if he would safeword. He could do it, too, even claim he was still rattled by his recent torture. She would understand. She would be disappointed but wouldn't show it or try to guilt trip him. The problem was, he'd be disappointed in himself. He wanted to do this for her. He could take it because it would make her happy.

"No, ma'am." His voice sounded strained even to his own ears. His fingers clutched at the covers.

"Relax," she ordered, then leaned over and licked

her tongue up his flank.

Kyle shivered at the touch, and clever girl, she'd done it to distract him as she inserted her finger farther. His flesh quivered, but he otherwise managed to remain quiet.

She wiggled her finger around in blatant exploration. And then she proved more clever still by brushing against his prostate. She stroked it carefully, and he rewarded her with a startled gasp of pleasure bursting from his lips. Other than his doctor, no one had ever touched him there before, and certainly no one had ever done it in an effort to arouse. He'd heard it could be pleasurable, but he hadn't realized how electrifying it would be. It was like being goosed by a live wire. With each stroke, he quivered and writhed, his cock straining for release between his body and the sheet.

"That's it, boy-o. Feels good, doesn't it? See how, when you allow me to make the decisions, I won't disappoint you."

Hearing the words, Kyle let go of the last vestiges of concern. Regan was right. He knew she'd take good care of him. His complacency emboldened her to continue. She spent a few more minutes letting him get accustomed to her one finger before sliding it out and replacing it with her slightly thicker thumb. The larger digit caused a slight burn as it stretched his hole more. She stroked repeatedly, then moved on to two fingers, and once more there was a burn, a low level of pain that helped to increase his pleasure more than diminish it. She was careful to go slowly and wait until he was compliant. His muscles relaxed even more beneath her touch, his breathing became heavier, and his hole stopped squeezing the invaders.

He wasn't the only one turned-on by her control. She was wet against his leg where her body still straddled his and her breath came fast and hard over the small of his back. This mild invasion wasn't the end game, of course. She wanted to fuck him. And when she pulled her two fingers out, he knew the time had come.

As Regan moved to the edge of the bed, Kyle opened his eyes to slits in order to watch her. His eyes widened for a second as she pulled a strap-on out of the bag she had brought. Although the fake cock was no bigger than Kyle himself, he figured it was going to hurt some going in. Her preparation would help, but it wouldn't be enough. If he could stand the pain and allow himself to enjoy the stimulation, she would have truly conquered him.

She fitted the foreign devise between her legs, strapping it around her thighs. She looked surprisingly hot to him, given that he viewed himself as being firmly straight. Still, the fake cock added a dimension to the power emanating from her. There was a stubbly flap that hovered around her clit, guaranteeing she'd get some direct stimulation while she fucked him. She pushed it against her slit briefly, and her eyes closed in obvious delight. When she opened them again, he gave her a knowing smile, trying to hide any trepidation he felt.

"Close your eyes, boy-o."

It took a couple of seconds before he complied, a small war having raged inside him. On the one hand he wanted to obey and give himself up to her completely. On the other, he really wanted to keep track of where that dildo was. Once his eyes were shut, she ran through an abbreviated version of her previous foreplay. He relaxed and adjusted more quickly this time to the mild invasion, until a much larger, bluntness pressed against his hole. The dildo remained in place, just outside, not pressing. She was giving him a moment to say the word that would make her stop. Well, he was not going to say it, and before he could talk himself out of it, he pushed back.

The head of the dildo slipped in with that little bit of help. He grunted and started to rear up at the painful intrusion. Shit, no amount of prep could have made him ready for this. His hole convulsed against the dildo, while his hips rocked in an automatic effort to evade the thing. Regan pressed down with her hands at his waist forcing him to be still.

"Easy there, boy-o. I don't want you to accidentally take more before you're ready. You're my responsibility, and I'm not going to hurt you or let you hurt yourself."

Kyle forced himself to lie still, his breath coming in harsh pants. "Yes, Mistress. Sorry. I know you'll make this good for me."

"I will. I promise. Now rock with me, Kyle," she said as she began a slow rhythm of pushing and retreating. "Hump the bed in time with my thrusts."

He couldn't find fault with that plan. His cock wept with the need for release and hadn't softened even with the discomfort of the dildo. He complied with her command, matching her strokes, increasing the speed when she did.

With each push forward, the dildo gained greater entrance to his body, stretching him with an alien fullness that never quite stopped being uncomfortable.

But his mistress was enjoying this claiming of his body, so he reveled in his acceptance. She moaned above him, as her orgasm clearly built. Her knees squeezed his legs from the outside, trapping him beneath her.

Soon, she was truly fucking him, stroking them both to climax. The dildo hit his prostate even harder and better than her finger had, while the sheet beneath him coaxed his cock. He grunted and groaned in encouragement. Her increasing cries told him she was with him. They were one person, surging forward and back in a blind race to ecstasy.

"Oh, oh, God. That's it, Kyle, stay with me. Stay with me," Regan cried out.

He was mindless, reaching for the top. It was there, just there. He had it. The explosion ripped through him. He bucked up as Regan pumped furiously, digging her fingers into his flesh, grinding her hips against his ass. Kyle shuddered, and his cries echoed hers. His fingers clawed at the sheet. And when the last ripple went through him, she collapsed on top of him, her lovely weight a testament to how much he'd pleased his mistress.

Later, once she'd cleaned them both up and hugged Kyle close as they lay entwined in each other's arms, he could see the question in her eyes.

"I'm fine," he assured her. When she looked back at him skeptically, he wiggled his ass a bit. "Okay, I'm a little sore, but the force of the orgasm was worth it." He kissed her temple. "And, it made you happy, so it makes me happy, too."

"I thought you might safeword for a minute there."

Kyle chuckled. "No way. I'm all yours, Mistress Regan. I know you'll take good care of me always." He hesitated a second. "I love you."

Regan's breath caught. She'd thought she'd never hear a man say those words to her and had convinced herself she didn't need to hear them. A smile spread across her face as she pulled him tight. "You're mine, and I love you, too."

About the Author

I'm a corporate lawyer, happily married for over twenty years with three kids and four dogs. No white picket fence, but we do live in the burbs west of Boston. While my husband and I still do occasionally lick chocolate off each other, our more typical evening involves lying in bed once the kids are in theirs and reading separate books. Mine of course are romance. I started reading them as a defense against all those boring legal documents. Once I started, I couldn't stop.

I've also loved erotica since I was old enough to appreciate what sex is. I've been publishing erotic romance since 2009.

Besides my family, writing, and reading, my loves include the sight, smell, and sounds of the ocean (I'm a New England girl through and through), chocolate (naturally), prime rib (bloody), and good bourbon on the rocks.

Visit Samantha at
http://www.samanthacayto.com

To chat with Samantha Cayto and other Wild Rose Press authors of erotic romance, join us at www.groups.yahoo.com/group/thewilderroses.

Coming Soon

Internal Affair
Book Four
Boston's Brave

by

Samantha Cayto

As the oldest of the Callaghan brothers, Daire picked up the pieces of his family when his parents were murdered. With his brothers grown and out of the house, he is finally able to truly deal with his loss—and his loneliness. But he's out of practice when it comes to dating. Best to bury himself in his new position as police lieutenant.

Parker Li works in internal affairs. Having experienced bad cops, she is determined to weed them out from the inside. Proud of her Chinese heritage and her mission, she refuses to be intimidated by the hostility she encounters on the force. She has also decided to put her personal life on hold, unwilling to settle down with the guy her family has chosen for her.

While investigating a corruptions charge, Parker stumbles upon the Callaghan file. Because she cares about the truth, she reopens the case. Daire is, at first, dubious about the intent of the sexy dynamo who pushes her way into his office and his life. But her dedication to duty wins him over. A stickler for propriety, Parker resists the temptation of the steamy lieutenant with the chip on his shoulder.

The case might be cold, but heat rises as, together, they are forced to face the desire between them as well as the danger of solving the decade-old murders.

Also Available

Double the Risk

Book Two
Boston's Brave

by

Samantha Cayto

http://amzn.com/B00O5VPKL4

After the deaths of his parents and having to raise his younger brother, Detective Ronan Callaghan looks for three things—a good time, his next case, and when time allows, the man who murdered his family. The jury is still out on his new partner, but the hot new medical examiner at the first crime scene they share does it for him hands down.

Diego Nieves hopes his new job in Boston will allow him to shake the painful memories of an on-duty shooting. Haunted by the event, he takes his job seriously and isn't certain he can work with a cavalier partner. He sure as hell wants to work more closely with the pretty ME standing over his first homicide vic.

Newly free from a long and boring engagement, medical examiner Cassidy Barnes is finally free to cut loose with her sex life. She's determined to break old patterns and start taking new chances. When two sexy cops catch her eye, she can't resist either—the charming rogue or the serious romantic.

Just when Ronan and Diego begin to click as partners, their simultaneous relationship with Cassidy pits them as rivals. As each man vies for her attention, Cassidy struggles to choose between them. Solving the case and keeping Cassidy just might mean Ronan and Diego must to learn to work together...in more ways than one.

Prologue

"What are you going to do, Rory?" The fear in his mother's voice was obvious to Ronan.

"Sheila, my love, don't worry about it." His father tried to put his arms around her, a look on his face he only wore when he was about to cajole his wife of more than twenty years.

His mother deftly avoided the hug and moved to the other side of the kitchen. "Don't tell me not to worry when I can see as plain as day how much *you* are."

His father sighed heavily and ran his fingers through the head of black hair still thick in his middle-age. "I'm not so much worried as pissed, honestly. I thought better of these men. Hell, I went through the academy with some of them. I thought they were good cops, honest ones. They're tarnishing the badge," he added, his voice lifting.

His mother glanced around. "Lower your voice, Rory," she admonished. "Finn will be home any time now, and Ronan is coming for dinner. I don't want them to hear any of this."

Ronan was already home, lacrosse practice having ended early when Bobby McCoy broke his leg. That's what he got for showing off, not that Ronan would ever say as much out loud. Standing quietly in the hall, he listened to his parents talking, understanding quickly that something was up. He'd seen the tension in his father these last few months every time he came home from college looking for a better meal than they offered up on campus. Perhaps now, he'd understand why.

"Neither do I," his father said in a quieter voice. "I've told them all their lives that being a Boston cop was the best job in the world. I hate to have to tell them there are worms eating at its core."

"It's not your fight, or at least not entirely," his mother amended quickly when his father scowled at her. "Please don't take this on yourself anymore. You need to tell others. You need to tell James."

His father's scowl deepened. "I don't want to go to James until I have more proof and know who all is involved. He's up for promotion again, and you know he's going places, Sheila. I don't want to put him in a bad spot."

"You do him a disservice by keeping him in the dark. He's as good a cop as you and would want to know the truth."

Running his hand down his face, his father said, "Maybe you're right. I'll bring him into the loop soon, I promise." He opened his arms. "Sweetheart, I don't want you to worry, though. I'm being careful, and I know what I'm doing. I promise."

"Oh, Rory." His mother walked into his father's arms and hugged him tight. "I can't stop worrying about you. You know that."

As his parents stood wrapped in each other's arms, Ronan stayed still so as not to disturb them. But his mind whirled with what he'd heard. Something bad was going on, and his father was in the thick of it. Whatever it was, it had his mother worried, and now he was worried, too.

Chapter One

The City of Boston clung tenaciously to summer, hot and humid already at six in the morning. It was going to be a scorcher, hitting near ninety, and as early as it was, the sweat had dripped off Ronan Callaghan before he'd gone more than a block. That was New England weather. It could be as cold as Montana and as steamy as Florida. Given that it was early September, the heat and humidity weren't a complete surprise.

Ronan didn't care or even notice that his T-shirt was plastered to his torso as he turned into the last block of his morning run. The college students were back in class so he wasn't the only one huffing his way down the sidewalk. He didn't mind that, either. When he'd finally moved out of the family home for good, he'd deliberately picked the Brighton area to be near his alma mater, Boston College, and its student body.

After his parents' murder, he'd been forced to return home and commute, having tasted college living for only one semester. That's what he got for deferring college until January. Someone had to look out for his kid brother, Finn, and with his older brother, Daire, working full time as a new cop, that someone had been Ronan.

He hadn't minded, not really. He'd done it without even being asked. Sure, a fourteen-year-old boy was a major pain in anyone's ass. One who was also mourning the brutal loss of his parents, even more so. It had been tough keeping tabs on the kid, making sure he got to school on time, did his homework, and cleaned his room, everything Ronan had loathed to do himself at that age and older. All this was while dealing with his own grief and anger and trying to adjust to being a college student and young adult with the angst that entailed. There hadn't been time anymore to go to parties or just hang out with other students after class. There was laundry to do and dinner to fix. The weekends had been filled with house cleaning and food shopping.

Yeah, Ronan had become the "mom" of the house, filling his mother's shoes to the best of his ability and always feeling as if he'd fallen short. One day he'd been lecturing Finn about missing dinner and not calling, and suddenly he wondered when in the holy hell he'd grown his mother's forefinger. The one she'd shaken countless times in front of his face. Still, he'd done it all because he was a Callaghan and Callaghans always took care of their own.

Those days were past him. He'd graduated from college and the police academy. He wasn't merely a cop but a detective, and knowing he followed his brother up the ranks, the way Callaghans had always done, filled him with pride. Finn didn't need him anymore, hadn't for years really. Finn had put on the badge months ago, and even had an undercover assignment under his belt, plumping up his file. And his brother was making a home of his own, living with another cop and raising a teenage boy to boot.

Just the thought made Ronan grin. Every time Finn bitched about the pain-in-the-assedness of teenagers,

Ronan told him to talk to the hand. Been there, done that, bro, and welcome to the club. Finn's partner, Michael, was a good guy, so Ronan didn't worry about Finn anymore. Sure, he still had bad dreams about the night they'd almost been too late finding Finn during the undercover job. He'd wake up in a cold sweat with visions of Finn's naked and bloody body in the grip of the leader of the pedophile ring they busted. On those days, it was doubly great to slip on his ratty clothes and hit the pavement.

Maybe it was kind of pathetic that he wanted to immerse himself in the community he'd missed out on as a student. He didn't care. It wasn't as if he was hanging out at frat parties or anything. He just liked the vibrancy of the location, and it wasn't as if at the age of twenty-six, he was some lecherous aging guy ogling the co-eds. He wasn't even into his age group. He liked slightly older women, seasoned ones who knew what they were doing and not necessarily looking for forever. Having spent much of his young adulthood being too much of an adult, he liked to play it easy and loose.

Ronan pushed his speed because he needed to burn off the stress already building within him. Normally, he loved his job and couldn't wait to get the day started. This one, however, could turn out to be a bitch. He was getting a new partner. He'd known it was going to happen as soon as Vicki told him she was pregnant. Only four months into her pregnancy, and she'd been put on bed rest. Twins, Christ Jesus. She and her husband would have their hands full. He couldn't begrudge her the need, of course, but they'd been partners for less than a year. As the older, more experienced detective, she'd been his mentor. Her steady and methodical manner had worked wonders at curbing his impulsiveness. Now, who knew what kind of cop he'd be paired with? He couldn't even think of anyone in the department that was currently solo. Maybe they'd give him a rookie detective. Then he'd be the senior man, and he wasn't so sure he was ready for that.

Shit, he'd rather have the twins. He'd rather be the one to *give birth* to the twins.

As his feet pounded the pavement and the sweat dripped into his eyes, he willed his mind to shut off. Worrying about things never helped. He'd just have to wait and see. He put in a burst of speed as he ran up the front stoop of the duplex he rented. A nice cool shower before heading into work would slap him more awake. Iced coffee on the way to the station was also a must. He needed to be on his toes today in particular.

Throwing himself into the shower stall, he leaned into the stream and sighed with the pleasure of it. His cock sprang up, much like Pavlov's dog. Living on his own meant he could spend as much time in the bathroom as he wanted and jerk off whenever he felt the urge. His morning showers had turned into play time given the dry spell he was going through date-wise. He pumped some body wash into his palm and clasped his dick. He teased himself with long, slow strokes that made him groan. With his other hand, he rolled his balls. The rhythm his hands danced to was automatic. He knew just how to coax his pleasure to climb at a steady pace.

No hurry, no one else to please or worry about. Just him squeezing his cock on the upstroke and sliding his thumb through his slit. He tugged his sack away from his body, grunting at the small bite of pain. They tightened in his grip, signaling his climax was near. He picked up the pace, jerking his dick hard and fast. As the first rope of cum shot out, he clasped more firmly with both hands and pulled himself through the orgasm. He gasped into the spray, choking on the water entering his mouth. When his knees threatened to buckle, he released his balls and braced his palm against the wall.

He stood panting for long minutes, until his brain kicked back into gear. He needed to get going so that he could meet his new partner. Now that he was a relaxed as he was ever going to get, it shouldn't be too bad. How much of a douche could his new partner be?

****

Diego Nieves parked his Harley in the precinct employee parking lot and debated whether he needed to bring his helmet in with him. Then he remembered the chance of being arrested never stopped anyone from committing a crime, and he tucked it under his arm. Man, Boston was as steamy as New York this time of year. Somehow, he expected it to be cooler because it was a little farther north and Boston Harbor wasn't as far inland as New York's, at least it seemed that way to him. Whatever, it was fucking ninety degrees with seventy percent humidity. He'd taken the risk of wearing just his suit on the bike and no leathers. If he'd gone down, the doctors would have been piecing his skin back in strips. Fortunately he was used to riding in the City, the real one. Boston drivers had nothing he hadn't seen before.

He entered the building and was grateful to get a blast of cool air. He flashed his credentials to the desk sergeant, a badge so shiny new it practically blinded him. The guy, an older man whose face was probably as red as it was all year round, gave it a quick look before buzzing him through. Diego nodded in thanks, a brief smile on his lips. He wanted this to be a good transfer, smooth, a new start. He was ready for it. Whether Boston was ready for a new cop, and a Puerto Rican one at that, remained to be seen.

If you ain't Irish, you're nothing up there.

His former partner, Julio, had been adamant about that, although he'd been keen on Diego staying in New York, so what he said had to be taken with a grain of salt. It seemed too nineteenth century to believe the Irish had a lock on the Boston police force. On the other hand, a lot of the name badges he saw as he walked down the halls of the precinct sounded Irish enough. He'd also wrangled the name of his new partner out of the lieutenant, and damned if it wasn't a guy named Callaghan. Ronan Callaghan. Of course he'd done an Internet search on the guy. Pure Boston cop royalty with a murdered father in the mix. He really hoped he was wrong, but his gut told him his new partner wasn't going to be to his liking.

His mother would say he was borrowing trouble. He tried not to dwell on his concerns as he found his way to the locker room and stowed his helmet. Taking a detour to the bathroom, he relieved himself and wet down his hair. He straightened his tie as well, because he took pride in his looks. He wanted to make a good showing for his new lieutenant if not his partner. Okay, and now he was just stalling. He forced himself out of the sanctuary of tile and quiet and headed to the bull pen.

Please, Jesus, don't let his new partner be a

douche.

Lieutenant Fuller seemed like a decent guy. As they waited for Diego's new partner to arrive, they sat in the lieutenant's office and chatted about Boston. His boss was obviously trying to put the new man at ease and give him pointers about getting around the area. So far, Diego had noted that he had to walk the Freedom Trail, but not to be discouraged if he crapped out somewhere around the Old North Church. Everybody did. Then there was the Aquarium, the Science Museum, and the Museum of Fine Arts, all of which sounded like places he'd go if he had kids or an appreciation for serious art. Neither of which he did. Fenway Park would be a great idea, if Diego wasn't a Yankee's fan. Sadly, from the lieutenant's point of view, he was.

The lieutenant was starting to branch out into Salem and Plimoth Plantation when Diego's partner finally showed up. To be fair, the guy wasn't late. Diego had a habit of always being early. He stood to greet Ronan Callaghan as they were introduced. As they shook hands, they sized each other up. Diego was taking Ronan's measure and could tell by the look in the other man's eye, he was doing the same. It rankled that the Boston man was a few inches taller, but while Puerto Rico had many things to recommend it, growing tall people was not one of them. On the other hand, Diego packed more muscle. Callaghan had that long, lean look to him, whereas Diego had played high school football.

"Have a seat, Callaghan," the lieutenant said. "I know having your partner go out so suddenly is disconcerting, but the timing is great in that Nieves here needs one."

Diego gave Ronan a sharp look. "What happened?" He hadn't heard of an officer going down.

Ronan gave him a wry grin. "Twins."

"Excuse me?"

"Vicki and her husband have been trying for a while to have a baby, and just their luck, it's twins. She's on bed rest."

"Oh. Well, please tell her congratulations from me, and I'll pray to Saint Margaret for her safe delivery."

Ronan narrowed his eyes. "I thought Gerard was the patron saint for pregnant women."

Diego shrugged. "Some say that, but my mother says that makes zero sense. Margaret was a woman and a virgin. She's a better saint for the job."

"A *virgin* is a better saint for the job?"

"Gerard was supposedly a virgin, too."

Ronan looked like he was ready for a Catholic throw down. A loud throat-clearing from the lieutenant cut him off.

"Gentlemen, if we are done with the religious instruction…? I'm sure we all wish Detective Sergeant Villas well in her pregnancy. In the meantime, you're going to be partnered. Do you have any active cases, Callaghan?"

"No, sir. We'd just wrapped one up when she started feeling bad."

"Fine, go help Nieves get settled in at Villas' desk for now and find something useful to do until you catch another case. Given the way this summer is going, that should be in about thirty seconds. Dismissed."

"Yes, sir," they said in unison.

"Oh, and Callaghan?" the lieutenant called out a

second later. "Nieves is primary as he's more senior even if he did get his experience in New York."

Ronan hesitated a second, casting a glance at Diego. His expression was unreadable. "Yes, sir," he finally said and walked out.

Diego let Ronan lead the way across the bull pen. He found himself looking at a messy desk. Ronan plopped down in the chair at the desk opposite his. It was equally messy. The guy picked up a large iced coffee and slurped on the bright orange straw sticking out of it.

Diego sat gingerly at his new desk and surveyed the paper and other detritus strewn over the surface. "I thought you said you'd cleared all of your cases."

Ronan looked at him over his straw. "We did. Vicki likes to hang onto stuff that doesn't have to go into the file. You know, background info, research, shit like that. Plus she's a squirrel and never throws anything away."

Eyeing what looked like stuff you'd find in Happy Meals, Diego understood exactly what his new partner was saying. "What am I supposed to do with all of this?"

Ronan shrugged. "Stuff it in a box. I'll take it to her house, and she can sort through it. It will give her something to do while lying around. She's already going crazy. Hates daytime television."

"I don't suppose as her former partner you'd like to…" He made a sweeping gesture at the desk and gave Ronan a hopeful look.

Ronan grinned back at him. "Not a chance. I have my own crap to deal with."

That was certainly true. "How do you stand

working with all that heaped up?"

Ronan only shrugged and went back to sipping his drink. There was no chance to push the issue. A uniform came up and handed Ronan a slip of paper. His partner's laid-back demeanor didn't change, but he stood up. "We've got a DB. I drive."

Diego stood up, too, his nerves jangling at the idea of going out into the field. He ruthlessly shut down the feelings. If he couldn't handle taking a case, then he was done being a cop. Besides, this was new territory. The whole point of moving to Boston was to take his therapist's advice to change up his environment, to change up his thought patterns. "Fine by me, Callaghan. I didn't think you'd want to ride bitch on my bike anyway."

As soon as he used the crude expression, he regretted it. His mother would have slapped him up the back of his head for being so disrespectful. He was letting his worry about his partner looking down on him put him in a defensive position. That was a stupid way to start their relationship and his new job. Not wanting to compound the problem, however, he didn't back track on his comment.

Ronan looked at him from the corner of his eye. "You have a bike? What kind?"

"Harley." He didn't add the "of course" although it was implied in his tone.

"Nice."

Okay, so points for him. He'd managed to impress his partner over his choice of ride. Juvenile to be sure. He'd take them anyway.

Ronan's car was a fairly nondescript, mid-sized standard issue coated in a fine layer of dust. The inside looked like the mobile version of Ronan's desk. Diego gingerly slid in and buckled his belt even as he kicked a fast food bag away. Ronan did the same and started the car, all while still sipping his coffee. Of course, the cup holders between them were jammed with change and crumpled napkins, but still.

"You want me to hold that for you?" While it was the last thing he wanted to do, it beat crashing.

"Naw, I'm good."

Ronan peeled out of the lot, working the steering wheel as if he was on a Sunday drive. The streets of Boston had earned their reputation, although as a New Yorker, Diego sneered inwardly at the idea it was the worst traffic in the country. Ronan hit the siren and maneuvered around the other vehicles with a skill Diego had to admire even putting aside the fact that it was done one-handed.

"Where are we going, exactly?" Diego asked, resisting the urge to cling to the dashboard.

"To the river, by the Hatch Shell."

New as he was to Boston, Diego understood that the river was the Charles and the Hatch Shell was the outdoor venue for concerts, most especially by the Boston Pops Orchestra on the Fourth. He decided not to ask any more questions and let his partner concentrate on not crashing.

The crime scene was easy to spot. A couple of marked cars and an ambulance were already parked on the side of Storrow Drive, a roadway too narrow and congested for parking. Traffic had started to back up even though it wasn't rush hour. A beleaguered uniform directed harried drivers away from the blockage. Diego got out on legs slightly shaky due to the ride over and those damn nerves of his. He took what he hoped was a subtly big breath and let it out slowly.

He could do this.

Ronan ambled up to the uniforms and the other responders, greeting most of them by name. The reaction from the others was telling. Big smiles and hand shaking told him that his partner was well-known and well-liked. He supposed that wasn't a bad thing. As Ronan stopped to question some of them about details, or maybe just to talk about sports scores, Diego continued on to the victim. Everyone moved away as he approached, giving him his first look at the DB. Male of so far an indeterminate age. A woman leaned over him on her knees. Diego saw blonde hair in a ponytail and a shapely ass.

He walked around the prone figure, taking in the visible details. Shoes barely holding together, grease stained pants that looked like they'd come out of a dumpster topped with a hole-filled T-shirt and grimy hands and arms. All that was immediately overshadowed as he caught sight of the gaping wound from ear to ear. The woman who was examining the corpse sat back on her heels and looked up at him. Diego's attention was immediately stolen by pale, flawless skin, high cheek bones, and vividly blue eyes.

The woman flashed him a smile. "Hi, I'm Cassidy Barnes, the new M.E."

The nascent smell of human decay wafted up to him. Despite that little horror, his body was on high alert, the lure of Dr. Barnes' gaze overwhelming anything else. It took a few seconds before Diego's mind and tongue started working enough for him to answer her.

"Um, hi," he said, squatting down on the other side of the corpse. Damn, he was usually smoother than that with women. "I'm Detective Sergeant Diego Nieves. I'm new, too," he added with a smile that usually resulted in at least a phone number. Not that he was trolling for a date over a dead body, but Holy Mother of God, this woman was too enticing to ignore.

"I'm thinking you're new to Boston and not just the force. Your accent is subtle, but I'd say New York?"

"Correct."

"Well, I'm Boston born and bred, just new to the coroner's office."

Her accent wasn't the thick stereotypical one he'd heard from some people in the area. She sounded more cultured, and he'd bet the diamond studs twinkling in her earlobes were genuine. She probably came from a section of Boston that was lined with trees and quiet. Classy and expensive, yet her expression was open and inviting.

Diego wrinkled his nose as he looked down at the body. "I hope this isn't your first." 'Cause that would suck. The man hadn't been in the water apparently as his body was dry and didn't look bloated. But that was a small mercy. It was an ugly corpse to view.

Cassidy sighed. "Not my first. Although I won't know for sure until I've had a chance to do a thorough autopsy, my initial guess is that this man died from having his throat cut."

The understatement and its dry delivery caught him off guard. It seemed incongruous with what he saw that she would be capable of cracking a joke while examining gruesome remains. He understood the impetus, of course. Gallows humor helped to keep the horror they dealt with every day at bay. He stifled a laugh as someone walked toward them and stopped at the head of the body. Glancing up, Diego saw Ronan. His partner had ditched his coffee, thank God, and was looking wide eyed not at the DB but at the ME.

"Hi," Ronan said, squatting down. "I'm Ronan Callaghan, Nieves' partner."

Cassidy gave him the same winning smile she'd given to Diego, so maybe she was just friendly with everyone and his shot at getting her to go out was a long one.

"Callaghan, huh? That's a name I've heard before."

"Oh?" Ronan's expression became guarded and his tone a little chilly. His body stiffened just a bit, as if he were bracing for a fight. That was odd.

"Yes, I met a Daire Callaghan on my first case."

Just like that Ronan's expression and body language changed again. "Oh, yeah, my older brother, emphasis on the *old*," he said with a charming smile that probably got him not just women's phone numbers but the women themselves.

Cassidy raised her eyebrows. "Really? He seemed younger than me."

Before Ronan had a chance to back pedal on his age comment, Diego jumped in. He was pretty sure he was older than Ronan, and while he might not be the doctor's age, he happened to like more mature women.

"Please excuse my partner, doctor. Given his young age, his frontal lobe just finished growing. He doesn't appreciate the appeal of maturity."

Cassidy grinned at the statement. Ronan's mouth opened for a retort. Figuring they'd wasted enough time, Diego overrode him. "So, the victim?"

Both Cassidy and Ronan shifted their attention to the body.

"Middle-aged male, or close to it, between forty and forty-five, I'd say," Cassidy began. "He's been dead for about ten hours, putting T.O.D. at around midnight. Looks like a single stroke of a sharp blade from left to right, so you're looking for a right-handed killer. I'll have to do a tox screen, but the lingering smell of alcohol indicates he may have been drunk when killed."

"I'm told he had no I.D. on him," Ronan jumped in, his tone all business and his look serious as he gazed at the corpse. "Appears he was a vagrant."

"That's certainly what his appearance indicates," Cassidy concurred.

Diego was about to weigh in on the observation when he focused on the victim's hands. He got down on his knees to take a closer look, and at the fingers in particular. He held out his own hand without looking up.

"Can I borrow some gloves?"

"Sure." Cassidy slapped surgical gloves in his open palm.

Sliding them on both hands, he picked up the victim's and held it up for scrutiny. With rigor already setting, it was hard to lift it too close, so Diego stayed bent down.

"What's up?" Ronan asked.

"Take a look at his fingernails." Diego moved to his left to give Ronan room to slide closer. "As dirty as he is, his nails aren't torn. They look recently groomed, you know like with a nail clipper."

Ronan dropped to his knees and hunched over the hand. He nodded. "You're right." Scooting back, he gestured to the head that was angled back given the gaping hinge across the neck. "Can you please pull back his lips?" he asked Cassidy.

She did so gingerly, and Ronan peered at the teeth revealed. Ronan looked at Diego and gestured with his own head. "Take a look at his teeth."

Diego braced a hand on the ground and leaned over. While they weren't the best set of choppers he'd ever seen, the victim appeared to have all of them and they'd been cleaned on a regular basis.

"If this guy was homeless, it was a recent event in his life," Diego observed.

Ronan nodded his head. "I agree. Interesting. How quickly can you do the autopsy on smiley here?" he asked Cassidy.

She looked back and forth between the two of them, a thoughtful expression on her face. "I'll put it at the top of my list."

Ronan shot her a megawatt smile that turned his boyish charm up to an eleven, the bastard. "Thanks. Let me give you my number so you can text me when you have the preliminary results."

As he watched the exchange of information, Diego reminded himself they were working a case, not a bar, and that his focus needed to be on the victim, not his sudden desire to pound his new partner's face into the ground.

Also Read

Bondage & Bureaucracy

by

Rynne Raines
http://amzn.com/B00OZQOHXG

After eight years married to the wrong man for all the wrong reasons, Fiona McBride is more than happy to sign on the dotted line, end the charade, and rediscover her penchant for kinky sex. She never thought the road to rediscovery would lead to her ex-husband's sexy political rival, Harrison Lancaster.

Harrison has promised his campaign manager he'll steer clear of the BDSM club until after the election, but when he runs into Fiona at a local cafe and starts fantasizing about taking the prim and proper debutante over his knee, he realizes abstinence is getting to him. Only a mad man would entertain the idea of sexually dominating his competition's vanilla ex-wife. When an old photo reveals she's not so straight-laced, he begins to wonder if it's possible to mix bondage and bureaucracy.